What Others Are Saying About Vickie McDonough and *Song of the Prairie*...

Vickie McDonough has a gift for weaving a story sure to delight lovers of the Old West. She's at the top of her form with *Song of the Prairie*, drawing her readers into this captivating tale about the bonds of family and friendship. McDonough's fans will enjoy this wonderful conclusion to the Pioneer Promises series, where love blossoms on the windswept prairie.

—*Carol Cox*
Author, *Truth Be Told, Trouble in Store*, and *Love in Disguise*

Vickie McDonough has outdone herself with the final story in the Pioneer Promises trilogy. *Song of the Prairie* is a heartfelt, heartwarming, and, at times, heartbreaking story of the lengths to which a woman will go to protect a child. Turning the last page was bittersweet for me. Although I sighed in pleasure at the resolution, I wished there were more than three Harper brothers so that I could look forward to another prairie adventure. More, please!

—*Amanda Cabot*
Author, *With Autumn's Return*

Song of the Prairie concludes the saga of three brothers with a story that snares the reader faster than the winds can sweep across the Kansas prairie. Vickie McDonough once again gives her readers a love story to lift the spirits and warm the heart.

—*Martha Rogers*
Author of the series Seasons of the Heart
and The Homeward Journey

This story is a wonderful conclusion to the Pioneer Promises series. As always, Vickie McDonough's westerns deliver action, emotion, and faith by the heaping handful. Her plots draw me in and keep me reading until the final punch.

—Susan Page Davis
Author of forty-plus novels,
including The Ladies' Shooting Club series,
Prairie Dreams series, *Captive Trail*, and *Cowgirl Trail*

This touching story of love, duty, and sacrifice set on the Kansas prairie is a pure delight and one you won't want to miss.

—Margaret Brownley
Best-selling author of the series Rocky Creek and
The Brides of Last Chance Ranch

In *Song of the Prairie*, Vickie McDonough delivers a memorable glimpse into the Old West, with realistic characters, vivid descriptions, and a romance that satisfies. I loved Janie, the courageous heroine who sacrifices so much to protect someone she loves, and Aaron, the strong rancher whose strength Janie comes to rely on. Any reader of historical romance will not only enjoy this book but will love the entire series.

—Miralee Ferrell
Best-selling author of the Love Blossoms in Oregon series

Vickie McDonough ends her Prairie Promises series on a high note with *Song of the Prairie*. A to-die-for hero, a charming heroine, a family who supports them through all their ups and downs, and a truly nasty bad guy who rides into their lives out of the past…what more could you ask for in a story? Well done, Vickie McDonough! I'll be watching for your next series.

—Dorothy Clark
Author of the Pinewood Weddings series

Once again, Vickie McDonough delivers a top-notch tale that grabs the heartstrings from the first page. In her true fashion, McDonough relentlessly tosses in heartbreak, loss, a touch of terror, and a wonderfully sweet romance, making *Song of the Prairie* an unforgettable, totally satisfying finale to the wonderful Pioneer Promises series. Highly, highly recommended!

—Delia Latham
Author of the Heart's Haven series

Vickie's done it again! *Song of the Prairie* delivers a sparkling romance at a steady clip, leading to a breathless showdown of an ending. Pure story and no fillers, this one's sure to please readers of the genre.

—Linore Rose Burkard
Author, *Before the Season Ends*

Filled with tension and delightful moments alike, *Song of the Prairie* is a true joy to read. Even though it's set in 1874, the parenting issues presented are still relevant today. Some of them will make you wince, while others will get you to grin.

—Diana Lesire Brandmeyer
Author, *The Festive Bride*, *Mind of Her Own*, and *A Bride's Dilemma in Friendship, Tennessee*

Song of the Prairie is another winner from author Vickie McDonough. The minute I started this novel, I knew I was in for a delightful read. All the characters spring to vibrant life, especially Janie. Her challenges captured my heart.

—Ann Shorey
Author of the series At Home in Beldon Grove and Sisters at Heart

Song of the Prairie is a fitting conclusion to Vickie McDonough's Pioneer Promises series. A new heroine brings both romance and a bit of suspense, and all the characters leapt from the pages straight into my heart. Even when I had to put the book down, which was very hard to do, they kept the story alive in my mind. The authentic setting and the details of 1870s society shone through every scene. I highly recommend this wonderful read.

—*Lena Nelson Dooley*
Award-winning author, *Maggie's Journey, Mary's Blessing,* and
Catherine's Pursuit

Song of the Prairie is both heartrending and glorious from beginning to end. With a colorful cast of characters, the author knits together a powerful, poignant story of sacrificial love and hope in the face of tragedy and trials. Be prepared to set aside your chores the day you start this book—it's a page-turner that you can't easily put down. Beautifully written!

—*Sharlene MacLaren*
Award-winning author of the series Little Hickman Creek,
The Daughters of Jacob Kane, River of Hope,
and Tennessee Dreams

Song of the PRAIRIE

VICKIE McDONOUGH

WHITAKER
HOUSE

SONG OF THE PRAIRIE
Pioneer Promises ~ Book Three

Vickie McDonough
vickie@vickiemcdonough.com
www.vickiemcdonough.com

ISBN: 978-1-62911-170-4
eBook ISBN: 978-1-62911-171-1
Printed in the United States of America
© 2014 by Vickie McDonough

Whitaker House
1030 Hunt Valley Circle
New Kensington, PA 15068
www.whitakerhouse.com

Library of Congress Cataloging-in-Publication Data

McDonough, Vickie.
  Song of the prairie / by Vickie McDonough.
    pages cm. — (Pioneer promises ; book three)
  ISBN 978-1-62911-170-4 (alk. paper)
  1. Single women—fiction. 2. Kinship care—Fiction. 3. Prairies—Fiction.
I. Title.
  PS3613.C3896S66 2014
  813'.6—dc23
                        2014012270

1 2 3 4 5 6 7 8 9 10 11 ɰ 21 20 19 18 17 16 15 14

Chapter One

September 1874

Juliet Fairchild bounced on her toes, nervous anticipation making her limbs quiver, as she waited off stage to hear her name introduced for the first time. Years of training and sacrifice had brought her to this moment—her debut performance in New York's Academy of Music opera house. A crescendo of applause heralded her entrance. A grinning stagehand winked, tipped his cap, and tugged the curtain open, and she walked onto the stage. Exuberant cheers and whistles joined the ovation. Smiling, Juliet curtsied and glanced up at the private box seating to her left where her parents sat, but shadows greeted her instead of their happy faces. The audience's clapping shifted, taking on a repetitive tempo.

Juliet blinked as her dream faded. Her eyes focused on the moonlight peeking through the opening between the curtains—her bedroom curtains. She wasn't in an opera house, preparing for her debut performance, but in her small rented room down the street from the music school where she taught voice lessons to young girls from affluent families. Though the chimes of the church down the street signaled five in the morning, the overly warm room was still shadowed in darkness. She bolted up from her bed, suddenly aware it wasn't applause she heard but knocking.

And she wasn't Juliet Fairchild but plain Jane Dunn, teacher at Boston Academy of Music for Young Women.

Yawning, Janie tugged her robe over her gown and hurried across the room. Who could possibly need her at this hour?

She unlocked the door and pulled it open just far enough for her to see out. "Who's there?"

"It's me, ma'am. Mazie."

"Mazie?" Her mind ran through her list of new music students and fellow teachers, but she couldn't remember anyone with that name.

The woman took a step back, and in the faint light of the lamp the landlady left illuminated on the hall credenza to help boarders to find their way downstairs to the privy, she recognized the dark-skinned young woman who worked for her cousin Carolyn.

Janie's heart pounded a hard staccato beat. She pulled the door back and motioned for the maid to enter, then lit her lamp. "Has Carolyn gone into labor?"

Mazie flipped back her cloak, revealing the bundle she held. Tears glistened in her eyes. "Yes, ma'am, but she done had d'baby." Mazie sniffled and held out the blanketed package.

"What this?" Janie shook her head and stepped back, fearful of the thought that charged across her mind.

"It d'baby, ma'am."

"What?" Janie crossed her arms. "Why did you bring it here?"

Tugging the bundle to her chest, Mazie puckered up her face and then broke into sobs. "She gone. Mizzus Carolyn died birthing d'babe."

Janie quickly shut the door, lest her guest wake the other boarders. She spun around, her mind refusing to accept the truth. "What?"

Mazie walked over to the bed and laid the bundle down, then slid a large satchel off one shoulder. She wiped her eyes and turned around. "Mizzus Metcalf is dead, ma'am."

Janie clutched her robe to her chest as pain lanced her heart. She dropped into the only chair in the room. "Dead? How?"

Mazie's features hardened. "That Mistuh Metcalf, it be his fault. He get mad 'cause Mizzus Metcalf wanted to go to d'hospital, and he pushed her. She fell down d'stairs and hit her head. She lived long enough to hold her baby once't."

Janie covered her face. "No! It can't be. I saw her just yesterday." The picture of her very pregnant cousin invaded her memory. Carolyn always had a smile for everyone, even though she often bore bruises and shadows under her eyes. Janie knew that her cousin's husband, Martin, manhandled her, but Carolyn always insisted that she'd done something to provoke his anger. Janie couldn't imagine her sweet cousin saying or doing anything to make someone angry enough to mistreat her. Carolyn was the kindest person she knew. Her best friend.

And now she was gone.

The thought created a stabbing pain in Janie's stomach, and she bent over. "Oh, Carolyn." *Why didn't you leave him?*

A squeak that more resembled a small animal than a human escaped the squirming bundle on the bed. In spite of the pain coursing through her, Janie stood and crossed the small room. She unfolded the edges of the quilt she'd watched her cousin lovingly stitch over the past few months and met her niece—or was it a boy?

Turning, she glanced at Mazie. "What is it?"

Mazie blinked, looking confused. "I done told you it was Mizzus Metcalf's babe."

In spite of everything, Janie couldn't help smiling. "Boy or girl?"

"It be a boy child."

Janie lifted the infant's perfectly shaped hand. Five tiny fingers, each with a diminutive nail. Blond duckling fuzz stuck up from his head, and he struggled to suckle his fist. "What's his name?"

Mazie shrugged. "Mizzus didn't say. Just to bring 'im to you."

Lifting a hand to her forehead, Janie grappled with her thoughts, trying to make sense of things. "Why would she say that? The baby doesn't belong to me." Although, the tiny imp had already stolen a chunk of her heart.

Mazie shrugged, stepped away from the bed, and reached for the doorknob. "I gots t'get back before I's missed."

"No, wait!" Janie moved the baby to the center of the bed and hurried toward her cousin's maid. "You shouldn't go back, Mazie. Martin will know someone took the baby, and it won't be hard to figure out that it was you."

Eyes wide, Mazie started shaking. "I only did what Mizzus told me t'do."

"I know, but Martin isn't normally reasonable."

"Uh-huh. Don't I know." She bobbed her head, then a light flickered in her eyes. "I just remembered—Mistuh Metcalf left after he pushed Mizzus Metcalf. He say he be gone till week's end. I can go get my things then go t'my sister's in Allegheny."

"Don't leave yet, please." Janie grasped the girl's hand. "I know nothing about tending babies. How will I feed him? What will I do with him while I work?"

Tightening her grip on Janie's hand, Mazie looked up. "You cain't stay here, neither. Take that babe and go somewheres far away, where dat baby's daddy cain't find you. He kill you if he find you with his child."

Janie's heart lurched. "But I can't. My work is here. My home." *My dreams.*

Mazie glanced around the small space. "This your home? It be smaller than my room at d'Metcalfs' house."

Wincing, Janie looked at her chamber—her haven. It wasn't much but was all she could afford on her teacher's salary. "I can't go now. The school term just started. I can't leave Miss Carpenter in a lurch with no one to teach my classes."

Mazie grabbed her by the arms, something completely unexpected from the normally compliant maid. "You read Mizzus Metcalf's letter, then you go."

"Letter?"

Mazie crossed over to the bed, rifled through the satchel that lay next to the baby, and pulled out an envelope embossed with a scrolling letter *M*. She held it out to Janie.

With a trembling hand, Janie took it, then turned the lamp up and lowered herself into the chair. Why had Carolyn never approached her about keeping the baby if something happened to her?

The single page fluttered as Janie held it toward the light. She immediately recognized her cousin's neat penmanship.

Dear Janie,

I know this will come as a shock, but if you are reading this note, then I am more than likely deceased. I have had so many bad dreams of not surviving the delivery that I have begun to believe it may happen just as I fear it will. I dearly love this child I've yet to meet. Should I perish and the baby live, I want you to raise him. Yes, I believe I am carrying a boy. That is why it is crucial for you to take him and raise him. I cannot bear the thought of birthing a son who might grow up to be a cruel man like his father. Please find a way to take him away—far away—where Martin will never find him. I realize that doing so will mean sacrificing your teaching career and your dream to sing opera on a big stage. Forgive me for my selfishness, but there is no one else with whom I would trust the care of my child.

I would like you to name him. Martin and I have talked names on the few occasions where he was in a civil mood, and he might remember them. Please don't pick a Metcalf family name. I want nothing that can lead Martin to you.

I pray you can forgive me for the sacrifice I am asking of you.

Your loving cousin,
Carolyn

Janie leaned back in the chair, tears trickling down her cheeks. How could Carolyn be gone? She glanced at Mazie, who stood next to the bed, gently rubbing the baby's head. "Why didn't someone send for me when Carolyn went into labor?"

"It was near midnight when we'uns knew she was birthin'. Mizzus Metcalf, she didn't want us t'bother you in the middle of d'night."

Janie stood, crossed to the bed, and stared down at her new ward. She was a twenty-five-year-old spinster—ill prepared to take on the care of a newborn baby. And if she left town, how could she support both of them? She sucked in a gasp, receiving a sideways glance from Mazie. What if people thought *she* was the mother and had borne the child out of wedlock?

The baby began to wiggle. His face scrunched up, and he emitted another squeak. Janie fumbled as she picked him up, hoping to stop him from wailing. It would be hard to keep his presence a secret if that happened. "How will I feed him?"

"Mizzus Metcalf, she bought some canned sweet milk, but you'd best find a wet nurse somewheres."

How did one do that?

"We fed 'im before I left d'house, so he's probably jus' tired. Try rocking 'im."

Janie lifted the baby to her shoulder, cooing soft words of comfort and gently swaying. The infant turned his face toward her neck, blowing tiny warm breaths against her skin. Instant love for the babe surged through her like the moving finale of a concerto. Love welled up inside, and she knew in that moment that she would do whatever she must to keep him safe.

⁓

Martin Metcalf paused on his porch and stared at the boxwood wreath hanging from his front door. The wreath dangled from a foot of black ribbon with a big bow at the top. Had one of the servants died? He wouldn't put it past Carolyn to have put it up for a deceased friend. The vulgar thing certainly hadn't been there when he'd left several days ago—or had it been closer to a week? After the argument with his wife, he'd spent several days soothing his anger with a bottle. He shoved open the door, noting a faint foul odor.

"Chalmers!" Martin removed his coat and hat, annoyed at the black crepe covering the hall tree mirror. This was going too far. He yanked the fabric down and tossed it on the floor.

The butler rushed into the large foyer, his shoes clacking on the highly polished mahogany floor. Chalmers' normally stoic face looked pinched today. "Welcome home, sir." He reached for the coat and hat, hung them on the hall tree, and then picked up the cloth and draped it over his arm.

"Why is there a wreath out front?"

Chalmers spun around to face him, gray eyes wide. "Sir... uh...you mean, you haven't heard? We tried to locate you, but..."

Martin's patience was thinning. "Heard what?"

Shifting from foot to foot, Chalmers looked past Martin, as if searching for someone.

Stepping forward, Martin grabbed the man's lapels, jerking his surprised gaze back. "Don't dawdle. Spit it out, man."

The thin man swallowed, his Adam's apple pushing out. "I'm sorry, sir, but…it's Mrs. Metcalf. She…she died…in childbirth."

Carolyn was dead? Stunned, Martin loosened his hold and stepped back. "What of the child?"

The butler shook his head and looked down.

Martin had never wanted a child, but after months of watching his wife swell bigger and bigger, he'd finally decided an heir was a good thing. But now Carolyn had cheated him of that. Anger spiraled through him. He shoved the butler backward into the hall tree. Chalmers flailed his arms and landed against the mirror, cracking the glass.

Martin spun toward the stairs. "See that you get that repaired. The cost will come out of your pocket."

Chalmers cleared his throat. "As you wish, sir."

Storming up the stairs, Martin couldn't find it within him to grieve Carolyn. Any love he might have had for her paled in the face of what he now shared with Felicity. But with him now a widower, Felicity would hound him to marry her. Marrying Carolyn had helped his image, but if he wed Felicity, tongues would wag. Being a father would have improved his standing in the community, but obviously that wouldn't happen now.

Halfway down the wide hall, he shoved open the door to his wife's bedchamber and strode into the dark room. He yanked apart the draperies over the windows and looked around. The room carried a disgusting odor, and he covered his nose. Another heinous black wreath lay across the bed. He yanked it off and flung it across the room, where it slammed against the wall and fell to the ground in pieces. There was no sign of the baby blankets or infant clothing Carolyn had spent months making—clothing that had laid in piles last time he'd been here.

He yanked open the wardrobe and was greeted with the more pleasant scent of his wife—lavender and cedar. The colorful gowns of green, pale blue, pink, and purple brought back memories of escorting her to dinner and out to the theater. She'd made a lovely ornament on his arm, and he'd relished the admiration in the glance of nearly every man who glanced her way. He slammed the doors shut.

"Mr. Metcalf, is there somethin' I can help you find?"

He pivoted, and his gaze narrowed. Carolyn's maid. What was that little mouse's name? She hovered at the door, as if afraid to enter the room with him there.

"Where is my wife?"

Her eyes widened. "Chalmers didn't tell you?"

"Of course he did. Where is her body?"

Her gaze zipped to the bed and then back to him. "She was laid out for two days, but then the mortician came and took her away. With the heat we've been having, he said it was time for her buryin', but I can't tell you exactly where he took her."

He moved toward the door, and she backed up so fast, it was almost comical. He wanted to wring her neck to vent his wrath, but he may have need of her later. He started to turn toward the stairs but paused. "What did she die of?"

The maid clutched her throat, but he could see that her hand still trembled. "Why, birthin' d'baby, sir."

His fist tightened. "I know that," he roared. "But why? She was perfectly healthy when I left her."

The woman retreated further, fear widening her hazel eyes. "Maybe you should ask the doctor, sir. All I know is, she bled a lot and that she was injured when you—"

"When I what?" He took a step toward her, and she flinched.

"N-nothing. I—I should get back to my chores." She turned and hurried down the hall.

"Stop! Right where you are!" He stormed after her, and she spun around but continued backing away until she collided with the hall table. The crystal prisms on the lamp clinked.

He reached for her throat, his anger reaching the boiling point. "When I *what?*" he ground out through clenched teeth.

She shook her head. "Please…I can't."

He tightened his grip and gave her a shake. "You will."

"Mr. Metcalf, please. Don't harm the girl."

He glanced down the hall at Mrs. Burns, the head housekeeper. Martin muttered a curse and gave the girl a shove, sending her sidestepping until she fell.

Mrs. Burns hurried to the mouse and helped her up. "Go downstairs, Paula, and help in the kitchen."

"Y-yes, ma'am." She hurried away toward the servants' stairs like a rodent seeking a hiding place.

Martin's anger soothed a tad knowing he'd bested her. He adjusted his cuffs and gazed at his servant. "What happened to Carolyn?"

Mrs. Burns looked spooked but stood her ground. "She never recovered from your pushing her down the stairs. She went into labor the same night, but she was already weak, and then the doctor couldn't stop her flow, and she died."

Martin ground down on his back teeth and struggled to remember that night. He'd lost a lot of money in a Faro game, and as a result, he had been drinking more than normal. He wasn't a good drunk—he knew that. But could he have tossed his pregnant wife down the stairs and not even remember? Someone was making him the scapegoat. "You're lying."

Her nostrils flared. "You're accusing me of telling a falsehood, sir? If I was so inclined, I certainly wouldn't have told you what I did just now, knowing your penchant for going off in a rage."

Deflating, Martin chuckled. The old bat always did have the nerve to stand up to him, and for that, he admired her. But then he sobered. "Did you see me…do that?" He waved toward the stairs.

"Yes, and if you'll allow me to say so, sir, it was a deplorable thing you did to Missus Carolyn and her babe."

He glared at her for overstepping her bounds, but he remained where he was. "And the child?"

She pursed her lips and shook her head.

"Was it a son?"

"Yes, sir, with fine blond hair like his mother's. They were buried together. At least, that's what the undertaker said he would do." She dabbed the corner of her eye with a handkerchief she pulled from her sleeve, then recomposed herself. "We figured you'd want to hold a memorial service to remember her once you returned. Should I summon Mrs. Metcalf's minister so we can start arranging it?"

He didn't give a fig about a memorial service. Didn't want to parade himself in front of a bunch of phony mourners who were secretly glad something hadn't gone his way for a change. Just thinking of their smug faces sent his temperature soaring. But a service would be expected, or he'd come across as an insensitive lout. He cursed and swatted his hand at the hurricane lamp on the hall table, sending it flying onto the floor. The fine Italian glass shattered and scattered across the carpet runner in hundreds of pieces.

Mrs. Burns gasped and jumped back.

Martin spun for the stairs. He needed a drink—and Felicity's comfort.

Tomorrow he'd go to the cemetery to his family mausoleum, open the casket, and have a look at his son.

～

Three days later, after consoling himself with his mistress, Martin stood back as two cemetery workers opened his wife's casket. The pair set the top on the ground against the mausoleum wall, then shuffled outside as Martin moved over to stand beside the coffin. With a hand that shook more than he would have liked, he lifted the scarf covering Carolyn's face. Shocked at the sight of her ashen, blistered skin, he dropped the fabric and took a step back, pinching his nose closed at the horrid stench.

His stomach curdled. Carolyn had been beautiful, but no more. He hadn't been good to her. She was a kind, patient woman who deserved far better than him. Bile rose in his throat.

He'd seen enough. Just one look at his son, and he would never return to this place. Avoiding touching his dead wife, he carefully flipped back the yellow crocheted blanket she had meticulously crafted. He unfolded the other side and stared.

Nothing.

Using the sides of the blanket, he forced Carolyn's stiff arm back and opened the blanket fully. He sucked in a breath and was instantly sorry. Gagging, he nearly lost his breakfast.

The blanket was empty.

Where was his son?

Chapter Two

September 1875 · A ranch near Windmill, Kansas

Janie set a bowl of steaming potatoes on the table and took her seat across from her brother, Phil. Benjy, tied to a ladder-back chair, grinned as he gnawed on a bread crust. Janie shook her head as she spread her napkin across her lap. "I can hardly believe it's been a year since I came here."

Phil nodded. "Time sure has flown by, but it's been a good year. I'm really glad to have you here. Life was right lonely before you came. Shall we pray?"

Janie bowed her head, and as Phil said grace, the familiar feelings of guilt nibbled at her like a pesky mouse in the pantry. Phil had thought it best they pose as man and wife, to protect Benjy as well as Janie's reputation, but she hated perpetuating the lie. It hadn't been too hard at first, when she didn't know anyone, but now that she'd made many friends, she felt like a charlatan, especially whenever someone hinted at her having another child. What would people say if they knew the truth? But the truth would remain a secret to guard Benjy from detection by his ill-meaning father.

Right after Phil muttered "Amen," three sharp raps sounded at the door. His chair creaked as Phil stood, as if objecting to being moved too soon. He crossed the room in six long-legged steps and opened the door. "Aaron, what brings you here at suppertime?"

Janie's gaze shot to the open doorway, where she had an almost unobstructed view of Aaron Harper. Their neighbor never failed to intrigue her. With his uncommonly good looks and penetrating dark brown eyes, he was one of the most comely men she'd ever met. She ducked her head and chastised herself for staring. Those were hardly proper thoughts for a married woman, and they wouldn't help her preserve the façade.

"Evenin', Phil. I'm headed home to eat now, but I just remembered something." He pulled a wrinkled envelope from his pocket. "Ma's plannin' a shindig, and she's hoping y'all will come."

"Thanks for the invitation." Phil took the envelope and stepped back. "Why don't you join us? Janie prepared plenty, as usual."

Aaron glanced into the room, and when his gaze caught Janie's, he tugged his hat off and nodded.

Janie smiled, in spite of her nervousness. "Yes, please join us, Mr. Harper."

"It's Aaron, and if you're certain you don't mind, I believe I will. There's something I need to talk to Phil about, and you need to hear it, too. Just let me wash up first." He turned and disappeared from the doorway.

Janie rose from her seat and hurried across the room to retrieve another plate from the shelf. She grabbed a fork, knife, and napkin, then set a place for their neighbor.

Aaron entered, hung his hat next to Phil's on a peg near the door, and then took the only vacant seat at the table. The room seemed to shrink with his presence. Janie's brother wasn't a small man, but Aaron Harper was over six feet tall with broad, masculine shoulders. His tanned face was free of trail dust, and his dark hair, damp from his recent washing, dripped water where it touched his collar. She should have offered him a towel. Yanking her gaze from her guest, she picked up the platter of sliced ham and passed it to him. "Help yourself."

"Thank you, ma'am." He caught her gaze for a brief moment, then focused on filling his plate.

Janie sighed. She even liked the deep timbre of his voice. He and the rest of the Harpers, their closest neighbors, were some of the kindest people she'd ever met. She cleared her throat, determined to quit thinking about him. "How are your children?"

A shadow passed across Aaron's eyes, and she wished she hadn't asked.

But then he smiled. "Oh, you know young'uns. Corrie was excited to get back to town to start school again and see her friends and wear the new dresses her grandma and aunts made her this summer, and Toby fussed like a calf being separated from its ma about having to leave and go back to school. He said he didn't like wearing church clothes all week. At least he was excited to see his cousin Mikey again."

Phil chuckled. "I guess it's good Janie was a teacher. We won't ever have to send Benjy away for his learnin'. She can teach him herself."

As if the mention of his name required a response, Benjy squealed and tossed his soggy bread onto the table. Janie snatched it and handed it back to him. "We don't throw food, little man," she admonished him gently.

Blushing, she glanced at her guest, but his head was bowed in prayer. Maybe he hadn't witnessed Benjy's uncouth behavior. But then again, he had children; surely, he would understand a baby's antics—probably better than she. Being a mother was still new to her, but she was learning as she went along, and she was relieved to see how resilient children could be.

During the meal, Phil talked about his crops, and Aaron mentioned the horses he and his brother Ethan had been gentling. When Janie had finished eating, she fed Benjy some mashed potatoes with diced ham. Her son may be a full year old, but he still had only a few teeth.

When the men finished, she cleared away their plates and then cut them each a large slice of peach pie. Janie untied Benjy, washed his face and hands, and kissed his cheek. Love for this precious boy soared through her. She grabbed the baby's rattle, then took her seat at the table again.

Aaron smiled then leaned back in his chair. "That was a fine meal, Mrs. Dunn."

"Thank you. It was nice of you to join us."

"Believe me, the pleasure was all mine." He smiled at her.

Janie dropped her gaze, unable to look into his alluring eyes. What was wrong with her? She'd never been attracted to a man like she was to widower Aaron Harper. Maybe if not for the front she and Phil were keeping up, something might have developed between them. She'd wrestled so many times over pretending to be Phil's wife that she'd lost count. He'd come up with the idea, and while she had leaned more toward pretending to be a widow, in the end, she had agreed to his plan. He was the one who had taken her in, after all. Either way, she had to lie to people who were now her friends, and she despised doing that.

"So, what did you want to talk to us about?" Phil pushed his empty plate aside.

Aaron looked at him, his lips pressed into a thin line. "It's not good news. Did you hear how Jim Cooper's dog got attacked by a coyote several weeks back? 'Bout had his leg tore off?" He looked at Janie. "Sorry, ma'am, but the story needs to be told."

Phil nodded. "I did hear that. What happened? Did the poor thing die?"

Shaking his head, Aaron pursed his lips again, then blew out a sigh. "Might have been the best thing. The dog developed hydrophobia. One of Jim's boys took water to it one day, and the animal went berserk and nearly attacked him. Thank the good Lord the dog was tied up and the boy wasn't hurt. Jim had to shoot it."

"Rabies?" Phil ran his hand along his chin. "That is bad. Did they kill the coyote?"

"No, but it's dead by now. The problem is, we don't know what other animals it may have infected."

"You're right. We could have an outbreak of critters with the disease." Phil looked at Janie. "I don't want you going anywhere—the barn, the chicken coop, the privy—without a pistol. You understand?"

Eyes wide, Janie nodded. How would she manage her chores, Benjy, and a gun? She didn't like the thought of one so close to her son.

Aaron turned his gaze on her. "I don't want to overly worry you, ma'am, because you'll most likely be fine and never encounter an animal that's infected, but play it safe. Make sure you look around good before you even leave the house. Animals with rabies tend to hide and stay in the wilderness, but they have been known to come onto a homestead." The seriousness in Aaron's eyes made Janie shudder. "At least you don't have a dog to be concerned about."

No, but she had Benjy and Phil. This meant no more taking Benjy with her to hang laundry on the line or take it down. Maybe she should hang it in the house, like she had done during the weeks of snowfall last winter. She couldn't very well take the baby to the barn or outside and set him on a blanket atop a pile of fresh hay if there was the danger of a wild animal nearby. Life on the prairie was hard enough without something like this to worry about.

Phil drummed his fingertips on the table. "I wonder if I should move my cattle closer to the house. With my small herd, I can't afford to lose any of them."

Aaron shrugged. "Rabies in cattle is rare. And besides, I imagine you've got too much to do to keep an eye on them all the time."

Sighing, Phil leaned back in his chair. "You're right."

"If you're worried about them, you can drive them over to our place and let them run with our herd until this scare passes," Aaron offered. "Our ranch hands can keep a watch on them."

"No, but thanks. I'm sure my concern is unwarranted. The Coopers live miles from here."

"Just be watchful." Aaron stood. "I'd best be getting home to finish my chores."

Phil stood and shook his hand. "You're welcome any time. Thanks for dropping off the invitation. Janie, I'm sure, will be eagerly awaiting the party. She's been hankerin' for some women time."

Cheeks flaming, Janie glanced down at Benjy and smoothed his fuzzy hair. Aaron would think she'd been complaining.

"Thanks again for the fine meal, Mrs. Dunn. Our women-folk will enjoy your company, too."

She darted a glance his way and smiled.

He nodded, then walked to the door, retrieved his hat, and stepped outside. Phil followed and shut the door. Janie sighed as her heart slowed to its normal rhythm. Even if Aaron Harper didn't think she was married, it wasn't likely he'd give her a second glance.

⌣

Aaron sipped his cider and watched the dancers spinning to the lively music in his family's yard. The wide area between the house and barn had been raked clean and had finally passed his ma's inspection. A neighbor and two of the Harper ranch hands played fiddle, guitar, and harmonica, keeping the festively dressed guests swaying and sashaying to their tunes.

After several young widows had batted their lashes at Aaron, he'd moved downwind of the dancing, preferring dust to danger—and women were dangerous. They were pretty and soft and would steal your heart and then stomp on it, leaving you feeling half the man you were before you met them. At least, that had been his experience with his wife, Della, who had died in a tragic horse riding accident.

His two younger brothers seemed to have fared much better. His youngest brother, Ethan, grinned broadly as he danced with his wife, Sarah. She looked pretty in a blue dress that matched her eyes. Aaron had come close to marrying Sarah himself, until his lily-livered brother had finally found the nerve to declare his love to her. A wave of loneliness enveloped Aaron. He was the only adult Harper who wasn't married, and the only man not dancing, except for some of the shyer ranch hands.

Della would have loved this party. It would have been the highlight of the month for her. Aaron caught a glimpse of his other brother, Josh, slow dancing with his wife, Sophie. They stayed on the outskirts of the group, most likely to avoid triggering Sophie's asthma by the dust stirred up by the other dancers.

Both Sarah and Sophie had grown up in big cities, yet they were happy living on the prairie. Della hadn't been. Aaron's city wife had hated living at their isolated stage stop and would visit their neighbors on a regular basis, even though they lived miles from the nearest one. She had been dead over five years now, and he rarely missed her anymore. Still, times like this hammered home the fact that he was alone. He hadn't minded it so much until both his brothers married.

Aaron may not have a wife, but at least he had children. He searched the group for Corrie and Toby, relieved to see them both occupied with their friends. Toby was shooting marbles with Mikey and two other school-age boys just south of the food tables. Aaron grinned. Leave it to his son to stay close to the grub. Corrie danced with one of her girlfriends along the edge of the crowd. Aaron wanted to dance with her again before the night was over, but for now, he needed a little quiet. He backed away from the crowd, determined to check on the horses.

"I still say it's odd."

Aaron turned his head toward Floyd Jones and Brodie Palmer, two ranch hands from the Cooper place, who stood on the far side of a nearby carriage.

"What is?" Brodie asked as he lit up a cheroot.

"Them Dunns. One day, Phil Dunn is a confirmed bachelor, and the next, he's drivin' through Windmill, carting home a wife and a baby, and grinnin' like a possum."

Brodie shrugged, then took a deep puff of his cheroot. He blew out several smoke rings. "I don't see nothin' wrong with that. Lots of men out West get themselves a mail-order bride. At least Phil got a purdy one and not a long-faced hag like that Abel Zickenfoose did."

Floyd cackled. "Ain't that the truth. You think that Mrs. Dunn got knocked up and had to find a man to marry fast?"

Aaron gritted his back teeth together and stormed toward the men. "I'd appreciate if you wouldn't talk bad about our guests. And smoking isn't allowed here."

Floyd's hazel eyes went wide, and he straightened. "Sorry, Mr. Harper. We was just passin' time."

Aaron eyed both men. "See that you find a different topic of conversation. And make sure you get that cheroot put out. There's a lot of hay around, and we don't want a fire."

They nodded. Brodie dropped his homemade cigar and ground it out well with his boot before both men made a beeline for the refreshment tables.

Aaron's pa and ma danced over to him and stopped. Ma fanned her face.

"Whew!" Pa said. "I'm gettin' too old to move so fast."

"Aw, you're not old, Pa." Aaron smiled. His father may be fifty-three, but he still worked a full day—a hard day—just like they all did.

"I'm just not used to all this sashayin' around."

Ma whacked him on the arm, a mock glare gleaming in her eyes. "Are you saying you don't want to dance with me, Nick? After all our planning and preparations?"

"No, ma'am. It's just that my feet aren't used to movin' so fast—and at the end of the day, at that."

Aaron winked at his father. "How about we give your shank's mare a rest? You go sit down, and I'll take Ma for a spin."

Ma grinned up at Aaron and looped her arm through his. She swatted one hand at her husband. "You go on, Nick, and take a seat while I dance with my handsome son."

Pa nodded at Aaron and hobbled toward the porch, where several other men sat in rocking chairs.

Ma patted Aaron's arm. "That was kind of you to give your pa a break."

"You know I love dancing with you, but aren't you getting tired? You've been cooking and getting things ready all week."

Ma tugged him toward the dancers. "I can rest tomorrow."

He chuckled and followed her through the crowd. By the time the music had stopped again, he'd worked up a light sweat.

Ma laid her hand across her chest, breathing hard. "That was delightful, but I think your pa might be wiser than me. I'm going to relieve one of the ladies at the refreshment tables for a while."

"Would you like me to fetch a chair for you?"

"Oh, pshaw!" She swatted her hand at him like she had done at Pa not so long ago. "I'm just fine, Son. You go on and have fun. Find a pretty young gal to dance with."

As she walked away, she stopped and greeted a couple, then moved on to someone else. Ma never complained about the hard work at their ranch or the isolation as Della had, but now she had the company of Sarah and Sarah's aunt Emma, who'd recovered from the illness that afflicted her when they first arrived.

The musicians stopped playing and set down their instruments for a short break. All around him, people chatted. Aaron enjoyed spending time with his friends and neighbors, but he missed the quiet of the prairie. He saw Phil Dunn lead his wife toward the refreshment table.

A loud shriek sounded behind him, and he spun around. Corrie raced toward him, then grabbed his arm, and swung around his back. Toby charged forward, a toad in his hand, Mikey loping along behind him. When the boy noticed who his sister had taken cover behind, he skidded to a halt, and Mikey bumped into him from behind.

Toby stuck the critter behind his back and grinned. "Hi, Pa." His gaze flicked to Mikey's freckled face.

Aaron fought to keep his amusement from showing. "What are you boys up to?"

"Uh…nothin' much, Uncle Aaron." Mikey swallowed, his Adam's apple bobbing.

"Toby's got a toad, Pa," Corrie offered as she stuck her head around his arm.

He knew his daughter wasn't particularly frightened by any critter, so he wasn't sure what her game was. "What's goin' on here?"

Corrie stepped to his side. "I was just talking with my friends when these hoodlums wheedled their way into our circle and scared us all with that creature."

Hoodlums? Wheedled? Aaron stared at his eleven-year-old daughter. She was growing up, and he was missing out on a huge chunk of her life because he sent her and Toby to school in Windmill.

"It's true, Pa." Corrie batted her long eyelashes at him.

"Nuh-uh." Toby frowned. "I just wanted her to get me a piece of pie, but she wouldn't."

Corrie leaned toward her brother, her hands on her thin waist. "I was talking with my friends. You can get your own pie."

Aaron gently pushed between his children, watching Mikey back away. "That's true, Son. Why did you ask Corrie to fetch you the pie?"

Toby ducked his head.

Aaron reached out and tilted the boy's chin up, lifting a brow. "Answer me, young man."

Toby's cheeks flushed, and he twitched his mouth to one side. "Because that ol' bat at the table said I couldn't have any more."

Aaron frowned and took hold of Toby's shoulder. "You don't talk about your elders that way."

"But she—"

"No buts."

Toby scuffed his toe in the dirt. "Yes, sir."

"Now, tell me how many slices you've had."

"Three."

"Three!" Corrie exclaimed. "No wonder she told you no."

"I shared one with Mikey." Toby pursed his lips and glared at his sister. But when he looked for Mikey, he saw that his cohort had abandoned him. His hand slipped slowly from behind his back, but Aaron grabbed the toad to avoid another incident.

"Corrie, go on back to your friends. I'll come find you in a dance or two."

"Thanks, Pa. I'll look forward to that." She smiled up at him, then scurried back to the circle of girls. He caught a glimpse of the lovely lady she would one day be and swallowed back the lump building in his throat. With her mother's blue eyes, his dark hair, and her own fair complexion, she was a beauty. Every now and then, he caught a glimpse of Della in one of Corrie's expressions or mannerisms. She was growing up far too fast.

Aaron walked his son away from the crowd that was starting to gather back in the dance area. When they stepped outside the ring of lantern light, he set the toad down. He longed for the days when Toby had been small enough for him to hoist in his arms. Aaron could still manage it physically, but at nine, his son was well past the age of wanting his father to hold him.

"I was just hungry," Toby said. "And it was Mikey's idea, anyway."

"If you eat any more sweets, you're likely to have a bellyache tonight, and you don't want that, do you?"

"I reckon not."

"Now, are you actually hungry? Or did you just want more pie?"

Toby shrugged.

It was just as Aaron thought. The boy had a sweet tooth wider than the Kansas prairie. "If you do get hungry, let me or your grandma know. We'll find you something."

The boy nodded. "Can I go now?"

"One more thing." Aaron took hold of his son's shoulder. "Mikey is your cousin, now that Josh and Sophie have adopted him, but he grew up on the streets. He's still learning to make wise decisions, but you should know better. I expect you to be a good example to him and your other friends. You understand?"

"Yes, sir."

"All right. Go on. But stay away from your sister, toads, and the food."

Toby was running before the words left Aaron's mouth. Beside him, a chuckle sounded, and he swiveled. "Josh. When did you sneak up on me?"

"Right after those two yahoos ran up to you. I figure I might learn more about handling the children by observing you."

Aaron lifted an eyebrow, more than a bit alarmed by his brother's comment. Corrie and Toby had been living with Josh in Windmill and attending school for close to four years now. "Are my kids giving you trouble?"

"No, not any more than normal. Sophie's better with them than I am, although I really don't have many problems with them, either. Mikey is behaving better and better, at least most times." In spite of the shadows, Josh caught his eye. "Corrie and Toby are good kids, Aaron, but they still miss you."

"I miss them, too." For the ten thousandth time, he wondered if he was doing the right thing by sending the kids away for their education. But he kept coming back to the same argument. "Ma and Sarah are too busy working the ranch and tending Sarah's young'uns to teach school."

Josh cleared his throat. "Have you considered taking a wife again? It's been over five years since Della passed."

He rounded on his brother. "That's not a topic for discussion."

Josh ducked his head, making Aaron regret snapping at him.

"Sorry."

"It's all right, but there's something I haven't told you yet—haven't told anyone." Josh looked up again, his eyes reflecting a gleam of the nearest lantern. "Sophie is with child."

Aaron smiled and clasped his brother's shoulder. "That's wonderful news."

Josh glowed with pride. "Yes, it is. Sophie and I decided to wait until after the gathering to tell everyone. We'll do it tomorrow."

"Then why tell me now?" Aaron shifted his feet, suddenly feeling edgy.

Josh heaved a big sigh. "Because I don't know that she ought to be caring for Corrie and Toby, now that she's carrying a baby and also has Mikey to keep corralled."

"But she watched all those young'uns that stayed at her aunt's place."

"True, but she wasn't pregnant then. I'm sure you remember how hard that was on Della, and Sophie has her asthma to be concerned with."

"I hear you. So, what are you saying?"

"I don't know. I just thought we ought to talk about it while I was here."

Aaron would be glad to have his children back home at the ranch, but that would create more work for the womenfolk. Even Sarah's aunt Emma kept busy making much of the family's clothing and new quilts for their beds, as well as doing most of the mending. Who would have time to educate the children?

"Jeff, Sarah's oldest, will be starting school in another year or so," Josh said. "Maybe you could hire an older girl from town to come and teach them."

"Maybe. When is the baby due?"

Josh shrugged. "Doc says late January or early February."

"I'll keep thinking on it and try to come up with a good solution." He'd have to think *and* pray on things, because right now, he had no answers.

Chapter Three

Janie hummed as she danced the broom around the room. That party at the Harpers' ranch four days ago had been the most fun she'd had in a long while. Phil had danced a few tunes with her before she'd taken her turn at the food tables, although that hadn't been easy with Benjy in tow. Thankfully, many of the older girls and other women had taken turns watching the babies and small children so their parents could dance.

She swept her pile of dirt to the doorway, just as Phil pulled the door open. "Stop!"

"Yes, ma'am." He backed away, allowing her to push the dirt onto the porch and then over the edge. "Isn't that tune one of the ones those fellows played at the shindig?

Janie set the broom in the corner and wiped her hands on her apron. "Yes, it is."

"Why don't you sing it? You know how I love to hear your beautiful voice."

Janie shook her head and went inside with Phil following. Ever since giving up on her dream to be an opera singer in favor of raising Benjy, she'd given up on singing. "I don't want to wake Benjy."

Phil snorted a laugh. "That boy loves your humming."

Janie stirred the stew she had simmering for their supper. "That smells delicious, but I may be out late tonight."

She spun around. "Are you going somewhere?"

Phil opened the gun cabinet, reached for his rifle, then closed the door. "I'm going hunting this afternoon. With winter not far off, I need to fill the smoke shed."

"Once Benjy starts walking, you're going to have to lock that cabinet."

Her brother frowned. "I hadn't thought of that. I rather like being able to grab them quickly when I need one."

"Perhaps you could mount the cabinet on the wall, so it's out of his reach. That would work for a while."

He nodded. "I'll think on it."

"Be careful out there." Janie kissed his bristly cheek. "I wouldn't object if you found a turkey or some prairie hens."

Phil winked. "I'll see what I can do."

Janie stood at the door and watched him ride off. Though Phil was nearly ten years older than she, they'd always been fairly close. What would she and Benjy have done if they hadn't been able to live here?

She sighed and shut the door. There was too much work to do to dwell on "what if?" She peeked in the room she shared with Benjy. He lay sprawled in the bed that Phil had made for him. Janie smiled. She couldn't love him more if he'd been formed in her own womb.

But now, she had to hurry outside and gather the laundry off the line before he awakened. Since the rabies warning, she'd been too fearful to let him play on a blanket like he had in the past while she gathered up the clean clothing.

She grabbed her basket, shoved a pistol in her apron pocket, and stepped outside, shutting the door behind her. As she danced her way to the clothesline, she pretended the basket was her partner. She closed her eyes, and Aaron Harper stood before her, just as he had the night of the dance. He'd taken her hand with a warm smile and spun her around before moving on to the next lady in line. Janie blew out a sigh. When would she stop thinking about that man?

⁓

Aaron guided his horse along the narrow creek bank, still pondering his conversation with Josh. His whole family had been thrilled that Sophie was carrying her first baby, but no one had considered how that might affect Corrie and Toby. Josh was right that childbearing had been hard on Della, although Sarah hadn't seemed to have much trouble with it. Still, Sophie had health problems that neither of the other women had to deal with, and Josh was wise to be watching out for her.

But where did that leave Aaron? God had yet to answer his prayers or give him guidance about finding a way to hire a teacher for Corrie and Toby. Another thought was to find someone else in town who would be willing to let his children board with him, but the thought of leaving them with a person who wasn't family bothered Aaron. What if the people didn't treat his offspring as well as they did their own?

He slapped the reins loudly against his chaps, and his horse trembled but didn't spook. He patted the gelding. "Sorry, Outlaw."

Off to his left, an animal growled. Aaron yanked his pistol from his holster and reined the horse toward the sound. It came from the other side of the creek, but the trees lining the water blocked his view.

More snarls sounded. A man cried out. A gun blasted, and the animal yelped.

Aaron nudged his horse across the creek, and they cautiously wended their way through the wooded area. Beyond the tree line, the prairie leveled out again, and Aaron spied a horse trotting off—a horse he recognized. Phil's.

"Phil? Where are you?"

"Here."

Aaron swallowed hard at the scratchy sound of Phil Dunn's voice. He dismounted, tied his horse to a sapling, and hurried through the shrubs and tall grass, keeping watch for a wounded man.

Phil lay in a patch of clover, blood covering his thigh. Three feet away lay a dead coyote. Aaron's gut churned as he squatted beside his friend.

Phil's pain-filled eyes turned his way. "There's no help for me. I know that."

Aaron wanted to tell him that was nonsense, that it was only a bite—a bad bite, but it would heal. Yet the words wouldn't slip past his tight throat. He'd seen the foaming saliva surrounding the coyote's mouth. Seen the animal's wide, bloodshot eyes.

Rabies.

Oh, God. How could You let this happen?

Aaron fired two more bullets into the coyote's carcass to make sure it was dead.

"Don't waste your ammunition. I killed the beast." Phil struggled to sit. Claw marks trailed across the back of one hand, and his left thigh looked nearly chewed in half. Blood saturated Phil's pant leg and the ground around it.

Aaron's heart broke as he knelt down and helped his friend to sit up. "What can I do?"

Phil held on to his leg, above the wound. "Ain't nothin' to do. You and me both know that critter had the hydrophobia. I'm a dead man. Best thing you could do for me is to shoot me." Phil glanced up with tears in his eyes. "Janie doesn't deserve to watch me die a little each day until I go mad."

Aaron's gut clenched. He wanted desperately to do something to help his friend, but there was no chance he would shoot him. "I'll take you to Ma. If anyone can help, she can."

Phil grabbed Aaron's arm. "I need to know you'll take care of Janie for me, Aaron. It's a lot to ask, but she'll need your help." He squeezed hard. "Promise me you will."

Aaron nodded. "Of course. You don't even have to ask." He stood. "I need to get you home and then send for the doctor." And he had to bury the coyote's carcass as soon as possible before other animals got to it.

"Would you please go catch my horse? Janie will need him, and I don't want him runnin' off."

Wrestling with what to do first, Aaron took several steps away. He gazed out across the thigh-high grasses and saw Phil's horse, Smokey, in the distance. It looked as if it was grazing. "Your horse is just over—"

The blast of a gun ricocheted across the prairie. Aaron spun back to Phil and sucked in a ragged breath. His friend slumped over to his side, blood spilling out across his chest.

❧

Janie sat on the porch, rocking Benjy. The boy had been restless this evening, probably because Phil had yet to return. He had missed supper, and she prayed he hadn't run into any problems. Hopefully he had just wandered further from home than planned.

Crickets battled one another in song, and a light breeze cooled her after an afternoon of working in the warm kitchen. The sun had set, but the western horizon was painted in such a glorious display of pink, purple, and vermillion that it almost took her breath away. Sunsets were one thing she loved about the Kansas prairie.

The old rocker creaked out a tune. The wooden spindles Phil had attached from the porch floor to the railings, as well as the gate she could close where the steps reached the porch, allowed Benjy a place to play outdoors and added to her security. As did the pistol lying on the table beside her. Kansas may be lovely in many ways, but she never took anything for granted. Life was tenuous here. Danger existed around almost every corner, but she hoped—prayed—that she and Benjy would remain safe. That they were far enough from Boston that Carolyn's husband would never find them—if he were searching for them.

Janie glanced down at her boy and smiled. Benjy's thumb had fallen from his mouth as he relaxed in slumber. She kissed his soft cheek, then carried her precious bundle to the room she shared with him. After laying him in bed, she covered him with a blanket.

How could Martin Metcalf not want his son? If he knew the child existed. She wished she knew if he did, but she dare not write a soul to question it, for fear of him seeing the missive and tracking her down. She had no doubt he would kill her.

Janie shook off her somber thoughts and washed her supper bowl and spoon, as well as Benjy's. She stirred the stew pot that still sat on the stove. What could be keeping Phil?

Returning to the porch, she leaned against a post and stared out across the prairie. Phil's cattle and two big draft horses grazed on the far side of the barn among the tall grass that waved to her as the wind caught it. Lucy, their milk cow, stood at the pasture gate, bellowing. It was far past milking time, and now that Benjy was asleep, she'd better tend to the task. Phil would be tired and hungry after his long day of hunting, and this was one thing she could do to help him. She peeked at Benjy again, then shut the front door and hurried toward the pasture gate.

Twenty minutes later, Janie turned down the lantern and closed the barn door. She glanced around the dusky shadows as she headed for the cellar but still didn't see Phil riding in. Where was he? Her brother had left her alone at night only when he'd had to travel by train to Windmill for supplies. What if his horse had spooked and thrown him, and he was lying wounded somewhere?

Pushing back her apprehension, she carried the milk down the dark steps, set the bucket on the table, and felt around for the cheesecloth they used for a cover. With that intact, she secured the cellar door and hurried back into the house. Guilt nibbled at her for not putting the draft horses in the barn, but she prayed they'd be all right for one night. They always trotted away from her, and she wasn't about to go chasing the big beasts in the dark.

The quiet of the prairie no longer frightened her as it had at first, but she still didn't care to be outside alone at night. Too many wild critters roamed about in the dark. She hung a lit lantern from the hook on the porch to light Phil's way. Inside, she turned up the two lamps in the parlor and sat in her rocker. She picked up her mending, but with her mind running rampant, she couldn't concentrate on her work. "Please, Father, keep Phil safe. Watch over him, wherever he is, and let him know that we're all right."

She blew out a sigh, leaned toward the light, and lifted her needle. Someone stomped up the porch steps. Janie jumped, but then her heart settled. Phil was finally home. She tucked the needle through the button on her brother's shirt and pulled it out the underside.

A rap sounded at the door. Janie froze. Phil never knocked. She tossed her mending into her the basket and stood. She fumbled for the pistol that weighed heavy in her apron pocket, and nearly dropped it. "Who's there?"

"It's Aaron Harper, ma'am."

Relief at the familiar voice nearly made her legs give out. She laid the gun on the drum table beside the lamp and hurried to open the door. "Come in, Mr. Harper. Is Phil with you, by chance?"

He stepped inside and pulled off his hat, wringing the brim. His expression was more somber than she'd ever seen it. Anxiety churned in her stomach. "What's wrong? Did something happen at your ranch?"

"No, ma'am." He lifted his gaze, and the pain in his dark brown eyes nearly made her knees buckle. "It's your husband." He looked away, and she could see his throat move as he swallowed.

Janie's whole body trembled, and she tried to see past the man, but his large frame filled the doorway. "What about Phil? Is he hurt?"

"I'm sorry to have to tell you, but he's dead."

"What? How?" *Oh Lord, no.*

"He was attacked by a coyote." The grief in Aaron Harper's gentle gaze was her undoing.

Tears she couldn't stop flowed down her cheeks. "But surely he isn't gone. People recover from animal bites every day." She tried to push past him. "Let me see him. Phil?" she yelled.

Aaron took her by the arms and gave her a gentle shake. "Look at me, ma'am."

She didn't want to. Didn't want to see the truth in his eyes.

"Please, Mrs. Dunn."

At his soft appeal, she lifted her gaze, dreading what he had to say.

"The coyote that bit your husband was rabid. There's no recovering from a bite from an animal with rabies."

Thoughts of her gentle brother hurting and dying broke her heart. *Oh, Phil.* He truly was dead. She gulped back a sob, but the next wail refused to be squelched. "No. It can't be."

Aaron pulled her against his sturdy chest and patted her back. "Shh…you'll be all right."

In spite of how comforting his arms felt, she stepped back, angered at his efforts to pacify her. "How can I be all right? My br—Phil is gone. What will happen to Benjy and me?"

She didn't wait for his answer. She needed to get away—to hold her son. Janie fled the room, closed her bedroom door, and collapsed on the bed, crying.

What would she do now? How would she manage without Phil's quiet encouragement and support?

Why, God? Why did You allow this to happen?

Chapter Four

Aaron exhaled loudly as he led his horse and Phil's to the barn. Had he done the right thing? Maybe he should have waited to tell Mrs. Dunn about her husband until after his ma arrived and could have sat with her. She obviously didn't want *his* comfort, but he couldn't blame her. She barely knew him.

The cow bellowed at him as he entered the barn. He turned up the lantern and put his horse in the stall next to it. Outlaw could wait until he tended to Phil's body. The man ought to be laid out in the house, but then, where would his wife sleep? Aaron took the lantern to the back of the barn where the buckboard was parked. That would do for now. In the tack room, he found several old horse blankets. He laid out two of them in the back of the buckboard and then untied Phil's body from his horse. Aaron shouldered his friend's body and carried the man to his wagon, laid him down, and crossed Phil's arms over his chest.

Aaron's eyes blurred as he stared at Phil. The man's face was pale, and dried blood saturated his shirt and pant leg. His friend was gone.

He understood why Phil had chosen to end his life, but it still bothered him. Aaron could never do such a thing, even though, given the same circumstances, he'd be facing a slow, agonizing death. Even though his family would be forced to watch him deteriorate and eventually lose his mind. There was no recovery from a bite by an animal with hydrophobia. Phil knew that and had wanted to spare his wife from having to go through those agonizing days of watching his deterioration and waiting for his certain death. But by taking his own life, he had robbed Mrs. Dunn of the chance to say good-bye.

Aaron rubbed the back of his neck. Phil must have thought he was making the right choice to end his life so suddenly. But Aaron felt that taking a life—even one's own—was wrong. Still, what was done was done. All Aaron could do now was pray for Mrs. Dunn and her child, and see to things around the ranch until she could make plans.

Aaron covered Phil's corpse with the last blanket, then brushed down the horses and fed them. The cow had already been milked, so there was nothing else left to do. He secured the barn doors and stared at the house, illuminated by the moonlight. What would Mrs. Dunn do now? Would she return East to her family? Would she want to sell out? *Lord, comfort her and give her wisdom. Show her what to do.*

He sat in one of the porch rockers, glad that the night air hadn't chilled as much as it would in the coming weeks. The wind had stopped blowing, and the evening was peaceful, oblivious to the turmoil he and Mrs. Dunn struggled with. He considered checking on her, but the few females he knew preferred to be alone when they were distraught.

Resting his head against the back of the chair, he marveled at how fast life could change. If only he'd ridden in Phil's direction five minutes earlier, he might have prevented the coyote attack. He thought of his friend and how happy he had been, dancing with his wife just a few days ago. Aaron had been glad when Phil finally married and no longer had to live alone. In spite of what he'd said about being content as a bachelor, he'd smiled much more since the arrival of Janie and the baby. Too bad Phil never had a child of his own. Aaron supposed it was still possible that he could, if Mrs. Dunn was already expecting, but another baby would only make things harder for her.

Aaron shook his head to rid it of such thoughts. Phil had been a good friend who would be missed by all who knew him. Aaron hadn't lost someone close to him since Della died, and now the memories he had pushed into the dark recesses of his mind charged back with full force. He'd been angry with Ethan for a long while for not stopping Della from racing horses that day, but then, Aaron knew that no one could have kept his wife from doing something she was determined to do, no matter how frivolous. The truth was, Aaron felt responsible for her death. He never should have married the beautiful socialite, regardless of how fast and hard he'd fallen for her. She was never happy at the stage stop, which had been the family business before the Harpers had expanded to ranching. She craved interaction with people—not her children but neighbors, adults, anyone she could use as an excuse to get away from home for a while. He should have done more to make her happy, but there was always so much work to be done. And nothing he'd tried had satisfied her. Had he given up trying at some point? Was he to blame for her unhappiness?

No. Ma and even Sarah had lived a life similar to Della's before they married, and they were both quite happy. Even though Sarah had grown up in Chicago, she'd molded into a prairie wife with ease once she decided marrying Ethan was what she wanted.

Maybe the problem was Aaron. Maybe he hadn't been a good enough husband.

A horse whinnied from the direction of Phil's pasture, snapping him from his reverie. Aaron released his tight grip on the chair.

He'd prayed for God to send him another wife, but that hadn't happened. He knew he was forgiven for not being the best of husbands to Della, but a part of him still struggled with it. Maybe God didn't think he deserved another wife.

No, he wouldn't believe that. When the time was right, God would open that door. Aaron glanced in the direction of the Harper ranch, wishing to see a wagon bringing his ma and Sarah in the moonlight. Mrs. Dunn needed the comfort of other women, certainly not something he could offer.

The next few days would be busy as plans for Phil's burial were made. Tomorrow, Aaron would build a casket. Maybe he could send for Josh, who was more skilled in woodworking. Josh would want to attend the funeral, since he'd also known Phil, and would probably be happy to help.

Aaron blew out a sigh. What would happen to the Dunns' ranch? He surveyed the barn's silhouette. It wasn't as large as the Harpers' big barn, but it was adequate for a property this size. If Mrs. Dunn decided to sell, Aaron might be interested, but he sure wouldn't pressure her to decide any time soon. He had some money saved, but not enough to buy Phil's land. His father and Ethan might see it as a wise investment, since the Dunn ranch butted up next to Harper land.

The idea of having his own place appealed to him more than he would have expected. The Harper ranch had been home ever since his family left Ohio when he was young, but it seemed more his father's land than his. Sure, his pa would divide it up between the three brothers in his will, but there were many issues that would cause problems—even though his family was peaceable—like who would own the two houses. Josh and Sophie lived in town, but they might want to return to the land one day. Ethan and Sarah lived in the smaller house they'd all worked together to build when Aaron was preparing to marry

Della, so they probably felt the place was theirs. Aaron had thought over the scenario many times but couldn't work it all out. He and his brothers would never fight over the land, but there were practical, logistical questions to settle.

The glow of a lantern bouncing to his right and the jingle of harnesses pulled him from his thoughts. Ma and Sarah had finally arrived, with Ethan as escort.

⌒

The September sun heated Janie's shoulders, but its warmth couldn't find its way to her cold heart. She stared at the hole in the ground where her brother's body lay as the minister from Windmill droned on. The Harper men had fashioned a lovely casket—almost too pretty to hide in a grave, with its simple ivy scroll work surrounding Phil's initials.

The letters blurred. Janie sniffed, then dabbed at her nose with her damp handkerchief. The minister said a prayer and then closed his Bible. A woman she didn't know started singing "Amazing Grace," but Janie's voice refused to join in when the other attendees' did.

Her brother was dead—her last living family member. Janie felt as if she'd been orphaned again. Benjy kicked his feet and then expelled an angry squeal, and she realized she had been holding him too tight. But she needed his closeness—whatever small comfort a one-year-old could give when he had no idea of the sad circumstances of the day.

Even so, she could tell that Benjy missed Phil. Several times she'd seen him watching the door, and he had crawled over to Phil's chair and patted it, as if asking where he was. Her heart clenched. Benjy wouldn't remember Phil. Tears filled her aching eyes once again.

Karen Harper, sitting on her left side, passed her a clean handkerchief. She accepted the gift and nodded her thanks. The Harper women had been such a blessing. They'd cooked for a day and a half, done laundry, tended the garden, and even recruited their men to play with Benjy. How would she have managed without their help? What would she do when they went home this evening and left her all alone?

Janie jumped as a clod of dirt hit the top of Phil's casket. One by one, people stood, made their way to the grave, and added another handful of soil, until Janie was the last person remaining. She had to get through this last task, and then she could escape to her room with the excuse of Benjy needing a nap—at least until she'd have to join everyone for the meal.

Aaron Harper and his mother waited for her while the others walked toward the house. Benjy spotted them and cried out, probably for Aaron, but it was Karen who came forward with a gentle smile on her face. "Let me hold him while you say good-bye to your husband."

Your husband. Janie cringed on the inside at the reference to her spouse, but she passed Benjy to the older woman, then turned back to the grave. Two of the Harpers' ranch hands stood by, hats and shovels in hand, waiting with lowered heads for her to finish so they could complete the burial.

She stared down at her brother's fancy initials, partly hidden by the dirt strewn across the lid of the casket. Had her coming here brought him any happiness? She hoped so. He had fallen hard and fast for Benjy. Her throat stung as she fought the frustrating tears. "Oh, Phillip. Why did you have to die?"

An arm wrapped around her shoulder. Karen, again. "It's all right to cry, dear."

But crying wouldn't bring her brother back. And it wouldn't help her decide what to do now.

She tossed her wilting rosebud into the grave, said a silent good-bye to her brother, and turned away. Before she could reach Aaron, dirt resumed thudding on top of the casket. Aaron, holding Benjy, looked past her, frowned, and shook his head. The noise instantly stopped. His consideration touched her heart.

Benjy rested his head on Aaron's broad shoulder, his eyes fighting to stay open. For a second, Janie was jealous of the imp. But she'd just buried her husband—so the world thought—and she wasn't about to seek comfort from another man, even if he offered. Aaron's sympathetic gaze almost made her waver, but she leaned toward his mother instead.

"Let's get you back inside where you can lie down," Karen suggested. "You look as exhausted as your son."

Your son. Another lie. And yet, in all ways important, Benjy was her child, even though she hadn't birthed him. Still, she wished she could be honest with these kind folks. That she could quit telling falsehoods.

She had let Phil talk her into pretending to be his bride and had regretted it ever since. But the die had been cast. There was no turning back.

⌒

Aaron's heart ached for Mrs. Dunn. She looked so alone, even with Ma's arm wrapped around her shoulders. He knew some of what she was feeling, but things were far different for a woman who had lost a husband than the other way around. And Aaron had been surrounded by a big, loving family to help him and his children move past the hard days following Della's death.

As he walked back to the Dunns' house with the women, he patted Benjy gently. The poor child had lost two fathers in his young life—two fathers he would never remember. Phil had never told Aaron how he'd met Janie or what had happened to her before she arrived here, but she must have been a widow, because his friend never would have married a shady lady. Phil had been a good churchgoing man, and it was a shame that Benjy would never get to benefit from the man's wisdom. Maybe in time, God would see fit to send along another good man to help Mrs. Dunn and her son.

But then, God had yet to send Aaron another wife, and it was five years since Della had died.

Not that he'd been looking too hard for one.

As they approached the house, Aaron saw his brothers and their wives preparing to leave in the wagon. Josh sat on the wagon bench, and Ethan stood beside it, holding his wailing toddler, Mark, in his arms. He kissed Sarah, then climbed aboard. Sarah handed four-year-old Jeff up to Josh, and he settled the boy on the bench next to his uncle. Jeff waved when he saw Aaron.

Smiling at his nephew, Aaron stopped beside the wagon, while the women surrounded Mrs. Dunn, preparing to accompany her to the cabin. Mrs. Dunn turned back toward him.

"Go on inside, if you'd like," he told her. "I'll bring Benjy in after I talk to my brothers."

She nodded, then followed the other women into the house.

Mark reared back in Ethan's arms, sucked in a breath, and let out another yowl.

Josh teasingly covered his ears and grimaced. "Is that what I have to look forward to?"

Ethan grinned and pressed his son against his shoulder. "He's got good lungs, at least."

Aaron rested his hand on the rump of the nearest horse. "Y'all are headed back home, I reckon."

Josh nodded. "I need to be there for tomorrow's train. I'm anxious to get home to Sophie and the children." He held out his hand, and Aaron shook it. "Sorry about Phil, big brother."

Aaron ignored his comment about returning to the children, because it hurt that their uncle, not their father, was the one headed home to them. Aaron knew his brother was just stating a fact. "Thank you for coming on such short notice and helping with the casket. It looked real nice."

Josh nodded. "My pleasure."

"Guess we'd better get going," Ethan said. "Sarah thought it best that these guys take a nap in their own beds. She wanted to stay and help with the meal, so I drew the short straw." His grin indicated he didn't mind the task. "I'll get these yahoos settled, then check on things around the ranch. You staying awhile?"

Aaron rubbed his hand along Benjy's back. The boy lay limply, deep in sleep. "I thought I'd hang around here for the next week or so and help Mrs. Dunn with the stock. She may not realize it yet, but she's going to need assistance."

"Yep." Ethan pursed his lips. "Too bad about Phil. I know he was a close friend and a good man."

"He certainly was." Josh lowered his head.

Aaron's throat had tightened, so he just nodded.

"Mama!" Mark pushed against his father's chest. Ethan patiently patted the boy. "It's all right, little buddy. We're going for a ride. Wanna help me drive?"

"I do!" Jeff bounced on his knees on the bench. Josh wrapped his arm around the boy.

Ethan winked at Jeff. "Mark first, then you, pardner." He climbed aboard and handed Mark to Josh.

"Aww. Yes, sir." Jeff relaxed against his uncle's arm, his short legs dangling.

Stepping back, Aaron waved them forward. "See you later, maybe."

"Yep." Josh released the brake, jiggled the reins he held in one hand, and clucked out one side of his mouth. He turned Mark around on his lap, letting the toddler hold the end of the reins. The horse lifted its head and plodded forward, the buggy creaking as the wheels set into motion.

The sight of his youngest brother with his own children created a craving to see Corrie and Toby, but Aaron had thought it best they not miss school to attend the funeral of a man they'd met only a few times. Josh had come alone, helped with the casket, and left right after the burial service. Still, it didn't stop Aaron from missing his children. He rested his head against Benjy's for a moment, drawing comfort from the sleeping child. The boy's soft breaths tickled his neck and sent waves of fatherly love washing through him.

But he wasn't Benjy's father.

Maybe he could help with the boy, though. Give Mrs. Dunn some time to herself and teach Benjy to do boy stuff, like fishing and riding a horse—if his mother decided to stay long enough for him to reach an appropriate age for such things.

Aaron chuckled at his thoughts of the future. Benjy would need to learn to walk first.

Suddenly he sobered. Here he was, thinking of teaching things to Phil's son, when his own son and daughter had been sent away. His kids were growing up fast, and he was missing out on so much of their young lives. But they needed to have an education. And they needed a father. Their spotty weekend trips home weren't enough for him. He blew out a loud sigh. There were no easy answers.

Aaron nodded at a couple of his neighbors who stood outside the cabin talking as he climbed the porch steps. He felt

God leading him to stay at least a few days to help Mrs. Dunn. Pa and Ethan could well handle the ranch for a time without his help—and that fact both gladdened and saddened him. He knocked on the door, feeling confused and out of sorts, like a horse whose rider tugged both reins in different directions at the same time.

He was a father without his children. A man wanting to marry but without any prospects. A rancher tending someone else's land. And one of his closest friends had just been buried.

This wasn't the time to be making decisions. He just needed to get through each day, one step at a time, and God would show him what to do when the time was right.

Chapter Five

Janie lay in her bed, hugging her quilt. She didn't want to get up—didn't want to move. Today was the first day since Phil's death that not at least one of the Harper women would be there. She was alone. Just her and Benjy.

She sniffed and wiped her scratchy eyes. Every time she'd awakened last night, she'd been crying. What was she going to do? How would she get by without her brother? Should she sell the ranch and move to town? Was the ranch even hers to sell?

She forced herself to sit up. Phil never talked business with her, other than to mention the crops he'd planted or harvested, and to tell her when he'd bought more cattle. She had no idea how many head they had or how to care for them. What if the ranch was mortgaged? Would she lose her home? So many questions and no answers.

Benjy lay jabbering in his bed on the other side of the small room. She had to get up and tend him, or he'd be wailing before long.

A cranky cow bellowed. Time for milking. And collecting eggs. And that meant going outside. With the rabies scare, she'd been afraid to take Benjy outdoors, which made getting chores done much harder. Now she wouldn't have a choice. The pressure of all she had to do weighed down her shoulders to the point where she could hardly move. "Oh, Phil. Why did you have to die and leave us alone?"

A Bible verse about God giving her peace and an expected end came to mind. She knew she should have faith, but everything looked so hopeless. How could she get by without Phil and his ever-present smile and encouragement? And Benjy…he loved Phil so much.

A knock sounded at the front door, and Janie jumped. Who could that be? She grabbed her wrapper and shoved her arms into the sleeves, then snatched Phil's pistol off the vanity. Tiptoeing to the front door, she kept her ears alert. What should she do? Answer it? Ignore the unwanted guest?

"Mrs. Dunn, it's just me, Aaron Harper. I've got your eggs here."

Her heart lurched but then calmed. "Just leave them by the door, Mr. Harper, and I'll get them in a few minutes."

"Yes, ma'am." The basket thumped as he set it down, but he didn't walk away.

Benjy let out an excited squeal, probably expecting to see Phil. Tears stung Janie's eyes.

"I'll go milk the cow now, ma'am." His footsteps moved across the porch, then stopped. "If you'd like, I can turn my hand at a skillet. I'd be happy to fry up those eggs for you and the boy."

Janie shook her head. Talking to her benevolent neighbor through the door was ridiculous. She opened it and peered out through the crack. "Thank you for your kind offer, Mr. Harper, but I can manage breakfast. Please come back after the milking and join Benjy and me."

He offered a soft smile and a nod, then lifted the basket of eggs and held them out for her. The sympathetic look in his eyes brought fresh tears. She opened the door wider and accepted the basket. As he turned, she started to close the door, but then she paused and watched him hop down the steps and cover the distance to the barn in a smooth, long-legged gait. Finally, Janie closed the door. As much as the man intrigued her, she preferred to be alone. But the fact was, she needed help. What would she do when Aaron Harper tired of assisting her?

She rushed through her ablutions and getting her and Benjy dressed, then hurried into the kitchen, with the boy on her hip. She didn't want Mr. Harper to have to wait on her since she was certain he must have pressing work at his own ranch. After tying Benjy in his chair with the wide band she'd made, she pacified him with a bread crust.

Phil usually brought her some bacon or ham from the smoke shed to cook for breakfast, but this morning, she'd make do without. Scrambled eggs with fried onions and potatoes, along with some slices of the bread that Karen Harper had made before the funeral, should be enough—at least, she hoped it would. Phil wasn't too big of an eater, but a man the size of Aaron Harper… She pulled another large potato out of the bin.

As she was dishing up the meal, another knock sounded at her door. She set the large bowl on the table next to the plate of sliced bread, smiled at Benjy, and wiped her hands on her apron as she scurried toward the door. Her heart pounded. Inviting an unmarried man into her home wasn't exactly proper, but then, who would know? And he was helping her.

She pulled open the door and stepped back, pressing her free hand against her swirling stomach. Aaron stood at the door, holding a pail of milk, looking less confident than she'd ever seen him. Had something happened?

He peered inside, looking in the direction of the table, then at her. "Are you sure that you want me to join you inside, ma'am? I don't mind eating on the porch."

Besides being kind and so handsome he stole her breath, he was considerate. "It's fine, Mr. Harper. If it will make you more comfortable, I can leave the door open. The sun is burning off the earlier chill."

Benjy squealed.

Aaron's lips cocked up on one side. "I promise to be a gentleman."

Janie waved her hand toward the table. "I've never known you to be otherwise. Please come in."

He wiped his boots on the porch floor, then stepped inside. She propped the pig-shaped cast-iron door stopper in place, then reached for the bucket of milk. "I can take that."

"No need. Just tell me where you'd like it."

She pulled her hand back, her fingers tingling from touching his. She cleared her throat. "Um…the cupboard would be fine."

He set the bucket down and stepped back, looking at the table. He frowned. "You want me to sit in Phil's spot?"

Janie placed a piece of cloth over the milk pail and spun around. "I…uh…just put it there by habit. Do you mind?"

Aaron shrugged. "I don't suppose it bothers me if you're fine with it."

"I am. Please have a seat." She took the butter bowl and jar of jam off the counter and set them on the table, then lowered herself into her chair.

Benjy squealed. She glanced at him and realized that he was staring at her guest. The boy's face puckered, and he let out an ear-splitting wail. Janie jumped up and checked the band around his waist to make sure it hadn't pinched him. "What's wrong, sweetie?"

He tossed his gummy bread crust in Mr. Harper's direction and squealed once more.

"I don't think he wants me sitting here."

"He's probably wondering where Phil is." Janie untied the boy. "I'm sorry he's disrupting our meal."

Aaron shook his head. "He doesn't bother me. I'm a father, remember?"

Janie sat down, holding Benjy on her lap. He quieted and reached for her spoon. "Would you care to bless the food, Mr. Harper? Phil always did that."

"If you're sure you don't mi—"

"Please don't keep saying that. If I minded, I wouldn't have asked." As she bowed her head, she wondered what he must think of her. She'd had him take Phil's seat, and now, he was saying the blessing. She hoped he didn't think she was trying to replace Phil.

"Heavenly Father, we ask Your blessing over this meal and the hands that prepared it. Comfort Mrs. Dunn and her son and give her guidance and wisdom. In Jesus' name, amen."

He looked up but didn't start eating. He must be waiting on her.

"Go ahead and take as much as you'd like," Janie told him. "Your mother blessed us with more bread than we could eat in weeks."

He took two slices and glanced her way. "You have your hands full. Would you mind if I served you?"

Rendered unable to speak by his gracious offer, she shook her head and then watched as he spooned a generous helping of eggs and potatoes onto her plate, followed by a slice of bread. Aaron was a man of rare thoughtfulness. Janie's brother was always kind and generous, but he'd lived alone for so long that he didn't tend to notice things like, when she held Benjy, she couldn't serve herself very easily. Even her father hadn't treated her mother with such benevolence. But all of the Harpers she'd gotten to know seemed the same—selfless and bighearted.

"These eggs are mighty good with the potatoes and onions mixed in." He smiled and took another bite.

"Thank you. I'm sorry there isn't any meat. Phil brought some in from the smokehouse most mornings, but I didn't want to leave Benjy to go get it."

"I don't mind not having meat, but if you need something like that, feel free to ask me to get it."

She fed Benjy a bite of eggs, thinking how his comment made it sound as if he'd be staying for a while. The thought both comforted and unnerved her. "Might I ask what your plans are, Mr. Harper?"

He washed down his food with a sip of coffee. "I thought I'd ride out and check on the cattle today."

"Surely, you have things to do at your own ranch. I don't expect you to work mine."

"I don't want to be an intrusion in your life, but I promised Phil I'd watch out for you. That's what I'm doing—for as long as you need me."

Janie didn't know what to say. "I can't pay you, I'm afraid. I don't even know if Phil had any money."

Aaron gazed in the direction of the window. "I don't mean to intrude, but have you looked for his papers? He should have a bank book if he has an account—or at least a money box."

In spite of his help, she felt the conversation had taken a turn in a direction she wasn't ready to go—toward a subject he had no business asking about. "If you'll excuse me, I need to go change Benjy."

He stood when she did, his eyebrows tilted downward.

Footsteps sounded on the porch, and then there was a hard knock on the doorframe. A man stuck his head in the open doorway. He wasn't as tall as her neighbor but looked just as rugged. Whiskers covered his chin. "Anybody home?"

"Allenby?" Mr. Harper walked to the door. "You need something?"

There was an edge to his tone Janie hadn't heard before. Was there something about Mr. Allenby he didn't like, or was it the intrusion?

Mr. Allenby smirked, his dark eyes holding a glint that sent a shiver up Janie's spine. "Well, well. Looks like you've already staked a claim, Harper."

"Looks can be deceiving."

Janie knew she had to step forward, or Mr. Allenby would certainly believe what he'd said. She hoisted Benjy up on her hip and strode to the door, then stepped past Mr. Harper onto the porch. "Mr. Harper has been kind enough to help out here, but this is still my ranch. How can I help you, Mr. Allenby?"

He chuckled. "She sure put you in yer place, Harper." He tipped his grungy hat. "Mornin', ma'am. I sure was sorry to hear about your husband."

Janie could hardly think straight with Aaron Harper breathing down her neck. "Thank you."

Mr. Allenby looked past her for a moment. "I don't reckon I could talk to the widow alone, could I?"

"I don't think that's a good idea." Aaron shuffled behind her.

Irritated at the man's gumption, she spun around. "This is my house, Mr. Harper. I can talk to whomever I please, in private or not."

Aaron's expression turned steely, and he nodded. "Yes, ma'am." He stepped around her, and Allenby moved out of the doorway, a gleam of victory in his gaze.

Janie's stomach clenched. Had she just made a big mistake?

⌒

Aaron strode away from the house, angry at himself for caring that Mrs. Dunn had dressed him down in front of Deke Allenby. She had no idea what kind of man Allenby was. Halfway to the barn, he spun around and started back toward the house.

"We ain't been introduced properly," Allenby began. "My name's Deke Allenby, ma'am. I work at the livery in town." He glanced over his shoulder and scowled at Aaron.

Mrs. Dunn's eyes widened when she saw him approaching. Instead of going to the porch, he aimed for the side of the house and passed by without comment. He hoped they would think he was headed to the privy. The barn was too far away for him to listen in on Allenby's plan—and he had no doubt the man had one. Aaron opened the privy door, glad that it creaked, and then shut it harder than normal without going in. He hurried back to the rear of the house and then around to the far side, stopping when he reached the open kitchen window. He wasn't normally one to eavesdrop, but he'd made a promise to Phil, and he meant to keep it. And keeping it meant finding out what Allenby had up his sleeve.

"I know there ain't been much time that's passed since you lost your husband, but I reckon you've found out how hard it is for a woman to run a ranch on her own. I've managed to put back a hundred dollars. I reckon that's a fair offer."

Aaron thought he heard Mrs. Dunn gasp—and right she was to do so. One hundred dollars was closer to a quarter the value of a ranch the size of Phil's. He peered through the window and was able to see the right side of her, where Benjy sat on her hip. The boy reached up and grabbed one of the pins in her hair. She quickly shifted him to her other hip and took a step to the left. Aaron had lost his view of them, but now he had Allenby in his sights.

"I'm sorry, but I haven't had time to make any decisions. If I do decide to sell, I will consider your offer, Mr. Allenby."

"Has Harper offered for it yet?"

"That's none of your business."

Aaron had to admire the starch in her voice.

"He will if he hasn't. Why do you think he's hanging around here? He's trying to get the lay of the land and weasel in on your good side."

Aaron closed his fist. Talk about a weasel. A man couldn't get much lower than trying to swindle a young widow. He strode back to the privy, opened the door, and slammed it again. Then he marched back to the front of the house.

"Time for you to go, Allenby." Aaron untied the man's horse from the porch railing and handed him the reins.

"That ain't for you to say."

Aaron narrowed his eyes. "Well, I said it, so get on your horse and ride."

The man looked him over, as if weighing his chances of physically overpowering him, but Aaron had a good six inches on him. "I reckon my business here is done." He turned to Mrs. Dunn and tipped his hat. "Ma'am. I hope you'll consider my offer."

"I will. If I decide to sell."

Allenby mounted his horse, glared at Aaron with his lips turned up into a snarl, and then reined his horse around and kicked it hard. The animal jumped and trotted away from the house.

Aaron watched to make sure the man didn't return.

"You were quite rude to him, Mr. Harper."

"Rude?" Here he was, watching out for her welfare, and she thought he was rude?

She shifted Benjy back to her right hip. "You treated him quite despicably."

He strode toward her, and when he stepped onto the porch, her eyes widened, and she backed up. Guilt over frightening her gnawed at him, but she had to know the truth. "That man tried to swindle you. He offered you a fourth of what this ranch is worth."

She blinked her eyes several times, as if absorbing his words. "Is what he said correct?"

Aaron stared at her, unsure what she was referring to.

"Do you want to buy my ranch? Is that why you're here helping me?"

Aaron's mouth dropped open. Is that really what she thought? "I won't lie to you, Mrs. Dunn. If you decide to sell, I'd be interested in making you an offer—a fair offer." He stepped closer and saw her gulp. "But that is not the reason I'm here. You've lived on the prairie long enough to know that neighbors help one another. You need help, so I'm here. That's it."

Her expression softened, but before she could say something else to irritate him, Aaron turned around, descended the porch steps, and strode toward the barn. Maybe it would be best if he went home and sent one of his hands over to help for the next few days.

~

Martin Metcalf stared out the window, gazing down at Boston's business district, barely visible through the low-hanging pewter clouds. The dreary day mirrored his mood. Felicity had been whining and pushing him toward marriage, his business was on a downward slide, and the useless detective he'd hired to discover what had happened to his son had turned up precious little, other than to relay a report from the doctor that the boy—his son—had been born alive, although a bit on the small side. The doctor had stayed until Carolyn passed, and at that time, the baby was still breathing and doing fairly well.

That was Janie's fault. His son was out there somewhere, and he was already one year old. Did the boy resemble him at all? What had happened to him? Where was he now?

Martin kicked the chair leg nearest him. He hated desiring something that was out of his reach. He was unaccustomed to being denied what he wanted.

Three quick raps sounded on his door. He glanced at the mantel clock. Two in the afternoon—time for his meeting with the detective he'd hired to find his boy. "Enter."

Gerald Buckner strode into the office looking quite chipper in his black three-piece suit, probably bought with money that Martin had paid him. Martin took his seat behind his imposing desk, and Gerald sat across from him. The man pulled a small leather book from his vest pocket and opened it. "It's a rather ghastly day, isn't it?"

Martin curled up one side of his mouth and then cursed. "Dispense with the pleasantries, Buckner. Tell me what you've found—and there'd better be something good, or our deal is off."

Buckner leaned back, not looking the least bit worried. A slow smile crept across his angular face, and his hazel eyes gleamed. "As a matter of fact, I've found my best lead to date."

Martin's heart leaped to a gallop. He laid his arms on his desk and leaned toward the man. "Go on."

"You should be glad to know that your employees are quite loyal. I've been after a couple of the gardeners and stable hands for the past few months, but no one would talk. Then, one of them got into some trouble and needed money, so I offered him a tidy sum in exchange for information. You owe me a Double Eagle, by the way."

Martin glared at the man.

He coughed into his hand. "I believe you will be pleased—"

Martin slammed his fist on the desk. "Out with it!"

Buckner jumped, then nodded. "Your man Owens told me that your wife's cousin visited her the day her laboring began. Jane Dunn didn't come to the laying out. No one I've talked to has seen her since, which is odd, wouldn't you say, since they were so close?"

Martin nodded, and the anger he had been feeling suddenly fled as he savored this first real lead. "Of course. I should have thought of that myself. My wife loved her cousin as a sister." He tapped the desk. "What was her name?"

Buckner looked down at his book. "Jane Dunn. Do you think it's possible the woman could have taken your son? Is she the kind of person to do something like that? I mean, it doesn't seem too likely, since she was a teacher."

"No, it makes perfect sense. The wren is as plain as her name. She'll never find a man desperate enough to marry her; thus, she's not likely to become a mother, either, so she kidnapped *my* son." He would find her, one way or another. "Do you know where she is?"

"Not yet. I talked with the headmistress at the school where she worked, but she wouldn't tell me anything."

"What's her name?" Martin stood. "She'll talk to me."

"Naomi Carpenter." Buckner pushed to his feet. "Don't do anything rash. I plan to sneak into her office tonight and see if I can find an address for Miss Dunn."

"I'll give you until tomorrow, then I'll go visit the woman."

One way or another, he'd find out where that Jane Dunn took his son.

And he'd get the boy back.

Chapter Six

With Benjy down for his afternoon nap, Janie paced to the front door. She peered outside, wondering if Mr. Harper had returned. He'd ridden out shortly after their disagreement and hadn't come back at lunchtime. He'd obviously taken offense at her question of whether he was helping her because he was interested in the ranch. Mr. Allenby had planted a seed of doubt that had grown like wheat after a good rain. Why had she been so quick to believe a man she didn't know?

Phil would have been ashamed of her. She was ashamed of herself.

She stepped out onto the porch, took a quick glance around for any stray animals, then cupped her hands around her mouth. "Mr. Harper!" She watched the barn door, hoping he'd stride out in that confident manner he had. But he didn't.

She'd chased him away, and now she was truly alone.

Her lower lip trembled, and her eyes stung. She missed her brother. She'd taken him for granted, just like she had Mr. Harper, and now they both were gone.

Janie leaned against the porch post. Crying wouldn't accomplish anything. There was so much to be done. She needed to wash Benjy's diapers, weed the garden, check on the cattle, make plans.

She was accustomed to order. She remembered the days when she taught school. Every hour was regimented; each class had a goal to accomplish. She knew what needed to be done, and she did it. Life here on the Kansas prairie had finally fallen into a routine, once she'd gotten used to being a mother and learned how to better care for Benjy. She tended the house and garden, while Phil took care of the animals and ranch. Now she had to do it all, and she didn't know where to start.

She gazed up at the clear blue sky. "Help me, Lord. I just want to go lie in bed, sleep, and wake up to find Phil back home. Give me strength, for Benjy's sake."

Peace warmed her chest. God would help her get through this time, and He would show her what to do. Right now, she needed to get some water boiling so she could wash diapers before Benjy awakened from his nap. She stepped inside, donned her bonnet, and stuck Phil's pistol in her apron pocket.

She hauled wood from the side of the house and piled it like Phil had shown her, then set the heavy kettle in place and filled it with water. While it heated, she filled a wooden tub with rinse water, then went to her garden and began weeding. The beans and peas she'd planted last month were growing well, as were the cabbage, turnips, and beets. If the weather held, and they didn't have an early frost, she'd have a good harvest to fill the root cellar. The smokehouse was another issue.

Janie tossed a handful of weeds into the pile at the edge of the garden, then peeked in the bedroom window to make sure Benjy was still sleeping. Though her eyes hadn't adjusted from the brightness of the sun, she could hear his steady breaths. Good. Maybe she'd get his diapers cleaned before he woke up.

Quietly, she walked through the house, retrieved the porcelain pot of diapers, and returned to the fire. She wrinkled her nose as she removed the lid, then dropped the soiled cloths into the hot water, one by one. She set the pot down beside her, shaved off a few curls of soap, added them, and then stirred the mixture with a stick she kept for that purpose. A gust of wind cooled her sweaty body. Though she was warm, she was glad the weather hadn't turned cold yet.

As she reached for the empty pot to wash it out, she caught a whiff of burning fabric. Had she left a diaper hanging over the kettle?

She turned back to the fire and glanced down at the smoke rising up from her feet.

Her skirt!

⁓

Aaron felt out of sorts. It wasn't like him to get angry easily, but when Mrs. Dunn had basically accused him of helping her just to get an edge on buying the ranch, he'd lost his temper.

Now that he'd checked on Phil's cattle and moved them closer to the house, he had to decide whether to return home or go back to Phil's place. There was always work to be done at home, with a ranch as big as theirs, but Pa and Ethan could manage the hands well enough without his help. For a while now, he'd felt like a change was about to happen, but he hadn't known what that change might be.

With a sigh of resignation, he guided his horse away from the Harper homestead and toward the Dunns'. He looked behind him, checking on the dead hackberry tree trailing behind his horse. Mrs. Dunn would need firewood—a lot of it—to see her through the cold Kansas winter. Dragging a tree to the house and chopping it there was easier than splitting it up where it was downed and fetching a wagon to haul it back.

The barn came into view as he crested the hill. Mrs. Dunn was outside, tending a kettle. He didn't know what he would say to her.

Suddenly she squealed and jumped back. She bent over, whacking at her smoking skirt.

Aaron's heart lurched. He yanked his knife from its sheath and sawed at the rope tied to his saddle horn. Finally, he cut through the last strand. He threw his knife to the ground at the same time he kicked his horse—hard. The gelding broke into a gallop.

Aaron reined Outlaw back as they rode into the yard, and he jumped off before the horse stopped. He ran to Mrs. Dunn and tackled her. She cried out as they hit the ground. Aaron jumped up and started stomping on the flames. He rolled her over to access the back of her dress and crushed the remaining embers with his boot. The fire had burned away over a foot of her black skirt and petticoats. Large holes had also been scorched into her stockings, and her legs looked red, but no blisters had started forming.

"Are you hurt?" He bent down and helped her to sit up.

Her pecan-colored hair had come loose from its pins and now spread out around her like a shawl. She didn't respond but stared at her hands, then gazed up at him with pain-filled eyes. Angry red welts covered her palms. Aaron jumped up, ran to the well, and hauled up a bucket of fresh water. He carried it to the porch, then helped Mrs. Dunn to her feet and into a rocker. He turned over the large chamber pot he'd found near the fire and placed it at her feet, then set the bucket on top of it. "Here. Soak your hands. The cool water will help with the pain."

She did as ordered, staring out at the yard with tears running down her cheeks. "W-what am I going to do? How will I care for Benjy?"

She looked up at Aaron, and the desperation in her gaze tore at him. He was reminded of Phil's anxiety when he'd asked Aaron to watch over Janie. This accident wouldn't have happened if he hadn't stormed off angrily. He should have been here to help.

Clearing his hoarse throat, Aaron bent down on one knee. He reached out and cupped his hand over Mrs. Dunn's arm. "I'll help you. And I'll go get Ma. She'll be happy to assist you, too." He started to stand.

"No!" She reached for him, then winced and put her hand back in the water. "Please, don't leave me. I—I can't even lift Benjy out of his bed."

Aaron pursed his lips. "Let me get you settled in your bed and doctor your hands, and then I'll take the boy and ride for Ma. He'll enjoy it. Toby always did when I took him riding."

"I can't ask your mother to come back again so soon. She just left yesterday."

"You aren't asking. I am."

She nibbled on her lower lip and looked away. "I'm sorry for what I said earlier. I had no call to doubt you." She turned back to him. "You most likely saved my life. If you hadn't come back…" Her voice broke.

"But I did, so don't distress yourself. Go ahead and take your hands out of the water."

She did as told and laid her hands in her lap, palms up. Aaron set the bucket aside and reached for her upper arms. "C'mon. Let's get you inside." He wrapped an arm around her and helped her across the threshold. He knew the house had two bedrooms because he'd helped Phil build the second one. It was smaller than the other room and just the right size for a child or two. He aimed Mrs. Dunn toward the larger room, but she balked outside the door and shook her head. "Take me to Benjy's room."

Not one to argue with a woman any more than necessary, he guided her toward the smaller room. He noticed that a cot had been placed in there beside the boy's small bed with wooden bars. It resembled a jail cell, although there was no roof. Benjy lifted his head and smiled, then sat up and rubbed his eyes. "Mama!"

Aaron helped Mrs. Dunn onto the cot. Her pain was so great, she didn't even acknowledge her son's greeting. "Do you have any salve or bandages?"

"I'll get them." She started to rise.

Aaron pressed down on her shoulder. "I'll do it. Where are they?"

"In the kitchen. There's a round basket with a lid on the shelf over the stove."

When Aaron returned to the room with the salve and bandages, Benjy had pulled himself up in his bed and was jabbering away. He glanced at Aaron, studied him for a moment, then grinned.

Aaron felt as if the boy had accepted him. He knelt again in front of Phil's wife and reached for her wrist, turning her hand over. The bright red skin looked painful. "This will hurt some."

She nodded and pressed her lips together, as if in preparation. He cut a small square of fabric with scissors he'd found in the basket, then scooped a generous glob of salve from the tin and gently wiped it on her burns. She hissed at the pain, but she didn't pull back or cry. He admired her bravery. He'd been burned a time or two and knew it hurt like the dickens. After applying the salve, he wrapped her small hands in the fabric he'd found rolled up in the basket. Benjy watched the whole process without making a sound.

"What about your legs?" He didn't want to embarrass her, but if there were open wounds, they needed attention.

"I checked them while you got the bandages. I think they'll be fine." Her cheeks were as red as her scorched hands.

"Why don't you lie down and rest? What do I need to do for the boy?"

"He'll need to be changed." She started to lie down but then pushed up on her elbow. "Oh! The diapers. Please, could you get them out of the pot before they boil down to nothing, and put them in the rinse tub? They're all Benjy has, except for the few clean ones on the shelf above his bed."

"Sure can. I washed a few loads of diapers for my own young'uns a time or two." Standing, Aaron returned the medical supplies to the basket and set it on a small side table. He headed for the door, then paused and turned around. "Should I take Benjy now?"

"No, he seems contented for the moment." She smiled. "Go ahead and rescue the diapers, if you don't mind."

He nodded and rushed from the room. The space was far too small for three people, and if anyone had seen him in there with Mrs. Dunn, her reputation would be shot, as would his. The Harpers tried hard to be upstanding Christian folk, and he wouldn't want to tarnish his family's good name. The sooner he got Ma here, the better.

⁓

Janie watched Sarah Harper bustle about the kitchen, cooking the supper she should have been preparing. With her hands bandaged as they were, she could do almost nothing. Benjy sat on a quilt on the floor, contented to play with two spoons and a cloth ball Sarah had brought him. Janie couldn't even hold her son unless someone lifted him onto her lap. "I feel more useless than a conductor without an orchestra."

Sarah glanced over her shoulder, smiling. "What a charming comparison. Do you have a musical background?"

"Um…I do like to sing." The skin on Janie's face tightened as she realized her slip. She'd worked hard to keep her musical past a secret, for fear that if news about her got out, it might somehow filter back to Martin Metcalf. She had no idea if the man was looking for his son or even knew he had one, but she couldn't take the risk. The less people knew about her, the better.

Sarah stirred the pot of chicken soup, then poured in several cups of rice. The delicious aroma filled the room, making Janie's stomach gurgle.

After setting down the rice canister, Sarah turned around and leaned back against the cupboard. "My aunt Emma has a lovely voice. I didn't know that until we came to Kansas."

The statement intrigued Janie. "How could you not know she had a nice singing voice?"

Sarah carried her teacup to the table and sat. "It's a bit of a long story, but I don't mind telling it if you'd like to hear it."

Flashing a wry grin, Janie shrugged. "I'd love to. There's not much else I can do with my hands swaddled up like an infant."

Chuckling, Sarah lifted Janie's teacup. "Are you ready for another drink?"

"Yes, please." She took a sip of the sweet liquid, once again humbled because of her need for help, although Sarah seemed quite happy to be assisting her. "Do you miss your children?"

Her new friend smiled. "Of course I do." She leaned forward and glanced around, even though no one other than Benjy was in the house. "But I'm also enjoying my time away. My boys can be quite a handful. At just two and four, they still need me a lot."

"I hope it isn't too much for your mother-in-law to handle."

Sarah shook her head. "Ethan is staying close to the house and helping with them."

Janie glanced down at the tea leaves that had escaped the strainer and settled in the bottom of her cup. "I've disrupted your whole family. You and Aaron are stuck here helping me, and now your husband and Karen have extra duties, too."

Sarah reached across the table and patted Janie's arm. "Please don't think that. Do you know how rare it is for me to get to visit with another woman my age? This is a treat."

The soft tone of Sarah's voice and the glimmer in her blue eyes soothed Janie's guilt. "I've missed chatting with other women since moving here, too. Phil talked some, but it was usually about his crops or livestock."

Benjy babbled a string of unrecognizable words. Then he threw a spoon, rocked onto his knees, and crawled after it. Sarah hopped up, brought him and the spoon to the table, and sat him on her lap. She pushed her teacup and saucer Janie's way, to keep them out of reach of grabby little hands, then placed a kiss on Benjy's head. "He's such a sweet-natured little fellow."

"Yes, he takes after his mother."

Sarah's brow crinkled. "I know Phil wasn't his father. Was he a bad-tempered man?"

Janie's heart lurched as she realized what she'd said. She should have said, "He takes after me," but that sounded pretentious. "Uh...yes, his father could be quite cruel."

"I'm so sorry. It must have been difficult for you to live with him."

Janie wanted to slink under the table. Maybe she should feign fatigue tiredness and go to bed before she spilled her whole story to her friend. This was why keeping to herself was better. Safer.

"My uncle Harvey was a cruel man," Sarah shared. "He didn't treat my aunt or me very nicely." She pressed her lips together, then continued, "It's probably not polite to speak ill of the dead, but it's the truth. I think that's why my aunt never sang when he was alive."

"I think I remember Phil saying that your aunt and uncle raised you."

"Yes, that's true. My parents died when I was seven, and I went to live with Uncle Harvey and Aunt Emma."

Benjy banged his spoon on the table, and it flipped up and landed on the floor. He arched his back in an effort to get down. Sarah placed him back on the quilt and moved his toys within reach. He picked up the cloth ball and gnawed on it.

"Looks like someone is teething." Sarah ruffled his hair before taking her seat again.

"Ph—I lost my parents when I was twelve. My brother raised me, until I was fifteen. He was older and hankering to see the West, so I went to live with my cousin's family." Janie forced herself to relax. She'd almost blurted out that Phil and she had lost their parents.

"Where does your brother live? I imagine the two of you are close."

Janie swallowed the lump building in her throat. She had to get the focus off of her. "I believe Phil said you're from Chicago. How did you end up here?"

Sarah grinned. "I got stuck here—and I hated it at first."

"That sounds interesting."

"Uncle Harvey got a wild idea to move to Santa Fe."

"Isn't New Mexico a territory? Why would he want to leave Chicago and go somewhere so rugged?"

Shrugging, Sarah shook her head. "It's a man thing, I suppose. He was a watch repairman for years, until he decided Chicago had too many other watch repairmen, and he no longer wanted to compete with them for business. Santa Fe evidently didn't, so he sold the house, and Aunt Emma and I had no choice but to go along."

"That must have been hard for you to leave your home and friends."

Sarah nodded. "Very hard, but I intended to return to Chicago once I got Aunt Emma settled. But God had another plan—a plan by the name of Ethan Harper."

The warm smile on Sarah's face and the faraway gaze in her eyes made Janie squirm. Would she ever find a man to love like Sarah had? A picture of Aaron Harper intruded on her thoughts. She may be attracted to the handsome man, but he'd never given her a single sign that he felt the same toward her. He was merely keeping his vow to Phil by helping her. How soon before he felt that his vow was fulfilled?

Chapter Seven

Aaron rode into the yard of his family home, glad to be back, even if it was for a short time. Ethan walked out of the barn, carrying Mark, with Jeff trotting by his side.

"Uncle Aaron!" Jeff broke into a run.

"Whoa, cowboy." Ethan picked up his pace and jogged after the boy, grabbing hold of his collar and pulling him to a halt, as Aaron reined his horse to a stop. "Jeff, you know better than to run toward a horse."

"But Uncle Aaron's home. I wanna see him."

Aaron smiled. It felt great to have someone happy to see him after spending nearly a week with Mrs. Dunn. He had the impression she would be glad to see him go when he finally left for good. He dismounted, tied his horse to the porch rail, and then walked toward his brother and nephews.

Jeff wriggled loose from his pa's grasp and ran for Aaron. He scooped up the boy and tossed him in the air, eliciting a giggle, then gave him a hug. "You been behaving for your pa?"

"Yes, sir."

Ethan chuckled. "Uh-huh. You saw how well he's minding me. I don't know how Sarah manages to keep him in line."

Mark waved at Aaron but seemed perfectly content to stay in his pa's arms. Both of Ethan's boys favored Ethan and had brown eyes like his, but they had their ma's blonde hair—the same as Toby. Aaron's gut twisted. He loved children and would like more than two, but that wouldn't happen unless he found a woman to marry. Besides, what right did he have to want more children when the two he had were living in town with his other brother and his wife?

"Why so glum?" Ethan shifted Mark to his other arm. "You havin' a hard time over at the Dunns'?"

Shaking his head, Aaron set Jeff on the ground. "Not so bad, especially now that Sarah's there. I didn't know how I was going to tend Mrs. Dunn after her accident, care for little Benjy, and manage the ranch, too."

Jeff tugged on his pant leg. "When's Mama comin' home?"

"I don't know, scamp."

Mark scowled. "Want Mama."

"Uh-oh." Ethan eyed him. "Hey, buddy, how about some lunch?"

"Want bisset."

Aaron lifted one brow at his brother.

"*Biscuit*," Ethan mouthed.

The back door of the house opened, and Ma stepped out. "Aaron, I didn't expect you today."

He turned and walked toward the house. "I needed to talk to Pa and eat some of your wonderful cookin'." He gave her a hug. "Let me tend my horse, then I'll be in."

"If you'll take this guy, I'll see to your horse," Ethan said.

Aaron smiled at his brother and lifted Mark out of his arms. "I can't turn down an offer like that."

Ma turned to Jeff. "You may ring the triangle and call your grandpa in."

The boy spun to face his father. "Pa, I get to ring for Poppy!"

Ethan jogged up the porch steps after his older son and lifted him up. The boy grabbed the clangor and ran it around the inside of the triangle, making a pitiful clinking sound.

"Me do." Mark bounced in Aaron's arms, almost causing him to lose his grip.

"Next time, pardner." Aaron tightened his hold on his nephew and escorted his ma inside. "Mmm...sure smells good in here. What's for lunch?"

"Stew." She released his arm, took her grandson, and set the boy in a chair. "You need a good scrubbing. Clean up this little guy while you're at it, why don't you?"

Aaron washed up in the big porcelain bowl reserved for that purpose, then wiped Mark clean with a cloth, and dried both of their hands on a fresh-smelling towel. He needed to bathe while he was here and pack some clean clothes. He wasn't comfortable washing at the Dunns', nor did he want to ask Phil's wife to wash his clothes—a task he'd have to tend to before long unless his ma came to his rescue.

"How's Janie doing?" Ma shook her head as she placed the silverware on the table. "It's such a shame how she burned her hands, what with just losing her husband and all."

"It is. She was quite fortunate her legs didn't get blistered, the way her skirts flared up." He pursed his lips and thought about seeing her fighting those flames with her bare hands. "If I hadn't ridden up when I did, it would have been much worse."

"God put you where you needed to be to help her, Son."

"I know. I've thought about that several times, but I don't understand why God would allow such a thing, especially to a newly widowed woman."

"Me hung'y." Mark climbed up on his knees and reached for the bowl of butter. Aaron hurried over and grabbed the boy, putting him back in his chair. Ma handed him a plate of sliced apples, and Aaron gave it to his nephew. Then Ma pulled a pan of biscuits from the oven and set them on her worktable.

She turned to face him. "Aaron, you know we can't question why God allows bad things to happen to His people."

"It doesn't do any good to ask Him, anyway." He knew. He must have asked God five hundred times why He hadn't kept Della from racing her horse the day she died—or kept her from falling. She'd been an expert rider.

"You're not doubting your faith, are you, Son?" Ma looked more serious than she had in ages.

"No, of course not. I just meant that questioning why God allows bad things to happen serves no purpose. I have to believe there's a reason, even when I don't see one."

Ma nodded. "That's true. I sometimes think God is being kind to us by not answering our inquires and even our prayers. He sees so much more than we can."

"You're right. But it's still hard to make sense of why a mother would be taken away from her young'uns, or Phil from Benjy. That little guy needs a father."

Ma dished up a bowl of stew and handed it to Aaron, who set it on the table. "Just think about Janie," she said. "She's lost two husbands in less than two years."

He hadn't considered that. "I guess you're right." He accepted two more bowls from her and set them on the table. "Did she ever tell you about her first husband? She's never mentioned him to me, not that we talk all that much."

"I imagine she's still in a state of shock over Phil's sudden death. That was such a shame. Have you heard of anyone finding any other rabid animals?"

"No, but then I haven't been around too many people." With the bowls in place, he pulled out a chair, flipped it around, and sat, winking at Mark. The boy giggled and held out a soggy apple skin. Aaron wasn't sure how the kid had managed to filet the fruit like he had. He took the offering and laid the apple skin on the small bread plate at Ethan's seat. "Speaking of people, Deke Allenby came by the Dunns' place yesterday."

Ma carried the big bowl of biscuits to the table, her eyebrows lifted nearly to her hairline. "What did he want?"

"Made Mrs. Dunn an offer on the ranch."

She snorted. "I bet he tried to swindle her."

Aaron buttered a biscuit, then tore it in half and gave one part to Mark. He shoved the other half in his mouth while his ma's back was turned. The boy grinned.

"I saw that, young man."

Aaron shook his head. "Still got eyes in the back of your head."

"How do you think I managed to raise three sons?"

The back door banged. Pa, Ethan, and Jeff walked in and stopped at the washbowl in the corner of the kitchen. Pa washed his hands, then looked at Aaron. "How are things goin' at the Dunns'?"

"Goin'. But that's one of the reasons I'm here. I have a request."

Pa kissed Ma's cheek, then ambled over to the table and took his seat at the head. "What kind of request?"

"Phil was a good farmer, but I've realized he was lacking in some other areas."

"Don't be too quick to judge. Running a place on your own can't be easy."

Ma took her seat at the table, then looked to Pa, an unspoken request for him to say the blessing. He bowed his head, and everyone else followed suit.

After the prayer, Aaron glanced at Ma. "Miss Emma's not joining us today?"

"She took sick yesterday. She's better today but is still abed."

Aaron looked at Ethan. "Wouldn't Sarah want to be here, tending her aunt?"

Ma fed Mark a bit of stew and nodded. "That's why I'll be going over to the Dunns' after I get the kitchen cleaned. She needs to be here with Ethan and her boys, too."

"What about me? I need you here." Pa frowned, although Aaron could see the teasing gleam in his eyes.

Ma nudged him with her elbow. "You can get along without me for a day or two, old man."

Aaron loved the way his parents were comfortable joking with each other. He knew his pa would miss Ma, because he dearly loved her, but he would willingly share her with someone else in need. Aaron wanted a marriage like his parents had. His life with Della had been wonderful at first, but she quickly tired of the isolated life on the prairie. When they'd married, before the war was over, she'd been eager to get away from the craziness of the city. But she quickly started missing her family and friends and all the excitement of town.

"Aaron, did you hear me?" Pa stared at him with eyebrows lifted.

"Uh, sorry, Pa. I was just thinking. What did you say?"

"I asked what kind of help you needed at the Dunn place."

"Well, for starters, Phil didn't have much wood stored up for winter. I could use a man or two to help bring in some trees and help split logs. I've been thinking about the cattle, too. Would you be open to letting them run with ours for the winter?"

Pa nodded and then dabbed his mouth with his napkin. He glanced at Ethan. "What do you think? Can we spare a couple of men for three or four days?"

"I think so. We got the cattle moved to the south pasture now, so there's not a lot to do until we start branding the spring calves. What about Slim and Harley?"

"Those two work well together and are responsible enough to not need supervision." Pa sipped his coffee.

"I agree." Aaron nodded. "Are they free to ride back with me today, or do you want to send them later?"

"I assigned them to ride fences this afternoon, so I don't mind if they go back when you do," Ethan said. "Pa?"

"Fine with me." Pa stood and went to the stove to refill his bowl. "Anybody else want some more of this delicious stew?"

Aaron held up his empty bowl at the same time as Ethan. "If you're serving, I'll take some. I've missed Ma's cooking."

"I don't want no more stew, but can I have another biscuit, Pa?" Jeff pushed his near-empty bowl away.

Ethan eyed it. "Finish that stew, and if you're still hungry, you can have another biscuit."

"More bisset." Mark started to lift his plate, but Ma grabbed it.

"Eat this bite of meat first." She held out the spoon. He scowled but then opened his mouth.

Aaron enjoyed watching the antics of Ethan's children, but it made him miss Corrie and Toby even more. And it reminded him what a lousy father he was. He had to figure out a way to bring his children home *and* make sure they got an education.

❧

Janie held her breath as Karen unwrapped the bandage from her left hand. The blisters had popped, and her palms were less red than the last time they had changed the dressing. "It looks better than it did yesterday."

Karen smiled. "That's good that they're healing. Can you bend your fingers at all?"

She flexed them. "They feel tight but don't hurt much."

Taking her hand, Karen stared at it for a long moment. "I think we can leave the bandage off this one. Try the other one now."

Janie grimaced as she slowly curved the fingers of her right hand, sending stabs of pain shooting up the lower half of her arm.

"That's enough. I can tell by your expression it hurts. Let's go out on the porch and leave this unwrapped for a bit. The air might do it good."

More than ready to be out of the house for a while, Janie pushed up from the table using her elbow. She was disappointed her right hand wasn't further along, but at least it was healing—and now she'd have her left one to use.

"We should leave the door open. Benjy will wake up any minute now." Janie allowed Karen to hold her arm and help her to the door. The fresh scent of fall greeted her as she sat in the porch rocker.

"I'd like to take a look at your leg, if you don't mind." Karen knelt before her. "Burns are not something to ignore, and Sarah said one of them was quite inflamed."

"The fire ruined my stockings, but my leg wasn't badly hurt. Although I decided to dispense with stockings until I could put them on myself. I hope you don't find that scandalous."

Karen patted her shoulder. "Of course I don't. It makes things easier for you, so don't think another thought about that."

"Thank you for understanding." Janie looked around for Mr. Harper. "Do you know where your son is?"

Karen smiled. "He and two of our hands rode out to find some wood they could chop for your winter pile, so you don't have to worry about him seeing beneath your skirts. Besides, Aaron's a gentleman and wouldn't gawk at a lady."

Janie's cheeks warmed. "You're right. He's been nothing but gracious, and Sarah is so kind, too. You have a wonderful family."

She wished her own family had been bigger—that her parents hadn't died when she was young. If only she had another sibling she could live with. How would she ever repay the Harpers for all they'd done for her? Karen rearranged Janie's skirts, pulling her from her thoughts. She hadn't even realized Karen was checking her leg.

"That looks fine, even better than your left hand." Karen grunted as she straightened, then rubbed her back. She smiled. "I'm not getting any younger."

"And here you are, helping me, when you should be home with your family."

"I was just making a comment. I'm perfectly happy to be here." She pulled the other rocker close and sat. "How are you handling Phil's death, if I may ask?"

Janie closed her eyes and leaned back. "I won't lie to you. It's difficult. He was such a good man."

"Yes, he was. We were glad when he bought out the last owners. He was a wonderful neighbor. Always willing to help others."

"I don't know what I'd have done if he hadn't taken me in."

Karen remained silent for a while. Nothing but the creaking of the rockers and the whisper of the breeze could be heard. Janie enjoyed sitting with the older woman and imagined that if her mother had lived, they would have shared moments like this.

"Would you mind if I asked you about your life before you came here?"

Janie's heart jolted. "Um...there's not much to tell. I was a teacher for a time." She thought it best not to mention her music.

"It's a shame for a young woman like you to have lost a second husband. Were you married long to Benjy's father before he died?"

Pain shot through Janie's hand as she gripped the arm of the chair. How could she answer that? She longed to blurt out the truth, but what good could come of the Harpers knowing her background?

"I'm sorry, but I prefer not to talk of him," she finally said. And she prayed to God that she never saw the man again.

"Forgive me. I was just hoping to get to know you better."

"Why don't you tell me how you came to live in Kansas? I believe your son—or maybe it was Sarah—said you used to live in Ohio."

Karen launched into a tale of a young couple seeking land for themselves and their sons. Janie only half listened. She had to get well and decide what to do. Maybe it was best to leave this place. Friends talked to one another, and sooner or later, she'd once again be asked questions she couldn't answer. But if she moved, she'd only start getting to know other people. She and Benjy couldn't live completely alone. She didn't want to, and it wouldn't be fair to him.

And leaving meant never seeing Aaron Harper again.

Lord, show me what to do.

Karen stilled for a moment. "Was that your son I heard?"

"Yes. Sounds like Benjy is awake."

Standing, Karen smiled down at her. "You stay there, and I'll see to him."

"Thank you."

Before Karen stepped inside, a loud bang echoed through the house. Benjy's loud wails filled the air.

Chapter Eight

Aaron rode toward the rear of the Dunn house. While Slim and Harley finished loading the dead tree they'd found, he planned to sharpen both Phil's ax and the one he'd brought from home. The men could chop the wood while he worked on repairing the barn roof. He smiled, glad his pa had a whole passel of pine shakes in his barn so he wouldn't have to make any.

A sweet, lyrical voice rose in song, and he stopped his horse to listen. His ma's voice was deeper, so that had to be Mrs. Dunn. Like a mythical siren, the beautiful voice drew him. He dismounted, tiptoed to the side of the house, and stood there listening—afraid that if he made his presence known, he'd frighten her away like a spooked bird. He closed his eyes, taking in every nuance of her lovely soprano voice. Only once, when he'd been in Kansas City on business and had visited an opera house, had he heard a voice even remotely comparable.

Mrs. Dunn had never sung before—at least, he hadn't heard her. What compelled her to do so now?

Something sharp jabbed his shoulder, and he spun around. "Ma?" he whispered.

She leaned her head out the open window. "I taught you better than to eavesdrop."

"I'm not eavesdropping; I'm...mesmerized."

"She does sing awfully pretty, huh?"

Aaron nodded, feeling a bit guilty. He tipped his hat to his ma, then walked back to his horse, grabbed the reins, and led him around to the front of the house. As he expected, when Mrs. Dunn glanced his way, her eyes widened, and she clamped her lips shut tighter than a snapping turtle.

He yanked off his hat. "That was about the prettiest thing I've ever heard."

She ducked her head, cheeks flaming, but a tiny smile pulled at the corners of her intriguing mouth.

In her lap, Benjy fussed and sat up. Aaron noticed Mrs. Dunn's left hand was unbandaged, and she must be able to use it again, because she had it pressed against the boy's belly. Benjy, though, had white fabric wrapped around his head, and his face was red and splotchy. The boy reached for the bandage, but Mrs. Dunn pulled his hand away.

"What happened?"

"He must have tried to climb out of his bed, because it fell over with him in it."

Aaron put his hat back on, then climbed the steps and knelt in front of them. "Was he hurt bad? Hey there, pardner."

Benjy stared at him and reached out one hand. Aaron gently wiggled it, earning a small smile from the boy before he leaned his head back against his mother's chest.

"He had a scratch that bled some, so your mother wrapped his head. He doesn't like it and keeps crying. That's why I was singing. It seems to help."

"Next time I get hurt, if you sing to me like that, I guarantee I'll get well faster."

Her eyes shot to his and held. He read surprise and then confusion there. Finally Aaron realized he'd been too familiar with her. "Uh...I'll go take a look at the bed and make sure nothing's broken on it."

He stood and hurried into the house, unable to believe what he'd just said. Even though there was truth in his statement, he shouldn't have said it.

Ma turned from the table, holding a tray of teacups and a plate of some kind of sliced bread. "Whoa! Where'd you come from, and what's the rush?"

He skidded to a quick halt and reached out to help balance the tray. "Sorry. I'm headed to check Benjy's bed."

"Might be good if you could attach it to the wall somehow. Otherwise he's likely to do the same thing again. Males seem to have hard heads and have to do things several times before they learn what not to do." A soft smile tittered on her lips.

"Yes, ma'am." He reached out and snagged a piece of the bread, giving her an ornery grin. "Some of us are still learning."

"Shame on you."

He chuckled as he headed to the small bedroom. He shoved the bread in his mouth. "Mmm. Apple."

After hoisting up the bed, he checked it over for cracks but didn't find any. Phil had done a fine job crafting it. Aaron would have to show it to Josh the next time he came home, since he would be a father before long and liked making well-crafted furniture.

Aaron looked around the room, trying to decide how best to fix the bed so it wouldn't fall again. He would hate to ruin the look of it by hammering it to the wall. As he stared at the bed, an idea formed. In the barn, he'd seen a can of some nails and several latches. If he fastened a latch to the wall on either side of the bed, he could run a thin rope in and out of the bed's railings and then tie it to the latches. That should keep the piece from tipping.

He started to leave, then looked around the small room once more. Mrs. Dunn's dresses and a nightgown and petticoat hung from pegs on the wall. Aaron's gut twisted. He had stormed his way into her private quarters without even asking. She'd confused him with that look. He rubbed his neck, fled the room, and exited the house. He paused on the porch, watching the women.

"Let me hold him while you drink your tea." Ma clapped her hands together and reached for Benjy. He shrank back and turned his head away.

"I'm sorry," Mrs. Dunn apologized. "He doesn't know you very well yet."

"Don't worry about me. I've raised enough youngsters to know some are shyer than others."

Aaron cleared his throat and explained to them his idea for steadying the bed.

"That sounds good to me," Mrs. Dunn said.

"Do you want to move anything around before I attach it to the wall? It will be harder afterward."

She shook her head and smiled. "The room is so small that there's not much I could do to rearrange it."

Aaron wanted to ask her why she was staying in that room instead of the bigger bedroom, but that would be inappropriate, especially with his ma within range of whacking him. He knew Mrs. Dunn needed his ma's help, but he would be glad when it was just the two of them again.

Benjy stared at him, then sat up and smiled.

Aaron waved his hand at him again. "I'm just going to the barn for a few supplies," he told the women. "How about I take Benjy with me and let him see the horses while you ladies enjoy your tea?"

Mrs. Dunn looked down at Benjy, then at Aaron. "You sure he wouldn't be in the way?"

"Not at all."

"Aaron's good with youngsters. Remember, he's got two of his own." Ma picked up a slice of bread and handed it to him, her eyes twinkling.

He had a suspicion she was up to something, but he didn't know what it could be, so he accepted the offering and nodded his thanks.

"If you're sure you don't mind, it would be nice to enjoy tea without worrying that Benjy will grab a cup and break it."

Aaron exhaled a breath. She trusted him with her son, and the thought made him stand a bit taller. Now came the real test. He walked over and held both hands out to the boy. Benjy looked up but didn't lean his way. Aaron stooped down. "Hey, little guy. You want to help me put my horse in the barn?"

"Ha!" Benjy grinned and bounced on Mrs. Dunn's lap. Then he lifted his arms.

As Aaron hauled Benjy up into his arms, his gaze shot to Mrs. Dunn's surprised expression. "Do you think that was his version of 'horse'?"

Smiling, she nodded. "I believe so."

"Ha! Ha!" Benjy shouted, as if confirming Aaron's question. The boy bounced in Aaron's arms and reached for Outlaw. Aaron grabbed his horse's reins and headed for the barn before Mrs. Dunn could take Benjy back. A smile tugged at his mouth at the child's excitement, but then he pursed his lips. He cared for Benjy, but would he confuse the child if he stayed on here for long? He'd hate for Benjy to grow attached to him, only to lose him if Mrs. Dunn decided to move away.

And yet, what else could he do?

He'd made a promise—and he never broke his word to a friend.

Janie watched Mr. Harper mosey to the barn, Benjy nearly climbing over the man's shoulder in his efforts to get to Aaron's horse plodding along behind them. "Your son is good with children."

Karen smiled. "Yes, he's a wonderful father."

Janie nibbled her lip for a moment, then decided to voice her thought. "Might I ask where his children are?"

"They live in town with Josh, my middle son, and his wife, Sophie, so they can attend school. It's not the ideal situation, because I know it bothers Aaron that he must send them away, but they are getting an education."

"Maybe now that more families have moved into this part of Kansas, you'll soon be able to hire a teacher and open a school." Janie took a sip of her tea, enjoying the flavor. She'd hadn't seriously considered teaching again, even though that could be the solution to her problems. But then, parents this side of the Mississippi weren't exactly looking to hire a music instructor. They wanted their children to learn more practical subjects, like reading, writing, and ciphering. She could probably teach any of those, but she didn't have a certificate.

"I wanted to keep Corrie and Toby at home and teach them like I did my boys, but I got overruled. Sarah was expecting, and we still had stages coming through every few days. With all there was to do at home, everyone felt that it was best for the children to go to school in town, especially since Josh had moved there."

"Will Sarah send Jeff there when he's old enough?"

Karen refilled their cups and set the teapot on the tray. She stirred in some sugar, then handed Janie her cup.

Janie's left hand shook a bit, but she managed another drink without spilling it on herself. She got the impression that her friend was stalling, and she stared off at the tall sunflowers in the distant field, dancing in the breeze, while she waited.

"I don't believe she will. After losing her parents at such a young age and having a hard time living with her cranky uncle, God rest his soul, I can't see her parting with her boys, even though she knows Josh and Sophie would love them as their own."

"I can't imagine how hard it must be to send a child away." Guilt pierced Janie. Hadn't she done that very thing—robbed Martin Metcalf of the joy of raising his son? She'd never once considered that before. Instead, she'd always thought that she was saving Benjy. What if she'd been wrong? She swallowed hard. If Martin ever found her, would she be sent to prison for stealing his child? Would she be separated from Benjy forever? Suddenly, being half a country away from Martin Metcalf didn't seem far enough.

"You must be thinking of something awful, the way you're frowning."

Janie turned her head toward Karen, her heart racing. Karen couldn't know her thoughts, but what if she learned the truth? Would she still want to be friends?

"I was just thinking how hard it would be if Benjy was taken from me."

Karen reached over and laid her hand on Janie's arm. "Fortunately, that's not something you'll likely have to worry about, unless you work out an arrangement like Aaron's."

Janie shook her head. "No, I could never send him away. I'd teach him myself. Besides, I miss him now, and he's just in the barn."

Karen chuckled. "I know. A mother loves being with her children, and even though she enjoys the times they're not together, she still misses them. It's the nature of a mother."

The thought warmed Janie's insides. Though she wasn't Benjy's natural mother, she was his ma in all the ways that counted. And she loved him as much as Carolyn would have.

If Martin ever found them, Janie would fight with everything in her to keep Benjy.

Please, God, don't let him find us.

"I know Phil hasn't been gone long, and I don't want to intrude where I'm not welcome..." Karen angled her chair toward Janie's. "But I'm a practical woman who believes in doing what's needed. I've been wondering what you plan to do."

"Do?" Janie asked the question to give herself more time to think of a response.

"Do you plan to stay here? Move to town? Go somewhere else?"

Janie stared at her bandaged hand. Was Karen getting tired of caring for her? She knew the woman had plenty of work at her own home, and she hated being dependent on her neighbors.

"Forgive me if I've overstepped my welcome."

"No." Janie shook her head. "It's not that. I...I just don't know what I'll do. It's obvious that I can't stay here alone." The thought of her and Benjy in the house at night without Phil or Aaron around terrified her. Besides the rabies scare, there were so many other things that could happen. She thought of Mr. Allenby, who'd made an offer for her ranch. The man gave her the creeps. What if he decided to return when Aaron wasn't here?

Maybe she should pack up and take Benjy out West. But things were bound to be even more rugged out there. Maybe she should go to a large city. Martin would have a harder time finding her in a densely populated area, but how would they survive?

"Janie, look at me."

She swallowed hard and did as asked.

"You don't have to decide this minute. I can tell that you are struggling. Just know that we're your friends and will help you as long as you need us. But winter is coming soon, and I would encourage you to make a decision, stay or leave, before then. When the snow comes, it will be much harder for us to get here if you need us, and I don't like the idea of you and that sweet boy here by yourselves."

"You're right." Janie sighed. "It's just so hard to decide what is the right thing to do."

"When I have a difficult dilemma, I find praying is the best thing I can do. God has a plan for you and Benjy. Ask Him to show you what it is."

Janie had always believed in God and had gone to church weekly before moving to the Kansas plains, but she'd never heard anyone say He had a plan for her life. Could it really be true?

"You have a Bible, don't you?"

She nodded.

"Read Jeremiah twenty-nine, verses eleven through thirteen. I think it will encourage you."

"Thank you. I'll read it tonight after Benjy is in bed."

She stared at the opening to the barn and heard Benjy's excited squeal, though she couldn't see him. Her future wasn't hers alone. She had to consider what was best for her son.

The picture of Aaron holding Benjy popped into her mind. She'd been attracted to the man since she first met him. Did he feel anything for her? Or was he helping merely because of his promise to Phil?

Aaron would be a wonderful father for her son. Dare she hope—believe—that he could be part of God's plan for her?

Aaron grinned at Benjy's giggles. The boy was beside himself sitting on Aaron's saddle. He bucked up and down, as if trying to get the horse to go. Thankfully, Outlaw was well-trained and just ignored the excited child.

Watching Benjy reminded him of Toby when he was younger. That boy couldn't get enough of horses. If he lived at the ranch, Aaron would have bought him a pony or small horse by now. Given the chance, Toby would jump the moon to stay at the ranch, but Corrie was another issue. She loved her school friends and getting dressed in her pretty frocks. She wouldn't take staying home well.

But could he bring Toby home and not Corrie?

No, it would be both or neither.

Aaron gazed up at the barn ceiling. Dust motes drifted in and out of the rays of sunlight shining through the holes in the roof, probably left from the hail storms they'd had several times this past summer. He needed to climb the ladder and jab a piece of straw in the bigger holes so that he could see where they were when he was on the roof, ready to repair them.

Outlaw shifted toward Aaron and stamped his hoof. He was ready to be rid of the bundle of energy on his back. "What do you say we give Outlaw some feed?"

He tugged the boy off, and Benjy wailed.

"Hey, none of that. Here, help me hold this bucket." He lifted the wooden pail so that the boy could grip the handle, and was rewarded with a two-toothed grin.

Benjy sure was a darling child—and good, too. Most of the time. Aaron had almost forgotten about the bandage on his head and the scratch on his cheek, which still had the sheen of salve on it. Filling the feed bucket while holding the boy wasn't an easy task, but he managed, and while Outlaw ate, Aaron let Benjy sit on the horse again.

As he held on to the wiggly boy, his thoughts veered back to the child's mother. He couldn't remember ever hearing a woman who sang so pretty. Not even at church, on the Sundays when his family went to town.

Mrs. Dunn's singing did something to a man. It drifted in and wove its way around his mind and heart, entwining them like a vine. He wanted to hear her sing again. Over and over again.

He blinked, as if coming out of a stupor. Was he attracted to Phil's wife? He'd never really looked too closely at her, since she'd been married. But maybe he should. She was no longer married.

He shook his head and pulled Benjy down. "Time to go back to Mama."

"Ma!" The boy's brown eyes gleamed, and he lowered his chin to his chest in his effort to nod.

Aaron chuckled. With his fuzzy blond hair and dark eyes, he could pass as Toby's little brother.

His mouth suddenly went dry. What was he doing thinking such thoughts?

All because he enjoyed Mrs. Dunn's singing.

Benjy tugged on the brim of his hat and grinned. "Pa."

Aaron nearly stumbled. "No, son, that's a hat."

The boy lowered his hand and fiddled with one of Aaron's buttons, then patted his pocket. "Pa."

Confusion swarmed his mind. Did the boy mean "pocket," or was he calling Aaron "Pa"?

"Lord, help me out here."

Chapter Nine

Janie sat in the parlor rocking Benjy. A soft knock sounded at the door, then Aaron poked his head in.

"Ma said for me to bring in some more wood so you'd have it for breakfast in the morning."

"Come on in. She's gone to bed. I would have, too, except my little man seems to be afraid of his bed ever since it fell over on him."

As he passed by, Aaron smelled like the outdoors—fresh and manly. He placed the wood in the crate near the stove and then moseyed back to the parlor. "Would you like me to light a fire?"

"I don't think we need one just yet. The mornings are cool, but the house warms quickly once the stove is lit."

"That will change before long."

"Why don't you have a seat? I'm up anyway, and you must get tired of spending so much time in the barn."

He hesitated, then sat on the small settee, taking up a good portion of it. He stretched out his long legs in front of him and crossed his arms over his broad chest. Even in the flickering lantern light, he looked all man.

Janie sighed. He almost looked at home in her house.

"That boy of yours sure does like horses."

"I'll have to walk him out to the barn more often. It's been difficult of late."

"I know, but things will get easier."

She stared at him. "Will they?"

He worked his lips, as if wanting to reassure her but not quite sure he could. "I pray they will. I know life is hard for you now, but I don't believe that Phil's death took God by surprise."

Janie bristled. "Surely you're not saying God had anything to do with his dying?"

He rubbed his nape and then sat up, resting his elbows on his knees. "No, I didn't mean it like that. I don't believe a man's life is happenstance. God put us here for a purpose, and He has a purpose for you."

He sounded like his mother. "And what of Phil?"

He shrugged. "I don't have all the answers, Mrs. Dunn. I was raised in a family that honors God and believes in His goodwill. I know bad things happen to good people like Phil, and I can't reason why he died like he did, but I do believe good can come of it."

Janie wanted to be angry at the man, but the patience in his deep voice and the sense in his statement soothed her. "You talk like your mother."

His gaze zipped to hers. "How do you mean?"

"When you talk about God. I've never heard anyone talk about Him like you Harpers do."

"Anyone can have an abiding faith in God, if he—or she—believes in Him. God wants the best for His people, Mrs. Dunn."

"Do you think you could call me Janie—or Jane? Mrs. Dunn seems too formal when we see each other so often."

The warm smile he gave her heated her insides. Who needed a fire with him near?

She ducked her head at the forward thought.

"I'd be happy to, if you'll return the favor and call me Aaron."

She nodded, unable to say his name at that moment because she was certain her voice would crack.

Several long moments of silence passed, and then Aaron stood. "I reckon I should head on out."

"Um...do you think you could put Benjy in his bed for me before you go? It's still hard to hold him with one hand bandaged."

"Of course. It'd be my pleasure."

He crossed the room in two long steps, bent down, and lifted her son. As he straightened, she stood and raised her eyes, her gaze crashing into Aaron's. Her breath caught in her throat as he stared back. The flickering lamp danced on his cheeks, and his eyes looked dark as the moonless night.

The tired boy cried out and arched his spine, his head flying toward Janie's. She lifted her hand to his back to stop him from conking his skull against hers. Aaron's large hand flew up and covered hers. "I've got him."

She pulled away and crossed her arms. Here she was, a widow of barely over a week, and she was making eyes at another man. What must Aaron think of her?

She followed him to the small bedroom but didn't enter. With no light, she couldn't see, but she heard him patting Benjy. "Go to sleep, pardner."

He quietly slipped from the room and bumped into her, quickly grabbing her arms. "Uh...sorry."

"No, I shouldn't have been standing in the doorway."

"Well...uh...gotta go."

"All right." She stepped back and let him make his escape, but she trailed him to the door. "Mr. Harper?"

He paused with the door partway open. "Aaron, remember?"

"Um...Aaron, I found a box of Phil's papers, but I haven't had the nerve to look through them. I wondered if you might have time tomorrow to sit down with me and answer any questions I might have concerning them."

He nodded. "It'd be my pleasure, ma'am."

The door closed, and he was gone. Janie leaned against it, reliving the moment their gazes had collided. Why hadn't he looked away? Did it mean he had feelings for her?

Or was he only interested in the ranch?

⁓

Aaron lay in his bed of hay, staring up at the blackness of the night, unable to sleep. Janie had seemed so alone—so vulnerable—tonight. When he'd accidentally looked into her eyes, it was as if someone had lassoed them together, and he couldn't break her gaze. He hadn't wanted to.

What did it mean? He didn't love her. Yes, he admired her bravery. She wasn't a weepy woman like Della had been, crying whenever things didn't go her way. Janie certainly didn't have Della's beauty, but she wasn't hard on the eyes, either. Her hair was the color of doeskin, and her eyes also reminded him of a deer's. Seeking. Scared at times. She seemed ready to dart away if he said the wrong thing.

She loved that boy of hers with a vengeance, and that was something else he admired. Della had enjoyed her children for about two days, and then she'd wanted to get back to doing things her way. Ma had been mostly responsible for raising Corrie and Toby.

Aaron closed his eyes, remembering the beautiful sound of Janie singing that lullaby. He could have stood there listening for hours. Too bad his ma had seen him. He grinned, remembering Della's off-key voice. She couldn't carry a tune in a sewing basket.

He flipped to his side and blew out a loud breath. Why was he comparing the two women? It wasn't like he was going to marry Janie. She was a brand-new widow, for heaven's sake. Marriage would be the last thing on her mind.

Prayer. That was what he needed. Praying would help him get his mind off that young widow.

⌒

Janie helped Karen clear the breakfast dishes while Aaron entertained Benjy. She smiled at the sound of her boy's giggles and how he rubbed his belly after Aaron tickled it.

Benjy reached a hand toward Aaron's nose, and Aaron chomped his teeth, causing the boy to snatch his hand back and shriek. Then Aaron grabbed hold of Benjy's hand and brought it to his mouth. Benjy's brow's dipped as if he thought Aaron might take a bite of his fingers. Wanting to reassure the boy, he kissed Benjy's hand, making a loud smack. The worried look on Benjy's face fled.

"I'd never bite you, pardner. I'm just playing."

Again, Benjy reached for Aaron's mouth; again, Aaron's teeth clacked. Benjy squealed, then erupted in hearty laughter.

"Aaron does love children," Karen whispered while her son growled and tickled Benjy again. "He always wanted a houseful."

Janie pondered that as she refilled the coffee cups. She'd never really thought about marrying and having children. Her focus had always been on becoming an opera singer. But now she was a mother, and though there were times when she still wished she could sing opera, she wouldn't trade Benjy for a career. Not ever.

Life had a way of taking interesting twists one didn't expect. Aaron Harper was another of those unexpected turns. The more time she spent with the man, the more she liked him.

Yes, he irritated her at times, but for the most part, he was a good, hardworking man. And Benjy had taken to him like a bird to biscuit crumbs. Phil had loved her son, but he'd never done much more than hold him and give him hugs. He'd never kissed him, that Janie had seen, or elicited such excited laugher as Aaron did.

If she ended up leaving Kansas, Benjy would have another man in his life to miss.

"Well, the table's clear." Karen pulled out her chair and sat. "Are you sure you want us to go over Phil's papers with you?"

"Yes. I may have some questions one of you could answer."

Aaron set Benjy on his quilt on the floor, then rolled the ball to him. When Benjy grabbed it and stuck it in his mouth, Aaron sat up and turned his attention to Janie.

She swallowed, then opened the wooden box that held Phil's papers. She picked up the top few pages. "This is a receipt for twenty head of cattle, and this one is for supplies he bought the last time he went to Windmill." Janie thumbed through a stack of smaller papers. "Just more of the same."

Beneath that were several letters she'd written him—letters from Boston. She couldn't let the Harpers see those, so she left them in the box and looked beneath the envelopes. She found a bigger one with the name of an attorney written in the corner. Glancing up, she gazed into Karen's curious eyes and then Aaron's. Janie lifted the official-looking envelope and tugged out the document. She unfolded it. "This is his will." Her eyes quickly scanned the fancy lettering, and her heart tripped. He had left everything to Janie Dunn—his sister. The Harpers couldn't see that, either. Needing some time, she folded up the will and returned it to the envelope. She drew in a steadying breath, looked up, and smiled. "Phil left everything to me."

"That's good. As it should be." Karen reached across the table and squeezed her hand. "I know we recently discussed this, but have you decided what you want to do?"

Janie wanted to stay here and see if there was a chance this side of heaven that Aaron would ever look at her with the same loving affection her father had showed for her mother. But she certainly couldn't say that.

"Do you have family anywhere that might take you in?" Karen asked.

Janie shook her head and peeked down at Benjy to make sure he was all right. He sat with his back against Aaron's boot, examining something between his index finger and thumb. A dead fly? "No, Benjy!"

Aaron quickly leaned down and grabbed Benjy's hand, pulling it away from his mouth, then pried the insect loose. Then he stood, walked to the window, and flicked it outside. He turned back, grinning. "That boy will eat just about anything."

As Aaron took his seat again, his mother tapped her fingers on the table. Karen quirked her lips, then stared at Janie. "You said you were a teacher. Is there any chance you could teach again if you decide not to stay here?"

Aaron's heart bucked. "You were a teacher?"

Janie nodded. "Yes, but I've taught only one subject, and that was music—specifically, vocal lessons to young girls of wealthy families. I can't imagine there being many parents in this part of the country who could afford to pay for music lessons for their daughters."

"Might be up in Kansas City." Aaron took a long draw of coffee, studying her over the top of the cup.

"Possibly. But I believe I'd really prefer to stay here."

"It won't be easy." Karen stared into her coffee mug. "There were few people in these parts when we first arrived and started the stage stop. We had a rough time of it, and we had the whole family to work." Karen laid her hand over Janie's unbandaged one. "I'm not trying to discourage you, but you need to know what you're getting into. Tell her, Aaron."

He glanced down at Benjy, who'd pulled himself up and was standing with one hand on Aaron's thigh and the other on the table leg. He brushed his hand over the boy's head, receiving a long line of babble.

Aaron's smile nearly stole Janie's breath. My, but he was handsome.

He looked at her again, all humor gone. "You have to worry about rustlers, the heat, ice, wind, hail, and then there's grasshoppers that arrive and devour your whole harvest. Wild animals that eat your vegetables if you forget to close the gate, and others that will get in and steal your chickens. Then there's all manner of sicknesses and accidents, and the nearest doctor is half a day's ride away, unless the train happens by just when you take ill."

Karen chuckled. "You don't have to be so encouraging, Son."

He shrugged, looking a bit embarrassed. "I'm just telling it like it is."

Karen playfully wagged a finger at him. "You left out droughts and floods and freak snowstorms that dump a foot of snow."

"My apologies." He grinned, his dark brown eyes sparkling.

Janie had encountered several of the events they had listed, but not the majority. Would she face them all if she stayed? "How does anyone survive here? Phil never indicated things could be so difficult."

"People are hardy, and God gives us strength and often prospers us." Karen wrapped her hands around her coffee mug.

"It isn't easy, but with determination, a man—or a woman—can do just about anything they put their head to."

Aaron folded his arms on the table. "And neighbors help each other, in times of trouble, but also during good times, like with barn raisings, apple bees, quilting circles, and the like."

While Aaron told her everything involved in running the ranch, Janie pondered it all. How could she manage? Clearly, she would need to hire help. If she kept her garden and the chicken and cows, would she have enough food? How would she ever manage the cattle? And she hadn't ridden a horse since she was nine years old, when she'd fallen off and broken her arm.

"There is one other option."

Janie picked up Benjy, needing his closeness, and looked at Karen. "What's that?"

"You could keep the ranch for now but move in with us. We have an extra room, and that would allow you time to grieve Phil before you have to make such an important decision."

Chapter Ten

Aaron struggled not to fidget. Why had Ma offered their home to Janie? Staying the winter at their place wouldn't help Janie—or Phil's ranch. He supposed he could stay at the Dunns' and tend to things, but he didn't like the idea of being alone the whole winter or having to see to his own meals on top of all the work there was to do. A man could live on jerky for only so long. Yes, Ma would feed him, but that would require two hours of riding for each meal.

As Ma changed tracks and started telling Janie about the quilt she and Sarah were making and how Janie could help if she were staying with them, Aaron looked around the small cabin. It was typical of most in the area, with a nice-sized parlor that melded into the big kitchen. The bedrooms were small but adequate. He could be happy here. He'd been restless for some time now, and maybe being on his own would help him figure out where God wanted him. Not having other men to yammer with sure left a lot of time for thinking and praying.

"Aaron, how much would it cost to hire a man to work for me?" Janie stared at him with those big brown eyes, and he struggled to get his mind working.

"Uh...you don't need a man when you've got me."

Ma lifted a brow, and Janie's eyes widened.

"But you won't always be here. When you return home, I'll need someone else's help if I'm going to stay here."

Aaron pressed his lips together. He didn't like the idea of another man staying here, helping her. He'd made a promise to Phil that he would do that—and he took his promises seriously.

"What do you think, Aaron?" Ma asked. "Twenty or thirty dollars a month for a hired hand?"

"That sounds about right." He stood, took his cup to the stove, and refilled it with coffee. "But you'd have to hire the right man, or you'd only bring more trouble on yourself."

"What do you mean?" Janie gazed at him with an innocent expression. She had no idea of what could happen to a woman alone with an unsavory man.

"Do I have to spell it out? You here, alone, with a man you don't know or trust?"

Ma stood. "That's enough, Aaron."

He looked at her with one brow lifted. "She has to know what could happen, Ma. Many men would take advantage of such a situation."

"Well, that's not going to happen. We'll help her find a man she can trust."

He gulped down the last of his coffee, then set his mug on the counter. "I have chores to tend to." Without another look back, he strode out of the house. He had honored his promise to Phil. If Janie wanted to hire someone to replace him, so be it.

"Aaron, wait."

He turned and saw his ma heading toward him. The light breeze tugged at her graying hair and dark blue dress.

"What was that about?" She crossed her arms and gave him the look she'd always given him when he was young and she was surprised at his actions.

"What do you mean?"

"You acted like you were jealous that Janie might consider hiring someone else. I would think it would be a relief to you to know you won't have to stay much longer."

He shrugged. "I made a promise to Phil."

"You told me about that, but he wouldn't expect you to stay on forever. Is there more to this than meets the eye?"

"More to what?" He blinked, trying to understand what she meant. Most women had a way of saying one thing but meaning something else altogether, but Ma was usually more direct.

"I want to know if you're sweet on Janie."

"Ma! She's been a widow for less than two weeks."

"True, but you've been a widower for over five years. And you didn't answer me."

Aaron toed the dirt, not sure how to respond. "I reckon I like her and Benjy, but if you're asking if I'm falling for her, the answer is no."

Ma raised an eyebrow as if she didn't believe him. "Just be careful. Janie's lost two men already. I don't want you toying with her affections if you aren't serious about her."

He couldn't help staring at her in disbelief. "Is that what you think I'm doing here? Because I can assure you it's not. I'm watching over her and the boy because of a promise I made to Phil as he lay dying, and you're the one who taught me how important it is to keep your promises."

She laid her hand on his arm. "Just take care, Son. I don't want either of you getting hurt."

He nodded. "Are we done? I have work to do."

"All right. Go on."

He hurried to the barn, knowing she was still standing there, watching him. How was it that he, a man of thirty years, still squirmed under his ma's eye?

As he reached the recesses of the barn, Outlaw nickered to him. He stopped at his horse's stall and scratched the gelding's head, glad that the animal couldn't talk.

Was he attracted to Janie? Yes, he liked her, as he'd said, and he was enamored with her singing. But did he have feelings for her?

Had Ma seen something he'd failed to recognize?

⁓

Janie held her breath as Karen unwrapped her right hand. She felt little pain this time, and when the final piece of cloth fell away, she smiled.

"It looks much improved." Karen gently brushed her fingertips across the red spots where the blisters had been. "Does that hurt?"

"A little, but not too bad."

"Good. I think we can leave the bandage off now, but you'll need to be careful. Make sure you don't grab anything hot with it or lift anything heavy until it's healed completely."

"Oh, I won't. And I don't plan on batting any more flames with my hands."

Karen rolled up the bandage. "I always keep a pail of water nearby when I'm doing laundry, just in case my skirts catch fire."

Janie grimaced as she bent her fingers, trying to close them. They were stiff and sore. She glanced down at Benjy, who'd fallen asleep on his quilt on the floor. Would she be able to care for him on her own now?

"Keep putting the salve on it when you go to bed."

Janie wrinkled her nose. "What's in that stuff? It sure smells nasty."

"Hog lard and chalk, mostly." Karen smiled. "My boys never liked the smell of it, either."

Deciding to experiment, Janie cautiously lifted her water glass with her right hand and took a sip. It didn't hurt as much as she'd expected, which was a huge relief. She should be able to return to doing most things for herself now, but that would mean Karen would be leaving, and she'd be alone with Benjy again. And Aaron.

"Karen, do you know how long your son is planning on staying?"

Her friend shook her head and stood. "No. He hasn't told me."

"Don't you need him at home?"

Karen dropped the bandage wrap in the dirty laundry basket, disappeared into the big bedroom for a moment, and returned with her sewing. She took a seat on the sofa. "You don't need to worry about Aaron. Between Nick and Ethan and the hired hands, we'll be fine at the ranch."

Janie looked down at her hands, resting in her lap. "But he can't stay forever."

Karen raised her head and stared at her for a long moment. "Aaron's a man you can depend on. He'll stay as long as you need him."

"But what if I can't find someone to work for me before winter? I don't know many people in the area, and I haven't the least idea how to find an honorable man to hire. And Aaron can't stay out in the barn all winter. It would be far too cold."

"Hmm…that's something we hadn't considered. You don't have a bunkhouse. Before you can hire a workman, you'll need a place for him to stay."

Janie wrung her hands, thinking of the small stack of money in the bottom of Phil's box. She still had several of the jewels Carolyn had given her, but she didn't dare use them. She had to have them in case Martin ever found her, and she and Benjy needed to make a quick escape. "I'm not sure I can afford to have a bunkhouse built—or even an extra room."

Karen's knitting needles clacked as she began stitching the blanket she was making. "I'll talk to Aaron and see if he has any ideas."

Janie opened a book and stared at the page without reading. She didn't like the thought of staying on the ranch without Aaron. She'd come to trust him and even looked forward to seeing him regularly at mealtimes. It wouldn't be the same for someone else to be here instead. She realized Karen's needles had grown silent.

"Janie, I know Phil hasn't been gone long, but do you think you'd consider remarrying in the near future?"

Her eyes widened. Had Karen sensed she was thinking about her son? "I don't know. It's been only two weeks since Phil was buried."

Karen nodded. "I know, but out here on the prairie, life is hard. Hard enough for a married woman, but a widow with a young boy... I've been praying, and I keep thinking the best thing for you would be to marry again. That way, you'd have someone to share the work of the ranch with, a man to protect you and Benjy. And Benjy would have a father."

Janie didn't know what to say. How could she tell her friend the only man she would consider marrying was her son? Would Karen think her disloyal to Phil? Although she still grieved her brother's death and missed him terribly, it wasn't the same as losing a husband. "I'll think about it—and pray, but men aren't exactly busting down my door wanting to marry me."

A quick knock sounded at the door, and both women stared at each other, then chuckled. Karen set aside her sewing and hopped up before Janie could. When she pulled open the door, the same man who'd come calling the day after Phil's funeral stood there. Janie's heart clenched.

He yanked off his hat. "Morning, Mrs. Harper. Didn't know Mrs. Dunn would have visitors. The name's Deke Allenby, in case ya forgot."

"I know who you are, Mr. Allenby. What can I do for you?"

He stared past her at Janie, and she felt as if spiders were crawling over her skin. There was something shady about the man that made her nervous. She prayed Aaron had heard him ride up.

"Mrs. Dunn, I was hopin' you might have decided about sellin' your place t'me."

Karen moved sideways, blocking Janie's view of the unwanted guest. "You're aware, Mr. Allenby, that Mrs. Dunn just recently lost her husband."

Janie winced at the reference to her husband. She longed to tell Karen the truth but was afraid it might drive the kind woman away.

"I am, but she's got no business stayin' here all alone. She ought'ta move to town. I need a place and can give her a good price, so it makes sense for her to sell it to me."

Janie bristled. The man sure had a lot of nerve.

Karen turned toward Janie but still blocked the man's entrance. "Do you wish to talk to Mr. Allenby about your ranch, Janie?"

She shook her head. "No. I haven't made a decision yet." She rose and walked to the door. "I haven't forgotten your offer, Mr. Allenby." An offer far below what the property was worth, according to Aaron. "If I decide to sell you my land, I'll send word with Aaron Harper."

He smashed his lips together, exhaling a loud breath through his nose. Then he nodded and slapped on his hat. "Good day, ladies."

Karen shut the door and leaned against it. "That's why you need a man around here, Janie. There's no telling what someone like him would do if he found you alone."

"I was alone most of the time Phil was alive."

"I'm sure that's true. But folks knew Phil was around, and when word gets out that you're staying here alone, then you may have cause to be concerned." Karen crossed the room and took Janie's hand. "I'm not trying to scare you, but it's something you need to seriously consider. You have Benjy to be concerned with besides yourself. What if he got hurt, and there was no one here to help?"

Janie knew she spoke the truth. "Maybe it's foolish for me to even think of staying."

"I can offer advice, but only God can give you the guidance and wisdom you need, dear. Spend some time seeking Him."

Karen was right. Janie needed to spend less time worrying and more time praying.

∽

Aaron strode down the aisle to the back of the barn, spun around, and marched the other way. The idea of Janie hiring a man to work for her made his stomach churn like eating a piece of rancid meat. Sure, there were plenty of reliable men in the area, but most of them had work already. He couldn't think of one man he'd want working here after he returned home.

And where did that leave him?

They'd had a few chilly evenings already, but the nighttime temperatures would plummet in another month or so. He wouldn't be able to stay in the barn too much longer. If he had a cabin where he could light a fire, he might stay the winter. But he didn't.

He turned toward the back of the barn again as his thoughts drifted to the cozy bedroom where his ma was staying. Maybe he could stay there when the cold came.

He shook his head. That would be highly inappropriate. Even though he knew Janie would be safe with him under the same roof, her reputation wouldn't be.

Outlaw stuck his head over the stall gate and whickered. Aaron paused beside the big gelding. "Sorry if my agitation has disturbed you, boy." He patted the black horse's neck, then straightened his forelock. "How about a ride?"

It would do them both good, and he needed to check on the cattle, anyway. All his pacing was doing nothing but wearing a pit in the barn floor.

He opened the gate, and Outlaw moseyed out. The horse followed him to the tack room, where Aaron retrieved the bridle and saddle pad. After he placed both on the horse, he returned for his saddle. Yep, a long, hard ride would clear his mind.

The barn door creaked open and then shut. Ma sashayed in as if she belonged there. "You heading somewhere, Son?"

"Yes, ma'am."

"Where are you going?"

"To check on the herd." Aaron lugged his saddle out of the tack room.

"Did you happen to notice that Deke Allenby came by again?"

He tossed the saddle onto Outlaw's back and spun around. "When?"

"He left about fifteen minutes ago."

Aaron inwardly chastised himself. He'd been so lost in his thoughts that he hadn't kept a good watch on things.

"I'm not one to judge, but I've never cared much for that man." Ma shook her head. "I have no doubt if I hadn't been there today, he'd have pressed Janie to accept his offer."

Aaron snorted. "I wouldn't sell Allenby the south pasture for the price he offered. He thinks Janie's desperate, and he's looking for a deal."

"If he comes around here again, you make sure he looks for one somewhere else."

Aaron eyed his ma. She was like a she-bear when it came to protecting those she loved, and from the looks of it, she'd adopted Janie.

Ma walked over and patted Outlaw's flank. "If Janie decides to sell—mind you, I'm not sure she will—we should be able to make her a fair offer. I'll talk to your pa about it tomorrow."

"So, you're heading home?"

She forked her fingers through Outlaw's mane. "Yes. I removed the bandage from Janie's right hand, and it looks pretty well healed. Don't let her lift anything heavy, like a bucket of milk or water, and remind her to apply the salve in the evenings."

Aaron wrinkled his nose. "That stinky stuff?"

She nudged him with her elbow. "What else would I use?"

"I think you take delight in torturing us." Aaron chuckled to soften his comment, then waited for her to get around to the subject that had brought her out to the barn. He didn't doubt she had something on her mind. He cinched the saddle, dropped down the stirrup, and rested his arm across the seat.

Ma took a deep breath, then blew it out. "There's something I'd like you to consider."

He nodded, allowing himself a tiny smile. He'd been right.

"I think it's time you consider remarrying."

Aaron straightened. He sure hadn't expected marriage to be the topic of her conversation. "Anyone in particular you've got picked out for me?"

She gazed in the direction of the barn door, then looked back at him. For a moment, he wasn't sure what she meant. And then it hit him with the weight of an anvil. "You think I should marry Janie?"

"That's not what I said. I just think you should maybe think about it."

"Ma, she just lost her husband. I doubt she's ready to marry again."

"Being ready has nothing to do with it. She needs a man like you to protect her and care for her. And you need a wife. You're a good man, Aaron, but it's time to stop moping for Della and start living again."

He rubbed his jaw. "You think I'm moping?"

"Not always, but yes, I think you sometimes do mope. I see you watching Ethan and Sarah with their boys with longing in your eyes. Marrying Janie might not be your first choice, but she's a good woman, and if you did marry, you would be able to bring your young'uns home for her to look after and teach. Before you know it, they'll be grown. Why, Corrie will be of marriageable age in just five or six years."

Aaron pushed away from the horse and walked across the barn floor. "Don't even talk about that. I'm not ready to hear it."

Ma came to stand beside him and laid her hand on his arm. "All I'm asking is that you think about it and pray. I can't tell you if marrying her is the right thing for you; only God can. But I didn't think that you'd even considered the idea, so that's why I wanted to talk to you."

Surprisingly, the idea of marrying Janie sat with him better than the thought of her hiring someone to work the ranch. He nodded. "All right, Ma. I'll consider it and pray about it."

She smiled. "And please don't mention to Janie that it was my idea. She'd be mortified to know I talked to you about this."

As Aaron rode away from the house, the thought of returning home to Janie each night felt good. Right.

Maybe Ma's idea wasn't as far-fetched as he'd first thought.

Still, he wouldn't do anything until he'd sought God on the subject. His first marriage hadn't been very good, and he certainly didn't want a repeat. But Janie wasn't Della. She liked living on the prairie. She loved her little boy and was committed to caring for him.

Janie would never lie to him the way Della had, pretending to be contented with their marriage. She might have cooed sweet words, but her actions had cried the opposite.

He nudged Outlaw to a gallop, quickly eating up the distance to the cattle. With the wind hitting his face and whipping at his shirt, a thought smacked him in the face.

When had he started caring for Janie?

Chapter Eleven

Janie laid Benjy in his bed and patted his back until he settled, then covered him up and tiptoed out the door, closing it behind her. She wished she knew why he'd been so fussy tonight. Was it possible he missed Aaron?

The cabin was dark, except for the flickering light of the lantern she'd left on the table for Aaron. She carried the lantern to the stove and checked the food. The mashed potatoes were lumpy, the slab of ham dried out. With a ladle, she scooped some water from the bucket on her worktable and added a little to the skillet, hoping the meat would soak it up.

She crossed the dimly lit room carefully, not wanting to trip. Had Aaron decided to stay the night at his family home after he drove his mother back? The thought of her and Benjy being all alone sent a chill skittering down her spine. When she lived in Boston, there had been people everywhere. The school was rarely quiet unless it was nighttime.

She removed the bar that she'd put across the door when darkness had fallen, opened it, and gazed at the barn. Light showed through the open door, spilling out onto the ground. Had Aaron returned, or was someone else in her barn? She retrieved the pistol, then stepped out onto the porch and shut the door. The cool breeze made her shiver. While inside the house, she hadn't noticed how much the temperature had dropped.

The sound of whistling came from the barn. Surely that must be Aaron. What thief whistled while he went about stealing someone's horses? She considered sneaking out there and taking a peek, but if someone was after her stock, she'd rather he just take them than hurt her. If something happened to her, Benjy would be all alone.

It was times like these that she wished she lived in town. Maybe staying here was foolish. "Show me what to do, Lord."

The light dimmed but didn't go out completely, and a man walked out of the barn, illuminated by the faint moonlight. He shut the doors, then headed toward the house.

Aaron.

Relief made Janie's knees weak. She lowered the pistol. "I thought you weren't coming back tonight."

Aaron started, his hand going for his gun, but then he lowered it. "You gave me a fright. What are you doing outside so late?"

"I had trouble getting Benjy to sleep." She was sure he'd been waiting to see Aaron, but she couldn't tell him that. "Then I noticed the light on in the barn."

He stepped onto the porch. "I'm sorry I didn't get to tell Benjy good night." He smelled of dust and leather. Not an unpleasant scent on him. "Here, let me have that," he said, reaching for the pistol. "Do you even know how to shoot it?"

She heard a touch of amusement in his voice. "Yes, I do, as a matter of fact. Phil saw to it that I learned."

"Good. You need to know how if you plan to stay out here."

Talking outside in the dark felt odd—intimate. Normally the table sat between them when they conversed. She cleared her throat. "Are you hungry? I still have some meat and potatoes on the stove."

"I ate at home, but actually, I could eat a bit more. It's been a long while since supper."

She opened the door. "Come on in, then. It won't take long to heat up."

She turned up the lantern, and behind her, Aaron lit another one, brightening the cabin. She poured the little milk left in the pitcher into the potatoes and stirred the lumps out while the meat warmed. Aaron went over by the kitchen door and washed in the bowl she left there for that purpose, then dried off.

The atmosphere was cozy—much different from how it had been with Phil and her. Aaron made the difference. She hoped that he might take an interest in her, but her hopes had rarely panned out like she'd dreamed. She never thought she'd be attracted to a rugged rancher, albeit a kind, mannerly, gentle, handsome one. Over the years, when she dreamed of the man she would marry, she always thought it would be a citified businessman in a three-piece suit. But the first time she met Aaron Harper, she'd been intrigued. She formed a silent prayer that if there was any chance, that God would kindle an attraction for her in Aaron's heart.

Janie took a plate off the shelf, dished up the food, and carried it to the table. "The coffee's only lukewarm. Is that all right, or would you rather wait until I heat it?"

Aaron pulled out his chair but remained standing. "It's fine as it is."

She filled a cup with coffee, set it on the table, and took her seat, knowing he wouldn't start to eat otherwise. She clutched the glass of water she'd poured earlier. Aaron sat, bowed his head, and prayed silently, then dug into his food as if he hadn't eaten all day. He made cooking a joy because he seemed to like almost everything, always cleaned his plate, and never failed to thank her.

"How are your hands?"

She glanced at them. "They're much better. The right is a little sore when I do certain things, but the left is good."

"I'm glad to hear that. Burns can be quite painful." He took a sip of his coffee. "Ma said to remind you to apply the salve."

Janie wrinkled her nose. "Have you smelled that stuff?"

He chuckled and nodded. "I've had to use it a time or two." He glanced at his right hand and rubbed his thumb over his fingertips. "I accidentally touched the wrong end of a branding iron once. Ma kept me pasted up in that stinky stuff for weeks."

Janie smiled at his expression. She enjoyed the easy camaraderie they'd developed. Was this how a man and wife talked? Just the thought made her cheeks warm, but she doubted he'd noticed in the soft glow of the lanterns.

He cleaned his plate, then set down his fork. "Thank you for the nice meal. I appreciate that you kept it for me, and I apologize for getting back so late. I needed to talk to Pa about something."

"I didn't mind." *But I was worried.*

He rose and carried his plate to the dry sink, then refilled his coffee cup. After setting it on the table, he ambled into the parlor, took down the lantern that hung near the door, and carried it to the table. Janie blinked at the brightness of the two lamps, while the rest of the cabin fell behind a curtain of darkness. Aaron pulled his chair around the table and sat directly across from her—something he'd never done before. She swallowed the lump that had suddenly formed in her throat. Was he about to tell her that he was going to return to the ranch now that her hands were better? Was that what he'd talked to his father about? Just the thought made her eyes sting.

He glanced at her, then stared into his cup.

He was leaving. Janie twisted her hands, sending a sharp pain up her right arm. How would she manage without him?

"I've had something on my mind, and I talked to my pa about it tonight." He lifted his gaze to hers. "Before you say anything, I'd like you to hear me out fully."

She nodded, unable to break her focus on his dark eyes. Her heart beat like a frantic bird trying to escape a cage.

"I want you to know I've prayed about this, too."

She nodded, curious now. It didn't sound as if he were leaving.

"My marriage to Della wasn't the best. She was a city rose that I plucked and planted on the prairie, but she never flourished here. I loved her and tried hard to make her happy, and I thought she'd settle down once she had children…but she never did."

Janie's heart ached for him, and she longed to reach across the table and touch his arm, but she kept her hands locked together instead.

"I imagine you've heard that she died over five years ago from a fall off a horse."

She rubbed her arm. The same arm she broke when she fell off her father's gelding when she was nine.

He exhaled a sigh. "She challenged Ethan to a race. The snow had just melted, so the ground was soft. He tried to stop her, but there was no stopping Della once her mind was made up. Her stubbornness cost her her life."

"I can't imagine how hard that must have been on you." Janie clamped her lips shut at the odd look Aaron cast her way. What a foolish thing to say for someone who was supposed to have just lost her husband.

"It was hard. I felt responsible for not being more understanding. I still do, on occasion."

This time she couldn't hold back—she reached for his arm. "It sounds like there was nothing you could have done."

He shrugged, and she pulled her hand away, feeling self-conscious for having touched his muscular forearm. His hands, so much bigger and tanner than hers, lay flat on the table.

"Della isn't what I needed to talk about, but I wanted you to know what happened."

"Your mother told me a little but not the whole story." Needing something for her hands to do, she cupped her glass again.

"I figured as much. It's not a secret." He inhaled a deep breath and blew it out. "I know you just lost Phil, and you'd prefer to have more time to grieve him, but you've got to make some decisions soon. I'd like to bring my children back home, but in order for that to happen, I need someone who can teach them. Since you've been a teacher, I thought…"

Janie blinked, surprised by his insinuation. He wanted her to educate his children? "You do know I taught music, right?"

Aaron nodded. "Yes, but you're educated and could teach them what they need to know—reading, ciphering, maybe some history. We have plenty of books at the ranch you could use."

"Where would they live?"

He gave her an odd look. "With us, of course."

"Us?" She hated the way her voice squeaked out that word.

"I talked to Pa, and he said he could send a crew over here to build another bedroom on to the house. It'd be small, like the one you share with Benjy. I figured Corrie could have the new room, and Toby could bunk with Benjy." He smiled. "You know, put the boys together."

Janie's mind swirled, soaking it all in. "I guess I could sleep in Ph—the other bedroom." But that still left Aaron in the barn during winter.

He rubbed his neck. "We'd have to share the big one."

Janie jumped up so fast, her chair fell backward and clattered against the stove. Her eyes were wide. "What are you talking about?"

He stood, circled the table, and picked up the chair. Janie backed toward her room, ready to bolt if he made an advance.

"Janie, wait. I think I've botched what I meant to say." He reached out his hand but didn't approach her.

"What is it you mean, then?"

He scrubbed his nape again. "I'm trying to ask if you'd consider marrying me."

If he'd hit her with the chair, she wouldn't have been more surprised. "Marrying you?"

He nodded. "It's the only thing that makes sense. You could stay in your home, and I could have my kids back. I'd be a good father to Benjy and treat him just like my own. You could even keep the ranch in your name. I want you to know that the ranch has nothing to do with my proposal. It's just that marriage seems like the solution to both our problems."

Her heart thundered. Was this the answer to her prayers?

"I won't press you for a real marriage—um…you know. But I would like us to share the bedroom for the children's sake. Corrie and Toby are old enough to know something isn't right if we don't, and I want them to see us as a real married couple, like my folks." He shifted from foot to foot. Then he pushed the chair in, snatched his cup off the table, and gulped the last of his coffee.

Janie had never seen him so nervous. Could she marry him, when he didn't love her? Yes, she had feelings for him, but was it fair to lock him into a marriage when he didn't feel the same way toward her, especially considering how bad his first marriage had been? His was a business proposal, and she knew those happened often on the frontier; she'd just never expected it to happen to her.

"You'll need some time to think things through, and I don't blame you. It's a big decision. I'll...um...see you in the morning, Janie." He rushed for the door and was gone before she caught her breath.

She hurried after him and set the bar in place behind the door, lest he return and sputter something else to tear her mind from its moorings. She leaned against the door and considered all he'd said. Could she marry him without telling him the truth about her?

A part of her desperately wanted to be his wife, but before she could marry him, she'd have to tell him the truth. And once he knew, he wouldn't want to have a thing to do with her.

⁓

Aaron ran out into the night, glad for the coolness and the dark. He'd made a complete mess of things. He'd actually mentioned sharing the bedroom before asking her to marry him. How stupid!

He hadn't even told her he liked her or that he was attracted to her. Maybe he should have asked her to sing first, and then he would have found the nerve to say all that he wanted to—in the proper order.

He wouldn't blame her for packing up and heading to town by morning.

He should have waited. Should have given her more time to get over Phil's sudden death. Should have made a list of what he wanted to say, so his tongue wouldn't get tangled up like a coil of cut barbed wire. But then, if he'd waited, he might have lost his nerve.

He slowed his pace as he reached the barn and opened the door. Maybe in the morning, he could try again to say all that he'd meant to say.

⌒

Mid-morning, Aaron knocked on the door for the third time, but Janie didn't answer. He let himself in and carried the stack of wood inside, dropping it in the box next to the stove. From behind the closed bedroom door, Benjy still wailed, like he had when Aaron had brought in the milk and eggs. He remembered his young'uns fussing when they were small and how impotent it made him feel to not know what to do to help them.

Janie had been so tied up with the boy, she hadn't had time to fix breakfast, so he decided to ply his hand to the task. He couldn't make biscuits, but he could prepare coffee, scramble some eggs, and fry bacon. In short time, he had the meal ready. He knocked on the bedroom door. "Janie, I've fixed breakfast. Can you come and eat? I'll tend Benjy."

She pulled back the door, looking more haggard than he'd ever seen her, except for when she'd burned her hand. She hadn't yet pinned up her hair; it draped over her shoulders and hung past her waist. His mouth went dry at the sight. He'd thought it was just a plain brown, like a bay horse, but the variety of colors brought out by the sunlight coming through the window held him immobile.

"I don't know what to do for him." Janie's pleading gaze tugged at his heart. "He's never been a cranky child. He's not overly hot, but something must be awfully wrong."

Benjy cried again, rubbing his closed fist across his gums. He reached for Aaron, who grabbed the boy, pulling him against his shoulder. He carefully lifted Benjy's upper lip and saw his red, swollen gums. "Looks like this big fellow is sprouting another tooth."

"A tooth? Do you really think that's all that's wrong?" Janie gazed up at him, her dark eyes hopeful. Shadows had staked a claim under her eyes, and she still wore her dressing gown. Wisps of hair curled around her face, making her look softer than when her hair was pulled back. He smiled, knowing how exhausted she must be not to worry about him seeing her in such a state of disarray.

As if sensing his thoughts, she glanced down and then spun around, brushing her hand over her head. "I'll be out soon."

"Take your time. Benjy and I will eat then head out to the barn. It's warming up fast outside."

She peered around the door, her cheeks flaming as if she'd applied rouge. "Are you sure you want to take him? He's been crying all morning and was up half the night."

Aaron felt a stab of guilt that he hadn't heard Benjy once he'd finally fallen asleep. "I don't mind. Besides, he's quiet now. Must've worn himself out."

"Him and me, both." She leaned her head against the doorframe and yawned. "I could sleep for three days."

"But you need to eat first. Then you can lie down and rest while I take care of Benjy. If he falls asleep, I can put him in his bed."

She eyed him for a moment, then nodded. "Thank you for fixing breakfast. It smells wonderful."

He rested his cheek against the boy's head. "It's nothing but some bacon and eggs. I tried my hand at biscuits once, but my brothers and I ended up using them for target practice. Even the birds didn't want them."

A smile tugged at her pretty lips, and her eyelids lowered, then blinked open. She yawned again. "Guess I'd better eat before I fall asleep on my feet. Let me get dressed first." She closed the door, but not before he caught the red on her cheeks brightening.

Aaron smiled to himself and patted Benjy's back. The boy was plumb tuckered out, too.

A short while later, Janie shuffled to the table and sat.

Benjy shouted, "Mama!" and waved, which caused Janie's exhausted features to brighten. One-handed, Aaron dished food onto her plate and then set it before her. Benjy eyed the meal and mumbled something unintelligible as Aaron poured Janie a cup of coffee.

"You want something to eat, pardner?"

Benjy nearly laid his chin on his chest as he made an exaggerated nod, which brought another smile to Janie's lips, in spite of her exhaustion.

"Mmm...this is good." She took a sip of coffee, then dabbed her lips with her napkin. "Since his mouth is hurting, it's probably best if he just eats some eggs."

"Did you hear that, Benjy? You get eggs."

"Eck." Benjy reached toward the skillet. "Mm...mm...mm."

Aaron spun around, grinning. "Did you hear that? He said 'egg.'"

Janie nodded, her eyelids lowering again. How long had the little rascal kept her up last night?

Aaron sat down with his plate, spooned some eggs into Benjy's mouth, and then shoved several bites in his own. He'd learned that if he didn't eat fast when the children were cranky, he went without.

He sipped his coffee and watched Janie slowly eat. She hadn't said a word to him about his marriage proposal. Did she even remember that he'd asked her? Or was she merely avoiding a topic she found distasteful?

While Benjy gnawed on a bread crust, Aaron stared into his coffee cup. Out of the corner of his eye, he noticed Benjy bouncing and trying unsuccessfully to get the crust in his mouth.

Aaron stopped jiggling his leg—a leg he hadn't realized he was moving.

He should have waited. It was too soon for her to consider marriage to another man. But winter would arrive before long, and he didn't want Janie and Benjy stuck here alone. And he couldn't stay here forever—unless they were married.

It was the sensible thing to do. But then, women didn't always do what made the most sense to a man.

Chapter Twelve

Janie stood outside the chicken coop, holding on to Benjy as he stood at the fence, gazing in. The boy squealed, scattering the nearest hens, sending them, clucking, to the far side of the pen. He giggled and gazed up at her. "Ick'n."

She smiled. "Yes, sweetie, those are chickens, and that big one is a rooster." She watched the big bird to make sure he didn't come near. He hadn't tried to peck her recently—not since she whacked him with the feed bucket.

Benjy looped his fingers through the wire and held on, bouncing and jabbering. Janie kept her hand at his back and looked around, the gun in her apron pocket weighing heavy. There had been only one report of an attack by a rabid animal in the past few weeks, but she wasn't about to be taken off guard. Not after what happened to Phil.

She lifted her face to the sun, enjoying its warmth. As October quickly approached, the sun was setting sooner and the evenings growing cooler. She was thankful to be able to get outside with Benjy and enjoy the lovely day. She had much to think about, and she'd found being outside in nature helped to clear her mind.

Benjy plopped down, and she looked to see what he was doing. A ladybug crawled across a weed, and Benjy pinched his forefinger and thumb, attempting to snag it. She lifted him up, lest he catch and eat the unsuspecting insect.

Benjy squealed and arched his back.

"You want to go see the horses?"

"Ha! Ha!" He reached toward the barn.

Now that she'd mentioned the animals, she hoped there was actually a horse in the barn. And what of Aaron? She almost dreaded seeing him. He'd been so kind this morning, fixing breakfast and caring for Benjy so she could rest. Any woman would be proud and blessed to marry a man like him.

And yet she was hesitating. Not because she didn't want to marry him, but because she didn't think it fair that he be locked into another loveless marriage. As she neared the barn, she slowed her pace, thinking of his engaging eyes and thick hair, both the color of freshly brewed coffee. He was a man who took control, and yet he made a woman feel safe and cared for. He wouldn't be hard to love—and maybe she'd already experienced the blossoming of affection for him. But he didn't love her. Could she be happy if he never grew to love her?

She swallowed, not sure if she could.

Would it be enough to be united in marriage for the sake of the children?

"Ha!" Benjy wriggled in her arms so forcefully, she almost dropped him. She fumbled for a second but regained her hold and hugged him to her.

"Hello!"

Janie spun toward the voice and saw a wagon approaching with a man and woman on the bench and a small red-headed boy standing behind them. Her heart dropped. *Not the Scroggins.* Even on a good day, she had to work hard to be hospitable to her nosy neighbors. She hadn't seen them since before Phil died.

"Who's that?"

Janie yelped, scaring Benjy, who jumped and puckered his lower lip. She looked over her shoulder at Aaron. "I didn't know you were in the barn."

"Sorry." He lightly touched her back with a hand that both calmed her and sent delightful shivers down her spine.

Benjy lunged for Aaron, and he grabbed the boy in midair. Janie was going to have to do a better job of holding him, or he'd jump clear out of her arms one day.

"Ah, I see. It's Elmer and Trudy Scroggins and that hellion of a son."

Janie chuckled, surprised by Aaron's description of the Scroggins boy.

The wagon slowed, and the boy hopped off the back before it stopped and ran over to her and Aaron. "Got anythin' to eat? I'm starved."

"Freddy! Mind your manners." Trudy stood, and her husband helped her down.

Janie guessed the couple wasn't much older than Aaron. They had an unkempt look, and a foul odor wafted off them. Elmer's faded overalls resembled a patchwork quilt, and his boots hadn't been polished in ages. Trudy's pale blue dress matched her eyes, and her curly red hair refused to stay pinned back, reminding Janie of a well-loved doll.

Trudy studied her and Aaron with a narrowed gaze, making Janie feel the need to squirm, but she wasn't sure why.

Freddy tugged on his mother's skirt until Janie thought it would surely rip. "Ma, you said we'd get somethin' to eat here."

Janie sucked in a quiet gasp at the boy's rudeness.

Aaron stepped past her and held out his free hand to Elmer. "Been a while."

"Yep, sure has. What'cha doin' here, Harper?" Elmer eyed Benjy, then glanced at Janie.

"Just helping out where needed."

"Looks a bit like you've made yerself at home."

Janie walked up to stand beside Aaron, already tired of the visitors. "Why don't I take Benjy inside, and Trudy and I can have some tea while you men talk?" She thought of being alone with Trudy and her son, then reconsidered. "Of course, you're welcome to join us, if you'd like."

"We may come inside in a bit." Aaron winked at her, as if he'd read her thoughts.

Janie nodded, took Benjy from him, and turned toward the cabin. Freddy yipped and ran for the porch, while Trudy fell into step with Janie.

The woman clucked her tongue and shook her head. "What is Aaron Harper doin' here mere weeks after your husband passed?"

Janie clenched her jaw but forced it to relax. "I'm sure you can imagine how difficult it would be to run your farm if Elmer died."

"Oh, don't say such a thing. If that ever happens, I'll sell out and move in with Mama." Trudy sidled a glance at her. "How's about you? Are you thinkin' of leavin'?"

Janie didn't know how to respond. Aaron's proposal rested foremost in her mind, but she still didn't know if accepting it was the right thing to do.

"Freddy!"

Janie jumped and realized the Scroggins boy had opened the door and walked on into the house, ignoring his mother's yell. She shifted Benjy to her other arm and struggled not to be irritated. Having visitors was usually a blessing, since she saw other women so rarely, but she found it hard to enjoy the Scrogginses and prayed that God would help her to treat them hospitably.

As they entered the house, and Janie's eyes adjusted to the dimness, she saw Freddy at her worktable, lifting the towel off the apple bread she'd baked yesterday for tonight's dessert.

"Git away from there, boy," Trudy yelled. "Sit yerself down at the table and behave, or you'll get nothin'."

The five-year-old frowned and climbed onto Phil's chair but then slid off it again. Janie put Benjy down on his quilt and handed him his ball, then washed her hands in the porcelain bowl while Trudy plopped into a chair at the table, not bothering to clean up.

After setting her teapot to boil, Janie sliced the apple bread and arranged the pieces on a plate, which she set on the table. Freddy stood in his chair and reached across the table, grabbing two slices, which he promptly shoved into his mouth at the same time. Crumbs clung to his lips and dropped to his clothing, the table, and the floor. Janie grimaced at the child's deplorable manners. She would make certain Benjy knew how to act, both at home and when visiting someone else's house.

"That Aaron Harper is a pleasin' man to look on." Trudy stared at Janie as if daring her to disagree.

Janie wanted to say she hadn't noticed, but she wouldn't lie. "That's true, and he's a hard worker. I don't know what I would have done without the Harpers' help after losing Phil."

"It ain't right that you have a man as comely as Aaron workin' here."

"What do you mean?" What difference did it make if he was handsome or not?

"I'm just sayin' that a man like that might tempt a woman outta her mournin'." She eyed Janie's brown dress. "And you ain't even wearin' widow's weeds."

She felt like moaning aloud at the woman's crass comments. "My only black dress caught fire when I was washing Benjy's diapers." She rubbed the scar the burn had made on her right hand. "I don't have the money to buy fabric for another one, and there aren't exactly any stores nearby."

Trudy stuck her nose in the air as she pulled another slice of apple bread onto her plate. "Well, you don't have to get huffish."

The water in the teapot bubbled, and Janie hopped up, glad to make even a brief escape. She prepared two cups and then carried them to the table. As she set them down, Benjy let out a squeal.

Freddy appeared on the far side of the table, holding Benjy's ball and grinning like a possum. Janie waited for Trudy to scold him, but she didn't, so Janie circled the table. She hated the thought of Benjy's ball being in that boy's dirty hands. She held out her palm. "Please give me the ball, Freddy."

The boy frowned and glanced at his mother, then looked back at Janie with an ornery gleam in his pale blue eyes. "No. I want it."

Benjy crawled to Janie, fussing, and pulled himself up on her skirt. She lifted him, patting his back.

"Give that baby his toy." Trudy dumped two heaping spoonfuls of the sugar into her cup—sugar that Janie was running low on.

As usual, Freddy ignored his mother. He tossed the ball in the air and caught it, then stuck out his tongue at Janie. She knew her expression revealed her shock, but the next time he tossed the ball up, she was ready and snatched it. Wrong as it was, she couldn't help the smirk that tugged at her lips.

Freddy glared at her, then burst into a wail. He ran to his mother and laid his head on her bosom. "She took my ball."

Trudy scowled at Janie. "Was it hurtin' anything to let him play with the toy?"

Janie's ire mounted. "Wasn't it wrong of him to steal it away from Benjy? And besides, my son chews on that ball. I don't want it getting dirty."

Trudy jumped up from her seat. "Are you sayin' my boy ain't clean?"

Sighing, Janie tried to find a way to pacify her guest. "I don't let any other child play with it since Benjy puts it in his mouth. Surely you can understand that."

"No, I don't. Freddy is the guest and should be allowed to play with it if he wants."

Benjy whined, most likely upset at the woman's tone.

Trudy snatched up her teacup, slogged back the rest of the contents, and dropped it onto the saucer, making it rattle. "I think it's time we leave. Freddy, go find yer pa."

The boy flashed Janie a look that she wanted to smack off his face. She shuddered, dreading to think what he would be like when he got older. She'd heard the Scrogginses had lost several other children, but that didn't mean they had to spoil Freddy so much that he was unbearable to be around.

Trudy marched toward the door, then spun around. "I suggest you get rid of that Harper man." Her gaze shifted past Janie to Phil's bedroom door. "It ain't right that you house a man in your home, not with you bein' a new widow an' all."

Janie gasped and tightened her grip on Benjy. "He doesn't stay in here. He sleeps in the barn."

"Uh-huh. You two looked mighty cozy standin' there at the barn door when we drove up. How come he was holdin' yer boy?"

Janie wished the hateful woman would just leave before her whole day was ruined. "Because Benjy likes him and misses Phil. What harm does it do?"

"You don't want that boy gettin' too attached." Trudy shook her head. "No, sir. You'd best send Aaron Harper packin'." She eyed Janie with a harsh glare. "You don't want folks talkin' 'bout you two."

Janie sucked in another loud breath. Of all the nerve! "Aaron Harper has been nothing but a kind, considerate neighbor. And if there's any talk, I'll know you're the one who started it."

Trudy huffed and turned, her nose so high in the air that she would have drowned had it been raining.

Janie regretted her harsh retort, but she wasn't sorry to see the woman leave.

And she would pray that Trudy kept her mouth shut. Aaron's reputation shouldn't be tarnished simply because he was helping her.

She considered his proposal again. Was accepting it the right thing to do?

If they married, it certainly would have people talking, what with her being a widow of only a few weeks—in their eyes, at least.

Could it be God's plan for her to marry Aaron? Had He been trying to tell her that through Trudy?

Janie sighed. She supposed if God could speak through a donkey, as the Bible said He did, He could speak through Trudy Scroggins.

That evening, Janie dried the last of the supper dishes, with the exception of their coffee cups, and placed them on the shelf. Aaron tiptoed past her carrying Benjy to bed. While she'd scrubbed the dishes, he'd rocked the boy to sleep—something Phil had never done. Aaron had a special touch with children. Maybe she ought to marry him so that her son could benefit from his influence. Benjy already adored him.

Aaron walked back into the kitchen and poured himself another cup of coffee, filling the room with his presence. He smelled of leather, outdoors, and the fresh hay he slept on each night, and having him just three feet away made her heart pound like a percussion drum at a symphony. If she had only herself and Benjy to think of, she'd marry him in a moment.

But she had to consider his well-being—and that of his children. She wiped off the table and caught him staring.

"You're doing an awful lot of sighing. You must have something weighing heavy on your mind."

She swallowed back her apprehension. "Do you think we could talk for a bit?"

"Sure." He nodded, then pulled out her chair.

"There's some apple bread left. Would you like a slice or two?"

He smiled and dropped onto his seat. "Yes. That sounds delicious."

She prepared the dessert, thinking on what to say and how to start the conversation. Her hand shook as she leaned close to Aaron's shoulder and set the plate in front of him. Needing more time, she topped off his coffee cup and hers, then put the pot back on the stove. Finally, she sat, staring at the half slice of bread she would never be able to eat, thanks to her nervousness.

"Mmm…this is really good. I'll pick apples all day if you'll keep making this stuff."

In spite of her anxiety, she smiled at his boyish delight. "It's a deal. I don't like picking apples because of the worms. Same thing with shucking corn." She waggled her eyebrows at him. "Did I ever tell you that I make delicious corn fritters?"

Aaron chuckled. "Why do I feel like I've been assigned the job of picking and shucking the corn?"

Janie loved their light banter and the way the lantern light glimmered in Aaron's eyes. His hair had grown past his collar, making him look even more rugged. She longed to run her fingers through it to see whether it felt soft or coarse. As she lifted her gaze, his eyes collided with hers, drawing her in and making her heart thunder like a runaway horse. She looked down into her cup. If she kept having those kinds of thoughts, she'd soon be begging him to marry her.

But could she agree when she didn't know if she'd ever be able to touch him like she longed to? To hold him when times seemed uncertain. To fully be his wife.

"Why don't you tell me what's bothering you?" He glanced down for a moment. "Are you struggling because you don't want to marry me but don't know how to tell me?"

She hated the uncertainty in his deep voice—uncertainty that she had put there. Feeling the need to comfort him, she reached across the table and touched his arm. "No, that's not it, exactly."

His gaze shot up, capturing hers and stealing her breath. "Then what is it?"

She inhaled and, before she could lose her nerve, told him, "I'm not sure our marrying would be fair to you."

The surprise on his face was almost comical. "Not fair to me? How do you figure?"

"You already said your first marriage had problems. Do you really want to marry me, knowing it would be a business arrangement?" Just voicing that hurt. It certainly wasn't the kind of union she longed for.

Aaron reached for her hand, his touch warm, gentle, and callused. "I wouldn't have asked if I didn't think we could make a go of it. I've prayed about it—a lot—and I believe this is God's provision for both of us."

He rubbed his thumb across her wrist, making her tremble. She'd prayed, too, but hadn't gotten any answers.

"If we obey what God tells us to do," he said quietly, "I believe that love for each other will come."

She gazed into his eyes, hoping, daring to believe that was true. If she believed he could love her, she would joyously agree. "You don't think people will talk…I mean, since Phil passed so recently?"

He shrugged. "People talk no matter what."

He was right. She knew that. Wouldn't people talk if they knew the truth about her?

"I like you, Janie, and I even felt a bit jealous of Phil in the past for finding a woman like you without much searching. I'm ready to be married again, to have my kids home with me. You need help with your ranch and raising your son. It makes sense for us to marry, so what do you say?"

The embers in the stove popped, and Janie jumped. Aaron tightened his grip on her hand, as if to reassure her. Everything he'd said made sense, as long as she ignored the part he didn't know about—Martin Metcalf. She'd left Boston over a year ago, but she still felt his wolfish breath on her neck. Still expected to see him step out of the shadows one day.

"Whatever concerns you have, we can face them together." The warmth and encouragement radiating from Aaron's eyes were such a contrast to her thoughts of Martin. One was dark and frightening, the other bright and hopeful.

Janie found herself nodding. "All right. I'll marry you."

"That's great!" The brilliant smile on Aaron's face was almost enough to chase away all of her doubts.

Almost.

But not quite all of them.

Chapter Thirteen

Karen Harper stepped into the room Janie had slept in the past two nights—a room at the Harper home, one they used as an infirmary whenever someone was sick or wounded. "Oh, my! You look lovely."

Gazing down at the beautiful dress that Sarah had given her, Janie smiled. It was the first new one she'd had since coming to Kansas, and while yellow wasn't her favorite color, she was grateful to be able to wear something Aaron hadn't already seen her in for her wedding day—her one and only wedding day.

Sarah picked up the brush off the bedside table. "I still have to fix her hair, but we're close to being done."

Karen nodded. "Good. The train came, and everyone is here and excited."

Sarah squealed, her blue eyes gleaming like sapphires in the sun. "I can't wait to see Josh and Sophie and that niece and ornery nephew of mine."

Thoughts of the children made Janie wonder about her son. "How is Benjy doing?"

"He was a little fussy, but Aaron took him out to see the 'ha's.'" Karen chuckled. "I just love hearing Benjy say that. It reminds me of my other grandsons when they were that age."

The anxiety in Janie's swirling stomach stilled at the way Karen already considered Benjy one of her grandchildren. She'd known her son would be gaining a loving father by her marriage, but she hadn't considered the extended family that would become theirs. She'd been humbled by how Nick and Karen, as well as Ethan and Sarah, had welcomed her into their family when Aaron told them they were getting married.

Yes, there had been a couple of raised eyebrows when it was first mentioned, but soon everyone was smiling and patting her back. Then a rider was sent at a gallop to Windmill to fetch the minister and the rest of the family. The rider had returned yesterday with news that all were coming, and then the cooking and other preparations had flown into locomotive speed.

"I guess I'd better get back out there, or those young'uns will be snitching food when Emma isn't looking." Karen waved and headed out the door, closing it behind her.

Sarah patted Janie's shoulder. "Enough talk of children. Turn around and let me fix your hair. We want you to look stunning when Aaron sees you at the ceremony."

Janie's heart sank. She could never look stunning. Her figure was too flat, and her features too homely. At least she would no longer be Plain Jane Dunn. In less than an hour, she would be Janie Harper—Mrs. Aaron Harper.

Never in her wildest dreams could she have imagined marrying a man as kind and handsome as he—a man who loved with his whole heart and protected those he cared for. She could only pray that she would one day stake a claim on a small section of his heart, because he already owned most of hers.

⌒

Aaron stood in the barn outside of Outlaw's stall, trying to keep Benjy calm while fending off his brothers. "Ethan, if you had concerns about me marrying Janie, why didn't you say something two days ago?"

Ethan rubbed the back of his neck, much like Aaron did when he was flummoxed. "I was shocked, to be honest. Phil hasn't even been gone a month yet."

"Almost." Aaron pulled Benjy's hand away from Outlaw's mouth.

"Three and a half weeks, to be exact," Josh said, leaning against the stall gate next to where Outlaw was stabled. "It's rather scandalous for a woman to remarry that quickly."

"The situation is unusual, I'll give you that. But I'm worried about Janie being alone all winter, and I want my children home with me. We've been apart for far too long."

"Corrie and Toby have done quite well in town." Josh straightened, as if he took offense at what Aaron had said.

Aaron turned away from the stall to face his brothers, and Benjy attempted to climb over his shoulder to get to Outlaw. The boy whined. "Shh…Benjy."

Ethan and Josh eyed each other, then gazed back at him. He loved his brothers and highly valued their opinion, but in this matter, his mind was made up. "Josh, you've done wonderfully with Corrie and Toby, and it's no slight on you that I want them home. I miss them, and they're growing up so fast, I can hardly believe it."

Josh opened his mouth to say something, but Aaron held up his hand. "Hear me out first."

His middle brother nodded, his blue eyes serious and mouth drawn tight.

"You, Sophie, and Mikey deserve some time to yourselves before the baby arrives."

"We had all summer," Josh said. "Mikey's glad to have Toby back. They're two peas in a pod, and Sophie will dearly miss Corrie's companionship."

Aaron frowned. It almost sounded like Josh wanted to keep Corrie and Toby permanently. Benjy reached for the brim of Aaron's hat. He blew air on the boy's arm, distracting him and making him laugh.

"He sure has taken to you." Ethan crossed his arms over his chest. "I don't guess that's a good enough reason to marry the boy's mother, though."

Aaron pursed his lips and blew a loud breath out his nose. "Is that what you think? I'd marry Janie because I adore her son?" He shook his head, disappointed. "I figured you thought more of me than to believe that."

"I don't believe that. I was only making sure. It's not like you to rush into something."

"I'm not rushing. I've been concerned about Janie's situation ever since I discovered Phil with his leg half chewed off and promised him I'd take care of her."

"Hang on," Josh said, pushing away from the stall. "You aren't marrying her because of an obligation you feel toward Phil, are you?"

Aaron rolled his eyes and sighed. It was becoming a habit. "Of course not. Janie and I have talked about all the possible scenarios. I've prayed long and hard about this, and I believe marrying her is what God wants me to do."

The starch seemed to leave both of his brothers at the same time.

"So, do you love her?" Ethan asked.

Aaron searched his mind. Did he love her? Even a little? The memory of hearing Janie sing infiltrated his thoughts, and he knew he did love her—at least a bit. "Some."

Ethan grinned. "Well, that gives me a little relief."

Josh nodded. "If there's a blossom of love, more will come."

"You're speaking from experience?" Aaron knew that Josh's relationship with Sophie had gotten off to a rocky start.

"You know I am. But once that seed of love sprouted, there was no denying it." Josh gazed into Aaron's eyes. "If you love her even a little, and you're sure this is God's will for both of you, then you have my blessing."

The tension fled from Aaron's shoulders, and he nodded his thanks, then glanced at Ethan. His youngest brother smiled. "Same here, big brother. Sarah and I will pray that you have an explosion of love."

Aaron chuckled. "Who's waxing poetic now?"

Ethan slapped Aaron's shoulder. "You'd better get dressed. You're not gettin' married in your denim pants and work shirt, are you?"

Josh held out his hands to Benjy and clapped them. "Come here, little guy. You want to go see the horses again?"

Benjy glanced from Josh to Aaron and back again. "Ha?" He bounced and reached for Josh.

"Traitor." Aaron chuckled. "If he gets fussy, feed him something. That boy loves to eat."

"Sounds like my two." Ethan waved his hand. "Go on. Get dressed."

Aaron jogged out of the barn, more thankful for his brothers' support than he could say. His talk with Ma and Pa had gone better than expected, with Pa's only concern being that he was marrying a woman who'd been married and widowed twice. He'd teasingly cautioned Aaron that she might be marrying him for his money.

Granted, he probably had a lot more than Phil ever had, but if Janie was looking for a rich man, he didn't fit the bill. He knew she wasn't, because she'd never asked for a thing. Della was a woman who'd craved fine things, and although Janie had several nice dresses, they paled in comparison to Della's exacting taste.

Janie wanted a home, security, and the ability to raise her son in a happy family. And Aaron aimed to give her those things. The cabin would be crowded until the new bedroom was built, and even then, with all the young'uns in the parlor at the same time, things would be a bit cramped. Maybe next year, he'd think about building a bigger house—one that would belong to him and Janie with no ghosts of past husbands.

Aaron shifted his weight from one foot to the other under the huge maple tree that stood between his parents' house and the smaller one that he'd once shared with Della, now inhabited by Ethan, Sarah, and their two boys. A mixture of excitement and apprehension bubbled through him—excitement at having his kids home again and to forge a new family with Janie, and anxiety over whether he was doing the right thing, as he'd conveyed to his brothers. Yes, he believed God had led him to propose to Janie, and that was what truly mattered. If he obeyed God, this union would have His blessing, and they would make it.

He tugged at his tie, which threatened to cut off his breathing, and glanced over at Toby, who sat between Mikey and Jeff in chairs the men had brought from the house for the family. Sophie held Benjy on her lap, and Sarah's aunt Emma had perched on one of the two seats at the end of the row, leaving the closer ones for Aaron's parents and brothers. It meant a lot to have his whole family here to support him and Janie.

He searched the yard for Corrie but didn't see his daughter. She'd been moping and pouting ever since finding out that she would no longer be living in town with Josh and Sophie. She loved school and would miss her friends terribly. He prayed it wouldn't take her long to adjust to living with him and Janie.

Aaron's gaze snapped back to his wriggling son. Toby looked covertly around, then pulled something from his pocket and held his hand out to Jeff. The boy slapped his palm to his mouth, his eyes twinkling. Aaron narrowed his gaze, wondering what mischief his son was up to, and willed Toby to look his way. After a moment, he did, and his eyes widened. Aaron wagged his finger, and Toby, lower lip protruding, shuffled over to where Aaron stood, waiting by the preacher for his bride.

"What, Pa?"

"What are you holding behind your back, Son?"

The boy hung his head and toed the dirt, flicking it onto Aaron's shiny boots. He sighed and shook his head. Having a ma again would be a good thing for Toby, but then, his son had never really had a caring mother. Of course, Aaron's ma had showered the children with affection, and Sophie had nurtured them, too, but it wasn't quite the same. He prayed Janie was up to the task. Toby slung another cloud of dust his way. "Stop that, Son, and take whatever critter you have in your hand over there"—Aaron flicked his head to the left—"and release it. Then take your seat and behave. I won't have my wedding spoiled by your antics."

"Yes, Pa." Toby dragged his feet all the way to where he turned loose the toad—at least, that's what Aaron thought it was—and then he dragged his feet back. The boy was covered in dust from knees to toes, but there was nothing Aaron could do about that now. He wiped the tops of his own boots on the backs of his pants and stared at the rear door of the house. When it opened, his heart took off like a rabbit fleeing a fox. Sarah exited the house, followed by Ma.

It wasn't too late to back out.

Could he make Janie happy? He wished he could say he loved her more than a little bit. Over the weeks he'd spent at her ranch, he'd gotten to know her better, enjoyed her delicious meals, and grown to appreciate how she loved and cared for Benjy and hadn't wept and wailed when she'd burned her hands. She had gumption—far more than Della—and he fully believed she could survive as a prairie wife.

No, he didn't feel the overwhelming love-at-first-sight that had consumed him when he first met Della. Nor would it have been right for him to, since Janie had been a married woman when they met; but maybe this time, love would grow slowly, and the roots would take hold and burrow deep. That was what he would pray—that, in time, Janie would grow to love him dearly and that his affection for her would multiply. Whether it did or not, he would be the best husband he knew how to be, and he'd try with all that was in him to please his wife.

The fiddler started playing some fancy tune he didn't recognize. Then Ma, who still stood on the porch, waved her hand, and Corrie came outside.

"Here we go." James Douglas, the pastor from Windmill, nudged Aaron's arm and winked.

Aaron's gut churned. He didn't like standing up in front of people. Because he was the oldest Harper brother, it had fallen naturally to him to be a leader, but he preferred to do it man to man and not in front of an audience. He swiped his moist hands on his pant legs, just about ready to bolt and call the whole thing off, but then Janie stepped onto the porch—a vision of loveliness in a pretty gown of sunflower yellow. Her hair had been piled on top of her head in a mass of curls, flowers, and ribbon, making her look taller—and far more fetching—than normal.

Sarah waved for Corrie to join her, and then she grabbed Ethan, and the three hurried down the aisle to their seats. Ethan scooted Jeff over and sat Mark on the chair with his brother, the younger boy squealing in delight, and Josh dropped into the seat between Mikey and Sophie. Then Aaron's gaze snapped to the back, where Pa waited for Ma. She gave Janie a quick hug and whispered something—probably a welcome to the family— then scurried to her place next to Pa.

A group of the Harpers' cowboys stood behind the chairs on the right side, where several of the older hands sat, shifting their stance and looking as uncomfortable as Aaron felt. They were there to support him, and he appreciated it, because he knew they preferred to be on horseback, out on the prairie. At least they would get rewarded for their faithfulness when the food was rolled out. The smells from the kitchen had nearly driven him loco.

The fiddler's tune changed, and Janie caught Aaron's gaze as she started moving toward him. He swallowed the lump building in his throat. He was committing the rest of his life to a woman he barely knew, and yet he felt it was what God wanted him to do. At least, he sure hoped he'd heard God correctly.

His bride-to-be lifted her lips in an anxious smile, while her eyes held uncertainty. She was bound to be nervous, getting married for the third time. He could only hope and pray that the third time was a charm.

"Aaron, please take Janie's hand and face me."

He did as the pastor requested, noting how Janie's hand trembled. Was she afraid of him? He'd done nothing to warrant any reservations, but then, she really didn't know him any better than he did her. He squeezed her hand and smiled down at her, hoping to alleviate her concerns. Love or not, they were in this together.

He gazed at the preacher, ready to commit himself to a woman for the second time in his life.

Chapter Fourteen

Janie muttered the responses in the right places—at least, it seemed that way, since the minister continued on and didn't give her any odd looks. Her trembling had finally ceased, thanks to Aaron's gentle touch and encouraging smile, but her tongue had tripped over itself as she'd realized that she would soon be this wonderful man's wife.

And that thought set her to shaking all over again.

As she pledged to have and to hold, her cheeks grew scorching. She glanced up at Aaron, and he had the gall to wink at her. What did that mean?

She hurried to say the next line. "For better or for worse."

If Martin ever found her, things would certainly get much worse.

"In sickness and in health."

Aaron frowned. Had she said the wrong thing?

"To love and to cherish from this day forward until death do us part."

Unable to gaze into Aaron's dark brown eyes, she studied the buttons on his black frock coat as she committed her life to him. Could he sense her secret? Her fear?

The pastor nodded at them, then looked up at the audience. "Please bow your heads as I pray for the new couple."

Janie blessedly closed her eyes. Would God honor a marriage such as hers? Here she was, pledging to honor a man from whom she was withholding the truth of her past—a past that could potentially endanger him and his children. She should have told him long ago that she'd never been married. That she wasn't really Benjy's mother. That a vengeful maniac might come looking for her one day.

"Aaron, you may kiss your bride."

Her gaze shot to his, and his eyebrows lifted as if asking permission. Heart thundering, she licked her lips and gave a slight nod, and his face descended, stealing all breath from her. His lips—warm, soft, gentle—rested against hers, sending delicious sparks throughout her body like shooting embers of fire. She'd never experienced such a stirring event, and she didn't want it to end.

But they had an audience.

He pulled back, a self-satisfied gleam blazing in his eyes. One side of his mouth turned up in a confident grin. He knew the effect he had on her, and the rascal was proud of it.

Her cheeks heated. Was this part of the spark between husband and wife?

She knew so little about being a wife. She'd been so young when her parents had died, but she remembered her father holding her mother close and kissing her, and she could picture the contented expression her mother always had afterward. Was that how Janie looked after Aaron's kiss?

"Ladies and gentlemen, it gives me great pleasure in presenting Mr. and Mrs. Aaron Harper."

Aaron turned her to face the crowd of smiling people, and she wanted to duck behind her new husband. She didn't want everyone to see the fraud she was.

Karen ran forward and hugged them both, but her happy gaze snagged Janie's. "Welcome to the family, dear. You don't know how many prayers I've prayed for God to send Aaron a wife."

"Ma-a." Aaron's tone was abashed.

Karen reached up and patted her son's cheek. "Well, it's true—and now He has."

Swarmed by well-wishers, Janie allowed herself to be caught up in the excitement. This was her wedding, after all, and she wanted it to be a happy time for Aaron and his family, who had helped and blessed her so much.

She could only pray that when the truth came out, they wouldn't all desert her.

⌒

By the time they pulled into the ranch yard, the sun already hovered below the horizon, its invisible rays lining the bellies of the clouds in a lovely shade of pink. How odd that she'd left here two days ago as Mrs. Dunn—in actuality, Miss Dunn— and returned as Mrs. Aaron Harper. Karen had begged them to stay another day or two, but Aaron thought it best for them to start their new life together at their own home. He pacified his mother with a promise to return for dinner next Sunday.

The cow mooed for attention. The man watching the place had returned to the Harpers' ranch earlier in the day for the wedding. Aaron glanced out the corner of his eye at Janie. "I'll help you inside and get all this stuff unloaded, then Toby and I will see to the animals."

She nodded, feeling odd around him now that they were married. Would he expect more from her than she was willing to give, even though he had promised not to overburden her? As the wagon squeaked to a halt, the horses blew out a loud breath, as if they knew their work was over. Benjy slept in her arms, while Corrie and Toby rode in the back. The boy had chattered on and on about all manner of things, from lizards to the cake and treats they'd had after the wedding to missing Mikey to being glad he didn't have to return to town and attend school. Corrie said not a word. Janie could tell the girl was upset. Was it because she had a new mother? Or some other reason?

She'd taught enough girls to know that Corrie was at a temperamental age. Maybe after a few days, she would thaw and give Janie a chance to prove they could be friends.

Aaron stood and hopped off the side of the wagon. "Stay here until I light the lanterns."

Janie nodded, though he was already moving away from her. Back East, they'd called lanterns "lamps." That was one of many things she'd needed to adjust to when she crossed the Mississippi.

Toby slid to the rear of the wagon and scooted off. "This house isn't very big. Do I get ta sleep in the barn?" His tone rose at the end of his sentence, as if the notion excited him.

Janie swallowed. She had agreed to share the big bedroom with Aaron, and the thought frightened her more than coming face-to-face with a rabid wolf. How would they manage? What if—heaven forbid—she needed to use the chamber pot during the night? Her cheeks flamed, and she was grateful for the darkness.

Lights shone in the window, giving the cabin a cozy glow. As she studied the place, she realized that it was far smaller than the Harpers' huge house, and probably even smaller than Josh and Sophie's house in Windmill, because she'd heard it had two stories, like Ethan and Sarah's.

Aaron strode out the door and jogged down the porch steps. "Let me have Benjy."

Janie slid over on the seat and handed the boy to him, then prepared to climb to the ground unassisted, but he shifted Benjy to one arm then reached up, smiling. "Allow me, Mrs. Harper."

Corrie made a sound in the back of the wagon that resembled a cat coughing up a hair ball. Janie put her hand into Aaron's and let him assist her, wondering if Corrie was reacting to him calling her "Mrs. Harper." Did it bother the girl that her father had remarried?

Time would tell.

"Why don't I carry Benjy in while you bring some of the food your mother sent?"

He shook his head. "It's no trouble. Do you want him in his bed?"

Janie shrugged. "It's a bit early—and he hasn't had supper. Lay him on my bed—I mean, Corrie's—and I'll change him. That should wake him."

Toby followed his father into the house, and Janie turned to Corrie. "Aren't you coming in?"

In the waning light, she saw the girl shrug and then swipe at her eyes. Janie longed to touch her but didn't. "I know that change can be difficult, but you'll get used to living here. You'll see."

Corrie jumped up so fast, Janie recoiled. "I don't want to get used to it! I want to return to Windmill, where my friends are. I want to go back to school. I was never given a choice about coming here. Just an order." She hopped off the rear of the buggy, but instead of going to the house, she turned and ran toward the barn.

Janie heard Aaron coming down the stairs, then felt his breath on her neck. "I'm sorry. She's unhappy about not returning to Windmill, but she has no call to be rude to you."

"And she's probably distressed about having a new mother. Be gentle with her, Aaron. Girls her age have emotions that change more often than the weather here."

He squeezed her shoulder. "That's good advice. I knew God brought us together for a reason."

Janie smiled as he walked away, then hurried into the house to check on Benjy and Toby. Toby strolled out of the big bedroom and looked at her, his brow puckered. "There aren't enough beds for everyone. How come?"

Janie peeked at Benjy, who lay sprawled in his bed, slumbering, then turned back to her new son. "Your grandpa and uncle Ethan and some of their hands will be over next Saturday to build another bedroom. For now, we'll have to make do."

"Where's Pa?" Toby had his father's dark eyes, but his hair was dishwater blond. She suspected it would darken as he got older. Like his father, he was comely.

"Out in the barn."

"Guess I'll go help him." He shuffled toward the door, then paused and turned. "I'm glad you're my new ma, even if Corrie isn't." As if the announcement embarrassed him, he spun back toward the door and bolted through it.

Janie smiled, thankful for the boy's encouraging comment. "One down, one to go."

~

The barn door creaked as Aaron opened it, unleashing the familiar odor of hay and livestock. He groped for the nearest lantern, then lit a match, and the wick flamed to life. The cow mooed at him, obviously in need of relief, but he had to find Corrie first. If he hadn't been worried about the Scrogginses ruining Janie's reputation, he would have taken the time to ride the train into Windmill and tell his children that he was marrying again instead of sending one of the cowboys with a note for Josh and Sophie.

He drifted away from the light, listening. Hearing a sniffle, he walked over to one of the empty stalls and found Corrie leaning her head against the stall post. Heart aching, Aaron sent up a prayer for wisdom and wrapped his arm around his daughter's shoulders. She was taller than she'd been when he brought her home at the end of the last term, her head reaching his collarbone. "Hey there, punkin. What's wrong?"

She turned and burrowed her face in his chest. "I don't want to be here. I want to go back to Windmill—back to school."

He winced. "Don't you want to be here with me—to be a family again?"

Corrie wiped her face on her sleeve. "I do, but I really miss my friends. I didn't even get to say good-bye. We just packed up and came home—and you got m-married." Her sobs started again.

"Would you rather Janie and her little boy live out here all alone?" He couldn't believe he'd stooped so low as to use guilt to make her see reason.

"No, but why did you have to *marry* her?"

Because I heard her sing, and knew I wanted to listen to her voice for the rest of my life. He cleared his throat. "I...uh...felt it was God's will."

She flung her arms out and stepped back. "Oh, that's grand. You get a wife. Toby is thrilled to not have to go to school. I'm the one that has to pay by leaving my friends."

Aaron heaved a sigh and rubbed his nape. Why couldn't women see the practical side of a situation and just do what was needed? A shaft of conviction stabbed him. Had he been seeing to his own needs—uniting his family and putting a salve on his guilt over not being a good father—instead of thinking of what was best for his children?

Corrie sniffled. "I don't suppose you'd reconsider letting me return to Windmill to live with Uncle Josh."

Aaron felt as if he'd been shot. "You'd rather live with him than me?"

"No, Pa. It isn't that. I love school and my friends and doing things in town. There's nothing to do out here."

She sounded like her mother. Della had wheedled and whined, trying to talk Aaron into leaving the ranch and moving to town. He was a rancher. What would he do in town?

Now his daughter had taken her mother's place—and that irritated him more than a little. "You're not going back to town, Corrie. This is your home now, and the sooner you adjust, the happier we all will be."

She sucked in a gasp. "But that's not fair."

"Life isn't fair." He sounded like his folks, and he didn't like it, but he wouldn't bend to her whining and disapproval. "Go inside and help your ma unpack the food."

Toby crept into the barn, and Aaron saw him, but the stamp of Corrie's shoe drew his gaze back to her.

"That woman is not my ma."

"Corrie, that's enough belligerence from you. You'll do as you're told, or I'll take a switch to your backside."

She sucked in another breath of surprise, then frowned, folding her arms across her chest. "Yes, Pa." She slipped around him and marched out of the barn, taking much of Aaron's tension with her.

"Why's she so mad?" Toby climbed onto the stall gate.

"She misses her friends." *And doesn't want to be here and doesn't like her new ma.*

"Me, too. I miss Mikey most, but I'm glad I don't gotta go to school no more."

"Any more." Aaron ruffled this son's hair.

"That's what I said. When're we gonna eat?"

"After we finish the chores."

"But I'm starved."

"Well, the sooner we get done, the better. You can start with the milking." Aaron walked over to the cow's stall. "This is Lucy. Make sure you warm your hands, because she doesn't like cold ones."

Aaron set the milk stool and bucket in place while Toby rubbed his palms together. It had been a month or two since the boy had milked a cow, but he knew what to do. Aaron watched him for a few minutes, then walked out to the wagon, grabbed one of several crates of food and supplies his ma had sent with them, and carried it into the house.

Corrie sat at the table, spooning something into Benjy's mouth. When the boy saw Aaron, he slapped the table and squealed.

"Eww!" Corrie jumped up, scowling. "He just spewed all over my new dress."

Benjy scrunched up his face and started crying.

"Oh, I'm sorry." Janie grabbed a towel off her worktable and handed it to Corrie, then reached for Benjy. "Why don't you go into the bedroom and change?"

"Into what?" Corrie wiped off her hand and sleeve.

"I'll get your trunk." Aaron set the crate down and turned, hurrying toward the door. The peaceful home he'd enjoyed with Janie had turned into a crisis of upset children. He had a feeling things wouldn't be peaceful again for a long while.

⌒

"How come I gotta sleep on the floor?" Toby crossed his arms and glared at Aaron.

"Because you're a young man, and men give up their chairs— or beds—if a woman has need of them. Besides, it's only temporary. By next Saturday eve, you'll get to sleep on the bed."

Toby plopped down on the pad of quilts in the corner of the small bedroom. "How come Corrie gets the new room? Why can't I have it?"

Aaron rolled his neck, tension making it feel as if it was locked in a vise. "Because she's the oldest and the only girl, and she needs her privacy. There are two of you boys, so you'll bunk together. And Benjy needs to be close to Janie in case he cries at night."

"But if he cries, he'll wake me up."

Aaron seriously doubted anything could wake his son once he was asleep. "Say your prayers, Toby. Morning comes early."

The boy mumbled a short prayer, then flopped down with a loud sigh and turned his back to Aaron, who fled the room. He had known there would be adjustments for them all to make, but he hadn't expected this much of a fight from his son.

Wearing the nightgown she'd just donned, Corrie slipped out of the bedroom Aaron would soon share with Janie. Her long dark hair flowed around her like a cape, creating a pretty scene, but her puckered expression made it look as if she'd just chewed a stick of rhubarb. Behind Corrie, he could see Janie moving around in the bedroom, and his gaze latched onto her unbound hair. His chest tightened at the lovely sight, but he refocused on his perturbed daughter. Had Janie said something to upset her?

"Why do I have to share a room with those boys, Pa? It's downright indecent."

He blew out a loud sigh. "It's only for a few nights. After that, you'll have your own room again."

"Couldn't I sleep on the sofa? That way, Toby wouldn't have to bed down on the floor."

"No. You're sleeping in the bed, and that's final." He didn't want to mention that *he* might end up on the sofa if sleeping beside his new wife proved too tempting.

She made a huffing sound and stomped into the small room. Who were these children, and when had they become so argumentative? He longed to head to the barn and fall asleep on a soft bed of hay, but that would mean having to answer another round of questions from his kids. He'd better just do what had to be done. First, though, he headed outside to visit the privy, hopefully giving Janie the time she needed to get ready for bed.

A short time later, before returning to the house, he lowered the bucket into the well and hauled it up. He splashed the cool water onto his face, hoping it would help him keep his wits about him. He'd made a promise to Janie that their marriage would be a business arrangement, but he wasn't sure how to manage that long-term with his wife snuggled up next to him. "Help me out here, Lord. I'm in over my head."

Chapter Fifteen

Janie shivered as she crawled between the cold sheets. She probably ought to take the side of the bed near the wall, since she'd gotten in first, but if Benjy needed her, she wanted to be able to get out without having to crawl over Aaron. Her body wouldn't stop trembling—and it wasn't from the cold, because the sheets had warmed against her body. The thought of sharing a bed with a man frightened her more than just about anything, except for Martin finding her and taking Benjy away. Why had she agreed to marry Aaron? Agreed to share his bed?

Carolyn had been happy when she first married Martin, but things had soon changed. She couldn't please him and had shared with Janie that he wanted her to perform acts she wasn't comfortable doing. After she refused him, Martin started staying out late at night and became abusive when he was home. Janie never understood why her cousin didn't leave the cruel man.

She found it hard to imagine Aaron becoming mean like Martin. She'd once heard him raging at Carolyn in the hall while Janie was in her cousin's bedroom. Martin hadn't known she was there. What would he have done if he had discovered her?

She swallowed hard, thinking of the pain Carolyn had silently endured. Martin made certain to never hit her where it would show, and if not for her corset stays, Carolyn would surely have suffered a broken rib on more than one occasion.

The front door opened and closed, and as Janie turned to face the wall, the bed creaked. Aaron would know she wasn't asleep. She willed her heart to calm, lest he hear its frantic beating. Her eyes popped open when she realized she would be facing Aaron once he joined her in bed. And what did a man sleep in, anyway?

The last time she'd been this scared, she'd been sitting with Benjy on a train in Boston, waiting impatiently to leave the station. She'd been certain Martin would show up at the last minute, take the boy back, and have her thrown in jail. He knew many people who had power in that city. But as the train departed, she'd allowed herself to relax, knowing that, though Kansas was a strange place to her, Phil would take care of them.

Now she was depending on a man she barely knew.

Aaron rustled around behind her, making quiet noises. She heard his boots drop to the floor and imagined he was taking off his clothes. She squeezed her eyes shut, trying to still her ragged breathing. Maybe once he fell asleep, she could sneak into the parlor and sleep on the sofa. Would that be a horrible thing to do?

Aaron exhaled a loud sigh, then crawled up from the foot of the bed. At least he hadn't climbed over her. He wrestled around until he got under the sheets. His cold foot touched Janie's, and she jumped.

He had the gall to chuckle.

"It's not funny." She gasped that she'd spoken out loud—to the man who was in her bed.

"Sorry. This bed's rather small."

She wasn't sure if he was apologizing for laughing or for touching her. And the bed had seemed huge to her until he climbed in, filling it with his large body and radiating heat, warming her. Maybe there was one thing good about sharing a bed.

"I'm sorry, too, for the way my children have acted. It's not like them to be so fussy."

"I understand. Getting a new mother, leaving their school friends, and moving to a new place are big changes."

He wiggled around and settled on his back, propping his hands behind his neck. His elbow was only an inch or two from Janie's face. She was thankful to see, in the faint moonlight coming in the window, that he wore his union suit.

"I suppose I didn't fully think through how our marriage would affect Corrie and Toby. I just wanted them back home with me."

He remained silent for a while, lost in his thoughts, Janie assumed.

"They're growing up so fast...I just didn't want to miss another day of their childhood."

Carolyn had done what she thought best for the safety of Benjy, as had Janie. She might well be considered a kidnapper, even though she had her cousin's letter to validate her actions. "We often make difficult choices for the sake of our children."

"Are you referring to coming to Kansas to be with Phil—or your marrying me?" He turned on his right side, and she could feel his warm, coffee-scented breath on her face.

She wanted to turn over, away from this man—this husband of hers—but she was afraid that if she did, she'd roll right off the edge. Their conversation had quieted her nerves some. "I guess I mean both, as well as other decisions I've made." Ones she couldn't tell him about.

He reached over and found her hand, thankfully not touching anything else by accident in the process. She liked the warmth of his big, callused palm. It was comforting and reassuring.

"You're shaking. Are you cold?"

She didn't dare tell him he was the reason she trembled. "Maybe a little."

"Why don't you move closer, and we'll keep each other warm?"

Her ragged breathing returned. Was he going to pressure her to give more than she was willing?

"You have nothing to fear from me, Janie. I gave you my word that this would be a business arrangement, and, hard as that may be for me, I promise not to go back on it."

She blinked in the dark. What was hard on him? Being married to her? Or not having physical relations with his wife?

He released her hand and sighed. Then he trailed his fingers through her tresses spread out on the mattress between them. "You have beautiful hair. I like how it resembles finely hewn wood when the sun shines on it."

He liked her hair? She'd always thought it so plain. Brown. Just like a boring sparrow. "Uh...thank you."

"Thank you...for marrying me."

Again he surprised her. She was the desperate one. She should be thanking him.

"Janie, I'd like to ask one thing of you, if you're willing."

Her heart pounded in her ears, sounding like a woman kneading bread dough. "What's that?"

"I always liked to give my wife a kiss before leaving the house and before going to sleep. Would you allow that?" His deep voice rumbled softly in her ear.

Her thoughts shot back to his wonderful kiss at the wedding. She couldn't believe the emotions it had stirred in her, and she actually wanted to kiss him again. "I suppose that would be all right."

She was certain she heard him grin, if such a thing was possible. He rose up on one elbow and gently brushed the hair from her face. Then he leaned down, slowly, his breath mingling with hers. Janie thought her heart would burst out of her chest, but then his lips claimed hers, and all thoughts turned to mush.

He pressed his mouth against hers, harder than at the wedding but not in a hurtful way. No, it was scrumptious and sent scalding stirrings racing through her body. She found herself responding, pushing back with her lips. Suddenly, he pulled away and flopped down. Like a wave, the mattress tick shifted, sending Janie over the edge. She landed with a *thunk* on the floor and lay there, stunned.

Aaron chuckled. "That gives a whole new meaning to falling for me."

Janie stood, embarrassed to her toes. Of all the nerve. She reached for her pillow and slammed it against her husband's head. It barely muffled his laughter. She climbed back in bed, wondering if every kiss would rattle her so much. Could Aaron tell she'd never kissed a man before?

He moved her pillow back where it belonged, but when she reclined, she found his arm beneath it and stiffened.

"Come here, and let me keep you from falling again. No more kissing or anything else. I promise."

She scooted over and allowed him to pull her close with her head lying on his muscular shoulder. Her hand rested against his broad chest, feeling the steady *thump* of his heart. This husband of hers was all man, no doubt about it. All muscles and strength. She forced herself to relax and quickly discovered she liked being cocooned in his arms. She felt safer there than she had anywhere for a very long time. Not since before her parents died had she felt so protected.

And she was surprised to discover she was disappointed that he'd said no more kissing. She looked forward to tomorrow night.

⁓

Toby sat on the top of the stall railing while Aaron cleaned Smokey's hooves.

"Can I have my own horse now? I'll need one if I'm gonna help you with the cattle and stuff."

"I'll think about it." Probably wasn't a bad idea. Toby had been riding almost since he was Benjy's size, and he would need a horse for many of the tasks Aaron would expect him to perform on the ranch. He released Smokey's leg and straightened. "You'll be helping me only part of the time, though. Just because you don't live in town anymore doesn't mean you won't have schooling."

"Aw, shoot. But I want to work with you. I'm nine and nearly a man. See?" The boy flexed his arm upward to show Aaron his muscles.

Scrawny was the word that came to mind, but he kept that to himself. "I see them. You're growing up, Son, but it's important in these modern days for a man to know how to read and cipher."

"I already know that stuff."

Aaron leaned against the rail and tapped the hoof pick against it to clean it. "All right, then, answer this: If a sack holds fifty pounds of oats, and you give a bucket of oats to each of your horses twice a day, how long before the sack will be empty?"

Toby's brownish-blond eyebrows dipped as he pondered the question. His mouth quirked up to one side, and then his expression registered defeat. He shrugged. "I don't know."

"And that's why you need to continue your schooling. Ranchers and farmers are businessmen. They need to know how to calculate such things to avoid buying too much or too little. Your livestock could die over the winter if you don't have enough feed for them. You also need to be good at ciphering so that unscrupulous men can't take advantage of and rob you."

Toby sighed. He must have realized there would be no escaping school.

"But for today, you don't have to worry. You're my helper until Janie is ready to start teaching you two."

"Yee-haw!"

Smokey jerked his head at the sudden outburst, and Aaron reached over to pat the horse's rump. "Easy, boy."

The gelding resumed eating his hay, and Aaron eyed his son. "Sorry, Pa."

"Speaking of work, go fill the wood box for Janie, and see how much longer it will be until lunch is ready."

"Yes, sir." Toby swung around, jumped down into the empty stall next to Smokey's, and walked out the open gate. Then he stopped and turned. "Pa, what am I supposed to call her? Don't quite seem right to call her 'Ma.'"

This was a question Aaron should have anticipated, but he hadn't. "Maybe you should ask her. I think it would be good if you called her 'Ma,' but if you're not comfortable with it, I won't insist."

Toby nodded, then plodded out the barn door.

Aaron put the hoof pick back in the box where it belonged, and then grabbed a currycomb and started grooming Phil's horse. Last night, while he held Janie as she drifted off to sleep, he'd prayed for his new family. Prayed that his children would adjust quickly and not give Janie too much trouble. Prayed that Janie would adjust well to being a mother of three—including a stubborn, emotional girl on the verge of womanhood. Prayed that she would come to love him and that they could soon be a true married couple in every way. And he'd asked God to grant him the patience and wisdom he needed to care for his new family.

He rested his arms across Smokey's back as he thought about last night and how Janie had responded to his kiss. She'd been hesitant at first—almost as if she didn't know how to kiss a man—but that was just plain nonsense. What woman who'd been married twice before didn't know how to kiss?

But she had soon warmed to him and reciprocated, even grasping hold of the top of his union suit, as if to keep him from moving away. He grinned. Yes, sir, maybe there was hope for a real marriage.

In the meantime, he had his hands full with his children, helping them to get settled. Things would be easier when Corrie had her own room again. He doubted she knew how fortunate she was to be getting that. When his family first moved to Kansas, Aaron had shared not only a room but also a bed with Ethan and Josh. Of course, they were all fairly small then. Being together had been a comfort. They had left their home back East and moved to a strange, rugged place with no other people nearby. It had been a bit scary but also exhilarating. It hadn't taken him long to fall in love with the wild Kansas plains. He could only hope and pray Janie felt the same.

⁓

Sweat trickled down Janie's back, and she squirmed, trying to stop its flow. The pastry crust of the beef pie baking in the oven filled the room with a buttery aroma, teasing her stomach. It was a fancier noon meal than she normally prepared, but she wanted to make something special for their first lunch as a family. The extra wedding food Karen had sent home with them made things easier.

Some family, though. Benjy was the only one who seemed completely taken with everyone. Corrie had barely talked to her all morning, mumbling and muttering only when Janie had pointedly asked her a question. She'd done little to help and had stayed in her bed reading for much of the morning. Janie glanced over where Corrie now sat on the floor, watching Benjy play with his ball. At least the girl seemed enamored of him.

Give me wisdom with her, Lord. Help me to be a friend to her and the mother she needs, even if she doesn't know—

The front door banged open, and Janie jerked her head toward it. Toby lumbered in, carrying a load of wood that looked far too heavy for his slight frame. He hadn't developed muscles yet, but he seemed determined not to let that bother him. He dropped the load into the box and looked her way. "Pa wants to know how long before lunch is ready."

Benjy clapped his hands and squealed. Toby bent down and patted his head. "Howdy, little buddy."

Using her apron to protect her hand, Janie peeked in the oven at the lightly golden crust. "Probably another few minutes or so. You might tell him it's time to wash up."

"Good! I'm starved." He spun and ran out the door, leaving it open.

She smiled, glad that the boy had a healthy appetite, like his father. They would have to work on the door issue before cold weather set in. Corrie had merely picked at her food last night and at breakfast. Janie worried she might get sick if she didn't eat something soon.

"Corrie, would you please set the table?"

The girl sat staring at Benjy, her elbows on her knees and her face in her hands, ignoring her.

Janie didn't know whether to scold her or ignore her, too. But pretending she wasn't there wouldn't solve anything. "Corrie, I need you to set the table so we can eat."

With a loud huff, the girl rose and flounced over to where Janie kept the silverware. She snatched it out of the small basket, making a clatter, and glared at Janie with narrowed eyes. "You're not my mother, you know. I had one, but she died."

"Corrie!"

The girl gasped and whirled toward the door. "Pa! I didn't know you were there."

He walked into the house, frowning. "Obviously. Set the table, then I want to have a talk with you."

"Yes, sir." She ducked her head, completed the task, and shuffled outside.

Aaron walked over to Janie. "Something sure smells good."

"Beef pie—and it's nearly done."

He gazed down at her, his eyes filled with remorse. "I'm sorry about what Corrie said."

"It's not your fault." Janie laid a hand on his arm. "I know she doesn't want to be here. It will take time for her to get to know me and for us to form a routine."

"Thanks for understanding." Aaron blew out a breath that warmed Janie's face. "She misses her friends. I allowed her to live in town so long that she got used to it. Got soft."

"Girls are supposed to be soft." Janie smiled. The thought of how soft Aaron's lips had felt against hers last night made her cheeks heat. "Don't be too hard on her. We didn't exactly have time to prepare the children for this change, so I'm sure it was a big shock. We probably should expect some backlash."

"Maybe, but I won't have her being disrespectful." The stern look in Aaron's eyes softened, and his mouth tilted up on one side. He ran the back of his hand along her cheek, sending her heart tripping over itself. "For the record, this isn't the kind of softness I was referring to." He winked, then turned toward the door. Benjy squealed as Aaron passed him, and the big man stopped suddenly, picked up the boy, and tossed him in the air. Benjy's excited laughter warmed Janie.

"I'll take him with me," Aaron said over his shoulder.

She thought about asking him not to. He should speak to Corrie without the distraction Benjy might create, but Aaron knew his daughter better than she.

Janie pulled the golden-brown beef pie from the oven and set it on the table, alongside the jar of applesauce, bowl of butter, and basket of sliced bread that Karen had sent home with them. Steam rose from the pie, filling the house with its delicious aroma. Her stomach gurgled.

She filled the children's cups with milk and hers and Aaron's with coffee. Everything was ready. All she needed was for her family to come to the table.

To resist the temptation to tiptoe to the door and listen in, she reached for Benjy's bowl, then dug into the beef pie, pulling out some potatoes and carrots so they could cool. She cut them up, then decided to butter a slice of bread for each person.

With that done, she sat in her chair to wait. She bowed her head. "Father, please give Aaron wisdom. Help Corrie to adjust to her new life. Let us be friends, and show me how best to reach her. And please unite this family. Let Aaron and me be husband and wife in all ways."

Her hands lifted to her cheeks, which had warmed as she prayed. Was it wrong of her to want to be a true wife to Aaron? She loved him—at least, she was pretty sure she did. And while she was not certain what he thought of her, his kisses last night had held a promise of more to come. She smiled, and her body tingled at the mere thought of them.

How could Della Harper have been unhappy with her husband?

She may have never met the woman, but Janie knew one thing. Della Harper had been a fool.

Chapter Sixteen

Saturday afternoon, the pounding of hammers echoed through the house and throbbed in Janie's head. A chilly breeze blew cold air through the new hole in the back wall, which would be the door to Corrie's room. Yesterday had been warm and sunny, but by morning, a chilly northern wind had arrived. While she'd been making preparations for lunch, the stove had been hot, so she hadn't noticed the chill so much, but there was no ignoring it now.

After the last dish had been dried, Janie draped the towel over a chair. Benjy's wails matched the noise of the hammers, even with the bedroom door shut. Karen, who had been helping with the meal, had gone in to rock him, but he wasn't settling down. It was time to rescue her friend.

Janie opened the door to the room she shared with Aaron, and Benjy pushed up from Karen's shoulder, his cries increasing in tempo when he spotted her. He reached out his little arms, crying "Mama," and Janie lifted him to her chest, patting his back. He sniffled, his whole body shuddering. The clamor of construction had evidently disturbed him, too.

Karen rose from the rocker and smoothed her skirts, then wrapped her shawl around her shoulders. "I'm sorry I couldn't get him quieted. I suppose he just wanted his mama."

"I don't know what to do for him. I'm not sure if the noise and all the people traipsing in and out is what's bothering him, or if it's his teeth."

"Probably both. Have you considered taking him out to the barn?"

"The barn? Whatever for? He needs a nap."

"You could distract him with the horses, and it's quiet out there." Karen gathered the small quilt that Janie had laid across her bed for Benjy to nap on. "Take this to wrap him in, then lay him in a pile of fresh hay. He should be fine."

"I suppose it wouldn't be much cooler out there than it is in here with that big hole in the wall." Janie raised her voice to speak over Benjy's sobs.

"I'll track down Corrie and send her out to watch him until he awakens."

Janie shook her head. "Thanks, but I don't want her to feel I only need her to watch Benjy. Besides, we don't have to start supper for a few hours, so I'll just stay out there and enjoy the quiet." She walked toward the door, then paused. "I do feel bad running off when you were so kind to come and help with the food for the men today. Please feel free to lie down here if you'd like to rest."

Karen smiled. "I may do that, just to get off my feet for a while, but first I want to check on the children."

"I think they're hiding from me."

"They're both good children, and they'll swing around to your side soon enough."

Janie nodded, but she wasn't as sure as Karen seemed to be. She tucked the quilt around Benjy, glad his wails seemed to be winding down. At the door, Karen draped Janie's cloak around her shoulders. "Take as long as you want. I'll hold down the fort."

Karen opened the door, and a blast of cold air blew through the house like the bluster of a blizzard. Janie hugged Benjy tighter against her chest. The temperature might be cold, but at least they hadn't had any snow yet. That always made prairie life harder and isolated families even more. Her hood blew backward, admitting a chilly gust down her neck. She shifted Benjy higher, then snatched her cloak as the wind caught it and yanked it off one shoulder, lest the strong gale carry it to the neighboring farm.

Arms aching, she hurried to the barn. Thankfully, the men had left it open since they'd been going in and out earlier, carrying the cut wood to the back of the house. She found a clean mound of straw in the back corner, set her son down, then hurried to close the door. The inside of the structure was chilly but much better without the wind blowing in.

Benjy sat up as she made her way down the aisle. He wiped his red, splotchy face, gave a shuddering sniffle, and pointed toward the stalls. "Ha."

Janie smiled, grateful he'd finally stopped crying. She lifted him up and carried him over to see Outlaw. The big horse stuck his head over the gate, probably hoping for a treat. "Sorry, boy. I didn't think to bring you a goodie."

"Ha! Ha." Benjy sniffled and bounced in her arms. He reached for the horse's nose, but she pulled his hand back.

"That's Aaron's horse, Benjy. Say 'horse.'"

He grinned, although teardrops still clung to his lashes, and his eyes glistened. "Ha."

She chuckled. "I guess proper pronunciation will have to wait until you're older. Say bye-bye to Outlaw. It's time to take a nap."

She reached out, in spite of her fear of horses, and patted Outlaw's forehead—far away from his teeth. As she turned and walked away, Benjy started crying again. She patted his back and took him to a dark corner of the barn, swaying and humming.

His wails increased. "Ha...ha."

Desperate to calm him and get him to rest, she started singing the first thing that came to mind—"Joy to the World." She transitioned into another Christmas song, "Cantique de Noël," enjoying the release of lifting her voice in song. Benjy slowly quieted, and she felt his body growing heavy as he fell asleep, but she wasn't ready to quit singing. Next came "Hark! The Herald Angels Sing," a piece she had loved ever since first hearing it a few years ago.

She could have sung on and on, but her arms felt as if they would soon fall off, so she crept to the pile of hay, laid Benjy down, and settled beside him, once again humming and patting his back.

She yawned. A nap sounded pretty good right now, and since she couldn't leave her son alone, she lay down beside him and covered them both with her cloak. Sharp pieces of hay poked her cheek, but she brushed them away and rested her face on her arm, thinking of the words of the songs she'd just sung. All three heralded the birth of Christ, and she would have been teaching them to her students if she were still working at the school. Teaching paled in the face of motherhood, and yet it looked as if she would have the chance to do both now. If only Aaron's children would cooperate. Toby preferred being outside to studying, no matter if he had to shovel manure or carry wood. Corrie seemed interested in learning, but not from her.

Janie sighed. "Show me how to reach them, Lord."

She yawned again and felt her body relax. She was a terrible hostess to hide out in the barn and take a nap, but…

A noise jerked Janie awake. Her nose itched, and she reached up to scratch it, only to smear some foul-smelling substance across her face. Giggles sounded from across the barn, and she sat up, staring at her green-smeared hand. Horse manure? Her stomach revolted at the stench and the thought of what was on her face. Using her elbow, she pushed aside her cloak to keep it clean. Thankfully, Benjy slept on, snoring softly.

Janie lurched to her feet and glared at the stall where the children were hiding. "I thought you two were more mature than to pull such a childish prank."

"It was Corrie's idea," Toby whined. "She forced me to do it."

"Shh! I did not."

Toby ran out of the stall with Corrie close on his heels and bolted for the door. He was too small to open it, and when his sister caught him, she shook him. "Telltale!"

Janie searched for something to wipe off her hand and face but found nothing except for her cloak, Benjy's quilt, and the hay. She grabbed a clump of hay and brushed it across her hand. At the foul odor, her stomach lurched, still threatening to erupt.

The barn door flew open, and there stood Aaron. He looked down at his children, then lifted his eyes and found her. The expression of shock on his face would have been comical if she hadn't been so mortified. His surprised expression quickly hardened as he turned his gaze on his children again. "Did you two do that?"

"Corrie came up with the idea," Toby whined again.

"But Toby was the one who put the horse flop on her hand."

"This kind of behavior must stop. Both of you go to the house and wait in the parlor for me."

They trudged out of the barn past their father. Aaron hurried toward Janie, tugging his handkerchief from his pocket. He held it out to her. "It's clean."

Janie huffed a laugh. "It would hardly matter if it wasn't, with this on my face."

His lips twitched.

"Don't you dare laugh, Aaron Harper."

"I'm trying not to, I promise."

He lifted the handkerchief to her face and gently wiped it across her nose, folded it, then cleaned her cheeks, his eyes sparkling. "I must say, Mrs. Harper, you have smelled better."

"If you keep that up, I may be forced to kiss you."

His eyes widened for a moment. "Manure or not, I'll take a kiss from you any day."

Surprise belted Janie. "I figured you would back away."

"You figured wrong." He stepped closer, wiping off her upper lip. And then he dipped his head toward her, touched his lips to hers, and sent sensations like lightning bolts charging through her.

She reached around his back and hugged him, then started laughing, even though his lips still rested on hers. He pulled away and quirked a brow. Giggling, she stepped back and showed him the hand that had just touched his jacket—the hand that was still smeared with manure.

He smiled, eyes dancing. "Not the first time. My brothers and I used manure as slingshot ammunition when we were young."

"Eww. That's disgusting." She turned up one side of her mouth. "Must be a male thing."

"Must be."

"Thank you for rescuing me and allowing me the use of your handkerchief. And, just so you know, I was only teasing. I would never wipe that nasty stuff on your coat." She paused. "What would you like as a reward for coming to my rescue?" The moment she said the words, her heart flip-flopped. What if he asked for more than a kiss? She lifted her chin. If he did, she was ready. She loved this man was willing to prove it.

His gaze grew serious. "What I would love is to hear you sing again."

She blinked. Had he been listening outside the barn earlier? "When did you hear me sing?"

"I confess, I heard you that day that you sang to Benjy on the porch. It was the most beautiful thing I've ever heard." His eyes took on a dreamy look. "I was standing near a window, and Ma caught me and jabbed my shoulder."

"Well!" She feigned indignation, even though she was secretly pleased. "You deserved it for eavesdropping."

"Like I told her, I was only listening—mesmerized is more like it."

Her cheeks grew warm, and she lowered her head, happy that he'd enjoyed her tune.

"So, will you sing for me, Janie?"

"Now?"

He shrugged. "Now…tonight…sometime soon."

When Phil died, she'd thought she would never have reason to sing again, other than to calm Benjy, but her husband had given her one. "Not now, but soon."

He nodded, then leaned in for another kiss. When he pulled back, he sighed. "Now I've got to deal with those two yahoos. I don't know what got into them to make them do such a thing."

She watched him go, wanting to tell him again to go easy on them but also feeling they deserved whatever punishment Aaron saw fit to dish out.

Aaron sat in a chair facing his two youngsters, who sat on the sofa, heads hanging. He blew out a breath, unable to remember the last time he'd been so disappointed with them. Had they created trouble like this for Josh? Or for their teacher at school? Wouldn't Josh have told him if they had?

All the more reason they needed to be here with him. A movement to his right snagged his attention, and he glanced over and saw his ma standing in the doorway of the small room. He wished he could head back outside and leave the disciplining to her, since she was the one with more experience.

"You two stay here." He rose, walked across the kitchen, and entered the bedroom. "Janie could probably use a wet towel."

"Oh? Did Benjy make a mess?"

Aaron rubbed the back of his hand across his cheek. "No. My kids did."

His ma's eyebrows lifted. "Must be bad from the way you all are acting."

He stepped further into the room and shut the door behind him. "I went to the barn to check on Janie and Benjy after you told me where they were and discovered Janie covered with manure." His ma's blue eyes went wide, but he continued. "She said she fell asleep and woke up to a tickle on her nose, and when she scratched it, she spread manure across her face."

Ma's mouth dropped open, then she snapped it shut. "Surely they didn't."

He nodded. "I could see the guilt on their faces, and Toby said that Corrie made him do it."

"Shame on Corrie for considering such a thing and for getting her brother to do her dirty work."

Aaron lifted his hat and forked his fingers through his hair. "What am I supposed to do about this? I know Corrie is upset about leaving her school friends, but she has to learn this is her life now." He leaned one arm against the wall and shook his head. "I never should have sent her to that school."

Ma placed her hand on his shoulder and gave a gentle squeeze. "You can't think that way. You did what you believed was the right thing to do at the time—and I agreed that it was, then, but God has provided something different now. You have a wife to help you—to care for your children, to teach them the things they need to know, including their education."

"I know all that, but how do I get my children to understand? I can't force them to accept Janie as their new ma."

"Of course you can't. That will come in time as Janie and the children get to know one another better and their relationship deepens. You need to pray for wisdom. Ask God to show you how to help Corrie and Toby to accept Janie and for wisdom in how you should punish them." She leaned up, kissed his cheek, and gave him a wry smile as she patted his chest. "It wasn't all that long ago that I was asking the good Lord for wisdom to know how to raise you and your brothers." She paused at the door. "I'll take a wet towel out to Janie while you talk with the children, and I'll pray for you, Son."

His chest warmed. He was blessed to have been born to God-fearing parents. Dropping down onto the bed, he bowed his head and prayed. When he knew what to do about his children, he thanked God and rose.

Toby was half asleep on one side of the sofa, while Corrie had found one of her books and was reading. They both gazed up at him with wary expressions. Toby yawned.

Aaron sat in the side chair directly across from the sofa and remained silent, allowing them to squirm and consider what they'd done.

Tears filled Toby's eyes. "I'm sorry, Pa. I like Janie and didn't want to do that, but Corrie said I had to."

"You made the choice to go along with her, and that's where you mucked up." He shifted his gaze to his daughter. "I'm very disappointed with your behavior. Treating your new ma in such a disrespectful manner and coercing your brother to participate in your shenanigans. What do you have to say for yourself?"

Corrie's expression remained belligerent. "It wouldn't have happened if you hadn't brought us here." She scrunched up her face and blinked her eyes, probably hoping her tears would weaken him. When had she learned to use such wiles?

"I made the decision I thought best for you and your brother. You're not going back to town. This is your home now."

"B-but this house isn't even as big as Uncle Josh's."

"It's getting bigger as we speak." And he needed to get back outside and pull his weight. "Both of you will apologize to Janie. Toby, you will wash the dishes for a week."

The boy bolted up, all evidence of sleep gone. "The dishes? That's women's work. How come I hav'ta—"

Aaron held up his hand. "You will wash the dishes. That is your punishment."

Corrie smirked.

"And you, young lady, will muck the stalls and fill the wood box for a week."

She stiffened, eyes wide. "Pa! That's not fair."

He rose, trying to keep a lid on his anger. "You think it's fair to assault a sleeping woman—a woman caring for a baby—with manure?"

Corrie wilted. "I'm sorry, Pa. I thought if she didn't like me, I would be able to go back to school."

"You thought wrong."

Tears dripped down her cheeks. "But I can't clean stalls—it's not becoming for a lady."

He almost laughed at her reasoning. "Regardless, you will do as you're told."

She slouched back and folded her arms. "I hate this place."

Toby scooted to the edge of the sofa. "Not me. I like it." He frowned. "All except for having to wash dishes."

"While you're tending to that task, maybe you'll think hard about letting people talk you into doing something you don't believe is right."

He ducked his head. "Yes, Pa."

Aaron heard a shout and realized the hammering had stopped. "I need to get back to work. Toby, you come with me. Corrie, you stay inside and help Janie and your grandma. And make sure you apologize."

"Yes, sir."

Aaron headed for the door, more relieved than he cared to admit to have that confrontation over with. Give him two dozen rowdy cowboys to oversee any day instead of a pair of ornery kids.

Chapter Seventeen

Shh...you'll be better soon." Janie sat in the rocker she'd pulled into the room Toby and Benjy shared, trying to get the fussy boy to take his nap. His first eyetooth had broken through, but now the other one was preparing to make its appearance, and his gums were red and swollen. Janie's heart ached at seeing him in such discomfort. He rubbed his gums with his fist, whining.

She felt like joining him. This week had been one of the most uncomfortable ones she'd experienced—even worse than her first week of teaching at the girls' school. Toby had surprisingly settled in with his schoolwork, but she'd cringed every time he'd washed the dishes. After he broke two of her six coffee cups, Aaron told him that for every item he broke, he would have to wash dishes another day. Janie smiled. She'd thought the punishment a bit harsh at first, but the boy hadn't broken a thing since. He was talking to her more and seemed to have accepted the changes in his young life.

Corrie was another matter entirely. The only task she seemed willing to do was to help care for Benjy. She had apologized for the manure prank, but Janie didn't feel she was truly sorry for the deed. She'd complained about the food, griped about being a slave and having to do so many chores, and had even asked to return to her grandma's home if she couldn't live in Windmill.

It pained Janie to see the way Corrie hurt her father. Did she care more for her friends than for him?

Benjy arched his back and screeched, then shook his head while rubbing his hand over his mouth. If only they lived closer to town. A doctor would know what to do, or maybe there would be a syrup or concoction in the mercantile that might help. She'd heard tales of babies dying from teething, and that thought frightened her dreadfully. She knew of only one thing to do that soothed him—and that was to sing.

She hummed until deciding on a hymn she'd learned shortly before leaving Boston: "What a Friend We Have in Jesus." Janie glanced toward the ceiling. "Please let this work, Lord."

As Benjy's cries continued, she lifted her voice in song. After a few minutes of singing, his wails had lessened. She shifted into "Nearer, My God, to Thee," and then into one of her favorite Christmas songs, "Silent Night." With Benjy finally asleep, she rested her head against the back of the rocker, enjoying the freedom to just sing as the words ministered to her battle-weary spirit.

The door creaked open, and Corrie stepped in, her eyes holding a look of shock. Janie's heart lurched. What had happened now?

She lifted her index finger to her mouth, then rose, laid Benjy in his bed, and covered him with a blanket. Then she tiptoed out, leaving the door open so the room could receive warmth from the stove.

In the parlor, she was relieved to see Toby at the table, working math problems on his slate. She turned to Corrie. "What's wrong? Has something happened?"

The girl shook her head, still looking dumbfounded. "Where did you learn to sing like that? It's so beautiful."

Janie smiled, happy that Corrie had found something to like about her. "I guess I was born with this voice, but I had training to help me learn to use it better."

Corrie swayed with a dreamy look on her face. "I could listen to it for hours."

Chuckling, Janie waved her hand in the air. "I'm afraid that it wouldn't sound too nice after singing that long." But wasn't that what she had wanted when she'd dreamed of singing opera?

"Why don't you sing at church or other places?"

"Partly because we rarely get to go to church, since we live so far from one." And because she'd wanted to keep her singing voice a secret, since it was one way that Martin might track her down. It also meant she could never again sing opera, at least nowhere but here on the ranch, where only her family could hear.

"Do you suppose you could teach me to sing?"

Janie's insides clenched. What if Corrie had a dreadful voice? But even so, if it helped the two of them connect, it would be worth a try. "I'd be happy to give you music lessons after you finish your regular schoolwork."

Corrie nibbled her lip, then nodded. "All right. I'll work harder and try to apply myself better."

Janie smiled and touched her stepdaughter's shoulder. "That would make your father and me very happy."

"Done!" Toby hopped off the chair. "Can I go out and help Pa now?"

"Let me check your work first." Janie winked at Corrie, who flashed her the first genuine smile she'd seen, and hurried around the table to proof the boy's work before he escaped. She scanned the columns of addition problems. "Very good, Toby. You may walk out to the barn, but if you don't find your pa, you need to come back to the house."

"Yahoo!" He rushed to the door, flung it open, and jumped off the porch, then galloped toward the barn.

"So much for walking," Corrie mused.

Janie glanced at her, and they both burst into laughter. She couldn't wait to tell Aaron about the improvement in her relationship with his daughter. She prayed this was only the beginning.

That evening, after the kitchen had been cleaned and the children were asleep, Aaron sat on their bed and tugged off his boots, both of them thudding to the floor. Janie, comfortable in bed under the quilt, peered at his wide shoulders and back that tapered to his slim waist. He was a fine man on all accounts—handsome, strong, capable, good-hearted, and he taught his children about God and instilled morals in them. She'd expected him to ask about the difference in Corrie tonight, but other than a few raised eyebrows at his daughter's more relaxed countenance and talkative nature, he hadn't.

"The wind turned around this evening. It's coming from the south. If it holds, what would you think about riding over to Ma and Pa's tomorrow, then catching the train into Windmill the day after?" He unbuttoned his shirt and pulled it off. The bed creaked when he stood. He crossed the room and hung his shirt on a peg, then blew out the lantern, as he always did before removing his pants.

Was he having second thoughts about keeping the children with him? "Why would you want to take the children back to town when they are finally starting to adjust?"

He climbed onto the foot of the bed, crawled to his spot, and slid under the covers. "Guess I didn't explain myself well enough. We need to stock up on supplies before we get a heavy snow, and with the southern wind and temperatures warming, that's not as likely to happen. The children need some winter clothing and boots for working at the ranch, Benjy's growing and could use more diapers so you won't have to wash them as often during the cold weather, and you need some woolen dresses and…uh…stuff like that."

"Oh. You're quite a thoughtful man."

He slid closer and found her hand, which laid on top of the quilt. His leg touched the side of hers, and she could feel the heat of his body through the fabric of her gown. Her heart hammered—not because she was afraid of this man but because she loved him and wanted to be his true wife.

"You think so?"

"Mmm-hmm." She didn't want to speak, lest her voice come out sounding husky.

"I want you to tell me if there's ever something you need. If it's possible, I will get it for you. I don't want you going without."

She cleared her throat. "I don't need much to be happy."

He leaned over and trailed kisses down her cheek to her neck. "What makes you happy, wife?"

Feeling daring, she turned her face toward him. "That does. And kissing you."

He sucked in a little gasp, then claimed her mouth, sending a riot of feelings through her. She turned on her side to reach him better and wrapped her arm around his shoulders. She'd never known such delight. Never known that being with her husband could bring such joy.

He suddenly pulled away and rolled onto his back, his breathing ragged. "You're driving me loco, Janie. I can't keep kissing you like that—not unless you desire to be my wife in the full sense."

That *was* what she wanted, and yet now that her dream was within grasp, she was afraid. Not of him but of herself.

He blew out a sigh that sounded like resignation, and her heart nearly broke. She could give him this. He'd done everything for her, and she'd done so little. She took a deep breath and exhaled slowly. "And what if I do?"

He lifted his arm from his face. "What?"

She reached over, grabbed ahold of his union suit, and tugged. "Come, Aaron. I love you and want to be with you."

"Thank You, God." He turned onto his side again and caressed her head. "There's nothing I'd like more." He kissed her, lightly this time, on the lips, and then at the corners of her mouth. "But first tell me what happened between you and the young'uns. Things were much different tonight. Much improved."

"You won't believe it, but I was singing to Benjy, trying to get him to sleep, and Corrie came into the room looking a bit stunned. She wanted to know how I learned to sing like I do and then asked me to teach her."

Aaron continued to run his fingers through her hair, sending delicious chills down her spine. "I know exactly how she felt. The first time I heard you sing, I was stopped in my tracks. You're welcome to sing to me any time, Mrs. Harper." He leaned on one elbow so that his face was just over hers. "I've grown to love you, too, Janie. I don't know how it happened so quickly, but it did."

She leaned up and kissed him, loving the feel of his bristly chin and warm lips, his muscles and strength. Tonight, she would put away all worries and enjoy her husband—and pray that he couldn't tell this was her first time with a man.

～

Janie couldn't quit smiling, but no one seemed to notice because everyone else was smiling, too. Corrie and Toby stared out the train windows, excited to be returning to Windmill. Aaron sat beside her, holding a bouncing, slobbering, jabbering Benjy up to the window. Every so often, Aaron would look her way and smile or wink or lean over and hug her. She suspected his mother had noticed a change, but she'd only commented on how much happier the children seemed. Janie was tempted to suggest it was because they were headed to town, but she didn't. Overall, things had been more pleasurable the past few days.

She stared down at the book in her lap, not seeing the words, as she once again remembered the night with Aaron. Never would she have dreamed that the relationship between a man and his wife could be so...so... Words failed her. Aaron took her hand and squeezed it. Heat marched up her cheeks, as she wondered if he knew what she'd been thinking. She'd been so embarrassed at her wanton behavior that she'd had trouble looking him in the eye since that wonderful night.

He leaned over, and Benjy crawled onto her lap, knocking the book to the floor. Aaron retrieved it and placed it on the seat. "You look deep in thought, wife. Are you mentally checking off your shopping list to make sure you haven't forgotten something?"

She peeked at him around the brim of her bonnet and knew by his ornery smile and the gleam in his eyes where his thoughts were. She leaned over and whispered, as she wrestled to get Benjy to sit down, "Shame on you."

His grin widened, stealing her breath away. She bent down and kissed Benjy's fuzzy head to keep her smile hidden. How was it possible to be so happy, all because of one man?

Had Carolyn ever experienced the joy Janie felt with Aaron? Somehow she doubted Martin was capable of giving of himself in any way. He was a taker, not a giver. Poor Carolyn. She was such a sweet, gentle person. If only she could have found a husband like Aaron. But it was too late for her cousin now. At least Carolyn's child was safe and happy. Even his aching gums hadn't stolen his delight at riding on the train, and the rocking motion looked to be putting him to sleep. She tugged him closer, but he kept sliding down the silk of her dress—the only fancy one she owned other than the one she'd been married in.

"Here, let me take him." Aaron reached for Benjy again and held him so that the boy's head rested on his shoulder. Janie was almost jealous.

Before she knew it, the train pulled into Windmill. Corrie and Toby's excitement shone in their glistening eyes. Janie was a bit apprehensive about showing up unannounced at Josh and Sophie's with the expectation of staying with them, but Aaron had assured her that they would be thrilled.

After donning their cloaks and coats, they exited the train, Janie carrying Benjy, and Aaron, Toby, and Corrie each hauling satchels. She'd tried to pack light, since they would be staying only two nights, but with a baby in tow, she hadn't wanted to be unprepared.

"When can I go see my friends, Pa?" Corrie held the satchel in front of her and bounced on her toes.

"Not until near the end of the school day. I don't want you disrupting their studies."

"But they'll all be going home then."

He shrugged. "Be glad you get to see them at all. I could have left you both at your grandma's."

Corrie stuck out her lip in a pout. Janie hated seeing her disappointed, but Aaron was right—they shouldn't interfere with the students' classes. Aaron led the way, Toby struggling to keep up, with his shorter legs and the bag he carried.

Corrie fell into step with Janie and sidled a glance her way. "You make Pa happy. I haven't seen him smiling so much in…I don't even remember."

Janie felt a flush of warmth at her comment, which both excited and embarrassed her. "I like making him happy."

"Don't worry about Uncle Josh and Aunt Sophie. They'll be thrilled to see us, but I have to warn you, Aunt Sophie isn't the best in the kitchen. Her family had a cook when she was growing up, so she's still learning. She's much better, though, than she was when she first came to Windmill." The girl shuddered, as if remembering a vile-tasting dish.

"Thanks for warning me. I'll be careful what I say."

Janie surveyed the town. Last time she was here, she'd barely paid attention to anything except the large windmill in the square, which for some reason had captivated her. Its giant blades swung lazily, whirling on the light breeze and making a whooping noise.

They passed the bank where Josh had worked before starting his furniture business and the house he had once rented, and then they were there, at the house Sophie had inherited from her aunt.

Aaron knocked on the front door. After a few moments, Sophie opened it and blinked at them for several seconds before breaking into a big smile. "What a nice surprise!" She stepped back and waved them inside.

Corrie ran up and hugged her aunt. "I've missed you and Uncle Josh."

"The house has been so quiet with you two gone." Sophie embraced Toby, then glanced at Janie. "Do you need a place to lay Benjy down?"

"My arms are about to fall off." She grinned to show she was teasing. "This rascal gets heavier every day. Is there a bedroom downstairs where we could put him?"

Sophie shook her head. "No, sorry. They're all upstairs."

Janie glanced at Aaron, unsure if she wanted Benjy so far away in a house that was unfamiliar to him.

"Why don't you put him on the sofa?" Aaron suggested.

Janie eyed the beautiful floral sofa. "I don't know. It looks new." She shifted Benjy up a bit.

"Oh, don't worry about it. Toby already broke it in."

"What?" Aaron sent his brother's wife a look of alarm.

Sophie giggled. "I meant that Toby spilled a glass of milk on the davenport the second day we had it. But don't worry, I was able to clean it."

"If you're sure." Janie looked at Aaron. "His blanket is in his satchel. Could you get it, please?"

He nodded, then set the bags down, pulled the small quilt off the top of Benjy's things, and spread it on the sofa.

Sophie crossed the room to the sofa and moved the side pillows to a chair. "All set."

"Is Uncle Josh in his shop?" Toby placed his bag next to the ones Aaron had been carrying.

"Yes, and he'll be thrilled to see all of you. Did he know you were coming? He certainly didn't tell me if he did."

Aaron shook his head. "No. This trip was quickly planned. We decided to take advantage of the warmer weather to stock up on supplies before the snows come."

"I don't know how you manage to live so far away from town. I'd be beside myself if I couldn't dash down to the mercantile whenever I ran out of something."

Janie laid Benjy on the sofa, and then Aaron moved a side chair over and turned it around so that the back butted up to the edge of the sofa, to keep Benjy from rolling off. Janie smiled up at him and received a wink that set her insides dancing.

She was so glad she'd accepted Aaron's marriage proposal. She could not imagine her life without him.

Chapter Eighteen

The stacks of supplies kept growing larger. Janie wasn't certain Aaron had enough money to pay for all they had amassed, but she trusted that he wouldn't buy more than he could afford. He never talked money with her, like Phil had done occasionally. She'd had to pinch pennies for so much of her life that she couldn't imagine a person being able to buy anything he wanted. Not that they were doing that, but still, their purchases amounted to much more than Phil had ever bought. The piles of clothing would keep them all warm through the long winter, and she was eager to put to use the spices, nuts, raisins, canned vegetables, and other food items they'd bought. Yet, even with so much, she was now cooking for a family of five and needed to be sure not to use up her stores too fast.

Aaron re-tallied the bill that the clerk, Mr. Purdy, had already added up while the man loaded their purchases into crates. Janie liked that her husband was so cautious and doubted he'd ever been swindled. She couldn't wait to get home, put away the cans and jars of food, and start cooking.

"My calculations agree with yours," Aaron said to Mr. Purdy. "You'll have everything crated up, labeled 'Harper,' and at the depot well before tomorrow's train?"

"Sure will." Mr. Purdy nodded at Aaron. "Happy to do it, Mr. Harper."

Corrie walked over from the area near the stove, where she'd been seated with Benjy on her lap. "Now that we're finally done, can we go down to the school? Remember you said we could eat lunch there today?"

Aaron chuckled. "How could I forget when you've been reminding us every fifteen minutes?"

"Aw, it hasn't been that often, Pa." Toby peered through the glass counter at the selection of knives. "Can I have a knife? I'm old enough now."

Janie shivered at the thought of the nine-year-old with a knife, but Aaron just shrugged. "We'll see."

"See when? We're leaving tomorrow."

Aaron tugged Toby's hat off the rack near the door and handed it to him. "Patience, Son. It's a virtue, remember?"

Toby ducked his head. "Maybe so, but waiting is hard."

Janie smiled at Mrs. Purdy, who bustled out of the storage area in back, holding a small quilt. She snapped it open and spread it across the open space on the counter. "This just came in, and I had to show it to you. Isn't it the cutest thing you've ever seen?"

"It's darling." Janie studied the quilt, which had twelve squares printed with boys dressed in overalls and wearing straw hats that completely covered their heads and faces. Two boys held a fishing pole, two more stood with a shovel in hand, and other pairs were equally charming. With colorful swatches of blue, green, yellow, and red fabric, the quilt rivaled an artist's palette. "How did you come by this?"

"A woman made it for her son but needed money so badly that she sold it. She said she could always make another one, but her child needed food today."

Janie's heart ached for the woman who had been forced to part with the beautiful quilt. She fingered the edge, noting its thickness. The large quilt would keep Benjy warm as he grew for several years, but it was too much to ask for. If only she could sew this well.

Aaron walked over and pressed against her back as he looked at it over her shoulder. "Do you like it?"

She gazed up at him, afraid to hope. "Of course I do. I've never seen anything like it."

He smiled, then looked at Mrs. Purdy. "How much is it?"

"Six dollars."

Janie's heart sank. That was far too much money, even for something that took many hours to construct and was so lovely.

"Make it four, and you have a deal."

Mrs. Purdy quirked her mouth to one side as she considered Aaron's offer. "Five sounds fairer to me."

"You might want to consider all that we purchased today." Aaron turned and ran his gaze over the stacks of goods.

Mr. Purdy waved his hand in the air. "It's a fair deal, Myrtle. Give it to him for four."

She sighed, as if she'd lost a fight, but then she smiled. "That little boy of yours will stay nice and warm in this quilt, and I'll let the woman who brought it in know how much you liked it, Mrs. Harper."

"Thank you." Janie returned her smile, mostly because the woman had called her by her new name. *Mrs. Harper.* It was taking some getting used to after being a Dunn for so long, but she liked it. Mrs. Purdy moved the quilt to the counter against the wall, tore a sheet of brown paper off a roll, and began wrapping it.

Janie turned to Aaron and looped her arm through his, drawing his gaze. "Thank you. I love it, and Benjy will get a lot of use out of it."

Aaron's eyes lit up. "You're welcome, wife." He glanced around, then quickly dipped his head and dropped a kiss on her lips. Janie's eyes widened at the brazen act, but her embarrassment fled when she realized no one was looking their way. She inclined her head close to his ear. "Shame on you," she whispered.

His grin turned a tad wicked. "Be careful, or I'll do it again."

She ducked her head, secretly pleased at his teasing. "Why don't I head back with the children? I know they're anxious to visit with Mikey and their friends, and I can help Sophie prepare lunch for them."

"All right, but don't forget we're eating lunch at the café."

She nodded. "I'll remind Sophie, so she can make sure Josh is ready."

As she walked away, her husband chuckled. "No need to worry about Josh. He's the most punctual of us Harper brothers. He's never late, especially if food is involved."

Janie smiled. "Children, shall we go?"

Benjy reached for her, and she took him from Corrie. "Thank you for watching this little rascal so I could shop."

"I'm happy to take care of him. He's more fun and not as much trouble as Toby."

Toby pulled a face but then smiled, obviously sensing that his sister was teasing. "I'm starving. Let's go."

Corrie shook her head as Toby ran ahead of them. "He's always hungry."

"Just like his father."

They shared a laugh, and Janie marveled at how much her life had changed in such a short time. A little over a year ago, she was teaching music with no hope of marriage or motherhood on the horizon. Now she was married, a mother of three, and happier than she could remember being since the deaths of her parents. A picture of Martin Metcalf's angry face intruded on her thoughts, but she shook it away, refusing to allow him to ruin her joy.

She studied the peaceful town and thought of her home at the ranch. Life was good.

Please, Lord, let things stay this way.

⌒

The train shuddered to a halt at the Harper family's small depot. A light drizzle was falling, so Janie ushered the children inside the small building the family had erected to shelter those waiting for the train. Aaron turned the other direction and waved at Ethan, who waited beside the tracks with two wagons. Corrie sat on one of the benches, holding Benjy, who'd fallen asleep.

"Can I go out and help?" Toby gazed up at Janie with pleading eyes.

"Sorry, but your pa said to stay inside, out of the rain. We don't want you taking sick." She bent down and buttoned his coat.

"I won't. I promise."

Janie smiled. "That's not a promise you can keep, young man. We'll do as your father asked and stay here."

She moved nearer the stove that someone had been kind enough to light, although it must not have been lit long, because the room still held a chill. In spite of the dampness, thoughts of her delightful time in Windmill warmed her. She had befriended Sophie, and the two had confided in each other about their husbands—all good things, for the most part, although Sophie did share that Josh hadn't trusted her to care for Corrie and Toby when they first met. Janie could hardly imagine that, considering how demonstrative Josh now was with her. He couldn't seem to do enough for his pregnant wife, frequently touching or kissing her.

Janie was surprised to find herself a bit envious, especially since her dream had always been to sing opera, not to be a mother. But now that it was a possibility, she found herself hoping that she would bear Aaron a child, and soon. Yes, they had a houseful of children, but this one would be theirs—never having belonged to anyone else first. It wouldn't affect how she felt about her other children, but she still hoped that this new dream would come true.

Aaron stomped into the room and shut the door. "Ready to go?"

"So soon?" Janie asked.

He nodded. "I want to get you all to the house in case the rain picks up. Slim will drive you while I stay and help Ethan finish loading the second wagon."

Janie was disappointed not to ride with her husband, but the trip to the Harper home was a short one. "We're ready. Corrie, let me take Benjy. Your arms must be tired by now."

"Arms?" She grinned. "I have arms? I sure don't feel any."

Aaron chuckled and tweaked his daughter's nose.

She shrieked and pulled away. "Your hands are freezing!"

"Ah, that reminds me. I need to put my gloves on." He reached into his coat pocket. "I fished them out of my satchel and forgot about them when the train stopped." As he tugged them out, two letters fluttered to the ground.

Corrie bent and picked them up. "These are for you, Janie."

Aaron's cheeks turned a bit redder. "Sorry. With all that was going on, I plumb forgot to give those to you. Arlis Purdy gave them to me as I was leaving the store. You better tuck them away somewhere the rain won't ruin them."

"Good idea." She passed Benjy to Aaron, and the boy patted her husband's face and offered a slobbery kiss. Normally she would have smiled, but the letters held her attention. One was from the headmaster at the school where she used to work, but the other bore a return address she didn't recognize. Although she longed to tear the envelopes open and read the missives, she turned away, opened her cloak, and tucked the letters into the bodice of her dress. When she was alone, she would see what they had to say. As she herded the children out the door behind Aaron, she couldn't shake the ominous feeling that chased her.

Aaron passed another crate out the door of the train car to Ethan, then reached for the last item—a trunk that held many of the clothes he'd purchased for the family. He slid it to the door, then handed it down to a pair of porters before jumping to the ground. "That's it."

Ethan returned, grinning. "You must have made the Purdys happy. Looks like you bought out half their inventory."

"Not quite that much, but plenty. I wanted to be sure we're well stocked for winter."

"I'd say you are. We'll have to return with the wagon for that last load."

Aaron nodded, then climbed the steps to the platform to sign for his goods. The porter wrote something on the paper attached to the clipboard, then handed it to him. "Looks like that's everything, Mr. Harper."

Scanning the pages, Aaron nodded. He signed the paper, returned the clipboard, and shook hands with the porter. "Thanks for your help, Elmer."

"My pleasure, Mr. Harper." The porter nodded, then waved at the conductor, who stood beside the open passenger door, pocket watch in hand.

The conductor turned to the few passengers who had debarked from the train to stretch their legs. "Load up, folks. We'll be getting under way soon."

A young couple with a charming little girl headed for the train door, as did two older men. Aaron nodded at them, even though they were strangers. He started to turn but then saw another man push away from the building wall and head for him. The citified man looked like a gambler in that double-breasted black wool frock coat, black coachman hat, and boots. The hair on the back of Aaron's neck stood up, and he rested his hand on his gun.

"Excuse me, but I wonder if I might have a moment of your time."

Aaron tensed as the man reached into his pocket, but instead of a weapon, he pulled out a photo with ragged edges.

"I'm Detective Phineas Parker, of Boston. Would you please tell me if you've seen this woman? She is the wife of my employer, and I'm searching for her and my employer's son, who would be a little over a year old now."

Aaron's gut clenched as he stared at the picture of Janie. It was not the same Janie he knew but a woman in a fancy dress with her hair piled atop her head in an enticing manner. She looked several years younger. And she was married?

His chest tightened even worse than when he'd learned Della was dead. He had to tell this man something, but he wasn't about to give away Janie's presence.

The porter approached. "Sir, I must ask you to board, or you'll be left here."

"Just one moment." The man's gaze never left Aaron's face, and he lifted a brow. "You know this woman?"

He shrugged. "Just admiring her. She's quite lovely." He handed the picture back, his world tilting off its axis, and tried to maintain a neutral expression. "Good luck with your search."

Aaron turned away and headed for the stairs. Janie's bonnet must have shielded her face from the man, because he obviously hadn't seen her. In spite of everything, he was glad the detective was leaving Windmill. Evidently he hadn't inquired of the right people in town, or he would have learned that the woman in the picture was Aaron's wife—or maybe she wasn't. If she was still married to someone else when they had spoken their vows, then she was not legally wed to Aaron. And he'd shared his heart with her—and his bed.

Tears burned his eyes at the loss of the woman he'd so quickly grown to love. Had Phil fallen for the same sad brown eyes and lovely voice?

Oh, God. How do I fix this?

It wasn't in his nature to run from a fight, but this one made him feel as if he'd been plugged full of bullets. He ducked his head as he climbed onto the wagon bench beside Ethan, glad for once for the rain. As he huddled in his coat, the chill reaching the center of his bones, his mind raced. Why would Janie have run away from her husband? Or maybe she hadn't been married at all, and the man at the depot had some other reason for searching for her.

But if she wasn't married, then who was Benjy's father? Could she have had the child out of wedlock?

His gut churned, and he thought he would be sick. He leaned forward, his hand pressed to his belly.

Ethan glanced at him. "You all right, big brother? Your face has gone white."

"Must be something I ate."

"Whatever it is, it sure came on fast."

"Yeah." Aaron turned on the seat and tried to find peace. He couldn't go in the house feeling like this, and he couldn't face Janie until he knew what to do. He'd have to talk to her, but he needed time to wrap his head around what he'd just learned. He needed time to pray.

The train whistled, then screeched as it pulled away from the depot. He wished they'd never gone to Windmill now. Then his dreams wouldn't have been crushed. He lifted his face, and raindrops splashed his cheeks as he gazed up at the miserable gray sky that mirrored how he felt.

As Ethan pulled up to the barn and started to guide the horses inside, Aaron grabbed the reins. His brother looked at him with concern. "What?"

"I...uh...need to check on the ranch. I think I'll drive over and take this load now."

Ethan frowned. "In this weather? You're likely to get stuck halfway there."

"It's something I've got to do. Tell Janie I'll be back for her and the young'uns by noon tomorrow."

Ethan didn't move. "Care to tell me what's really going on?"

Aaron shook his head. "Not right now. I need to work through something."

His brother wrapped an arm around his shoulders. "I won't say you don't have me worried and that I'm not curious what's wrong, but I know you, and I understand how you need to think things out. Go on, but when you're ready to talk, I'm ready to listen." He slapped Aaron's shoulder and jumped off the wagon.

Aaron reined the horses toward home, his throat tight. He'd wanted to tell Ethan that he appreciated what he said, but his voice would have cracked. Besides, Ethan knew that already.

As much as he might have liked to tell Ethan about the detective at the depot and get his advice on how to handle the situation, he couldn't. Not yet. First he had to pray to God, and then he needed to talk to Janie.

A thought suddenly struck him broadside: Janie was from Boston, as was the detective. That couldn't be a coincidence.

Could the man's story be true? Was Janie someone's runaway wife?

Aaron clenched his teeth and shuddered in his coat. His life had been perfect the past few days. Why did that Detective Parker have to come and yank the rug out from under him?

⌒

Martin exited the train at the first town past the tiny depot where he'd talked to that cowboy. He was certain the man had recognized Janie and had lied about knowing her, because he had looked stricken when he'd mentioned that she'd run away from her husband. But now, as he thought back, the man never actually denied knowing her. He'd merely said he was admiring her loveliness, which was poppycock. Janie Dunn was plain as a board compared to Carolyn's beauty. He didn't know how the two women could have been related.

His gut told him there was more to this Aaron Harper. The conductor had been only too happy to reveal the man's name for a coin. If Martin hadn't been so wrapped up in pondering the man's reaction, he would have thought to show the photo to the conductor. He snapped his fingers and reversed directions, gaining scowls from the other debarking passengers.

"I forgot something. Excuse me." He pushed his way through the throng of men, women, and children going in the opposite direction, halfway tempted to pull out his revolver and watch them battle one another as they fought to get away from him. But he didn't want to draw the attention of the law. The last thing he needed now, when he was so close to his prey, was to get tossed in jail and for Janie to somehow learn of his proximity and flee again. If he hadn't had the good fortune of discovering the name of the town she'd moved to, he never would have known where to find the wren. But he'd not found a soul in Windmill who admitted to knowing Janie. A few people had reacted in a way that made him suspect they had seen her before, but they didn't admit to it. He'd become so discouraged that he'd hopped the train and headed to the next town in hopes of finding her there. But his luck had suddenly changed when he met that Harper fellow.

He worked his way to the side of the train and waited for the last person to exit the car he'd been riding in. Then he hopped aboard and located the conductor.

"Did you forget something, sir?"

Martin retrieved the photo from his vest pocket and another coin from his pants. "No, I just had another question. Have you seen this woman?"

The man squinted as he accepted the photo, then pulled a pair of spectacles from his coat pocket and peered through them at the photo. He turned it toward the light coming in the window, then nodded. "Of course. Aaron Harper's new bride. The man you asked me about. Why, she just got off at the last stop."

Martin tightened his grip on the seat he was leaning against. He'd missed her? The only woman who'd gotten off at the last stop had been one with three children. He hadn't even thought to check her face behind that ridiculous sunbonnet. "The woman I'm looking for has only one child—a boy a little over a year old."

The man nodded and handed him back the picture. "Those older two youngsters belong to Mr. Harper. Them Harpers ride the train back and forth to Windmill quite regularly. One of the brothers actually lives in town."

Hope swirled in Martin's gut, mixing with regret. He'd been on the same train as his son and hadn't known it. At least he was close. Very close.

Soon he would have his son and his revenge.

Chapter Nineteen

Janie crawled in bed exhausted, both mentally and physically. Aaron had avoided her most of the afternoon and had barely mumbled responses to her questions. Even the children had sensed that their father was out of sorts. Something was definitely bothering him, although she had no idea what it could be. Their time in Windmill had been wonderful, and even the return trip on the train had been fun. But something had happened shortly after she left her husband at the Harper depot, because he'd gone on to their ranch instead of joining everyone at his parents' home. The warm camaraderie they'd experienced after their physical union was gone. On the ride home earlier today, he'd been sullen, barely even responding to the children's comments and questions. She'd wracked her mind, trying to figure out what she might have said or done to upset him, but she was clueless, and she desperately missed her husband's affection.

She rolled her shoulders, every muscle in her back and arms aching. Even though they'd arrived at their ranch around two in the afternoon, it had taken almost the rest of the day to unpack the crates and put the items in their proper places. Her cupboards and cellar were stocked full and bursting at the seams, and she knew her family would have plenty to eat for a long while.

She muttered a prayer of thanks for the train. How had Nick and Karen managed when they'd had to drive their wagons all the

way to Windmill whenever they needed supplies or a doctor? The
long, tiring trip would have been especially difficult with children
along. Janie yawned and tried to relax, but the tension between
her and Aaron kept her from sleeping, and the unopened letters
called to her. Once she'd reached her in-laws' home, Karen and
Sarah had wanted to know all about the trip and hear how Josh,
Sophie, and Mikey were, so she'd decided to wait until she was
home to read her mail. Now she had no excuse other than being
tired and discouraged. Maybe the missives would cheer her.

Aaron was still hauling crates out to the barn, so he wouldn't
be in for a little while, if he came in at all. Janie crawled out of
bed, shivering as her feet hit the chilly floorboards. She turned
up the lamp, crossed the room, and opened the drawer where
she'd shoved the letters earlier, then hurried back to bed. Paper
rattled as she tore open the first envelope—the one from Naomi
Carpenter.

My dear Janie,

*I miss seeing your cheerful face in the hallways here at the
academy and hearing your beautiful voice as you train your
students to sing. They missed you for a long while, but now
we have a new term with some new students and instruc-
tors, and all is normal again. I hope that you've settled into
your new life on the Kansas prairie. I admire your pluck,
for I could never leave the city as you have. My home is here
in Boston.*

*I'm writing to you mainly to let you know that I had a
visit from Martin Metcalf.*

Janie gasped, her pulse galloping as she continued reading.

*What a horrible man! He pressured me for information
about you, but all I told him was that you'd gone West to*

*live with your brother. He claimed you kidnapped his son—
of all the crazy notions I've ever heard. You could never do
such a thing, and I told him so. I didn't so much as reveal
what state you're in, not even when he threatened me with
bodily harm. He's a vile, nasty man, and I hope never to see
him again. I don't know the nature of your association with
that heathen, but you were wise to get away from him, if
that is why you left so suddenly.*

*I wish you well and hope that you will write to me one
day and let me know how you are faring.*

With sincere regard,
Naomi Carpenter

Janie laid her head against the wall, shivering. How had
Martin known to go to the school? Carolyn must have told him
at some point that she worked there, because she was certain
she never had. Or maybe Mazie, the servant girl who'd deliv-
ered Benjy to her, had returned to work at the house and had
given up the name of the school when Martin threatened her.
She prayed nothing dire had happened to the girl.

At least Naomi had kept Janie's secret, although she rather
wished her friend hadn't told Martin she'd gone to live with
her brother. But he didn't know Phil and surely had no way of
finding the ranch. He was as likely to locate her as a specific
sunflower in a whole field of them. The isolation of the prairie
helped her to remain hidden, and God would protect her and
Benjy. Wasn't that why He'd sent her Aaron?

She laid Naomi's letter on the bed and opened the one from
Helen Richardson, a woman she didn't know. How odd. The
letter was dated just eight days after Naomi's and was on the
academy's stationery.

Dear Miss Dunn,

My name is Helen Richardson. I was informed by several teachers at Boston's Academy of Music for Young Women that you used to be employed here, and I thought that you would want to know that Miss Carpenter has met with a most unfortunate end.

Janie inhaled sharply and lifted her hand to her chest. No! Naomi was dead? How?

We had the misfortune of a break-in a week ago. At the time, Miss Carpenter was in her office, working late. The intruder killed her and stole the month's receipts for the girls' tuition. I am so sorry to be the bearer of such bad news, but since you were a friend of Miss Carpenter, I thought you would want to know. A lovely memorial service was held in her honor, with many of her fellow teachers, former students, and students' parents attending.

By the way, I found a letter addressed to you under Miss Carpenter's overturned desk and am mailing it the same day as this one.

Sincerely,
Miss Helen Richardson
Headmaster, Boston Academy of Music for Young Women

Stunned—that was the only word that described how she felt. How could Naomi be gone? And all because of a theft? Something didn't sit right with her. She snatched up Naomi's letter and reread it. Martin had threatened Naomi with bodily harm, and Janie knew within her heart that he was responsible for her friend's death. He had either killed Naomi himself or hired someone else to do his dirty work, most likely because she hadn't shared the information he wanted. And if he would go to such extremes, he wouldn't stop until he found her and Benjy. She bolted up. She had to get away. Maybe to California. Or Oregon. Many settlers traveled to both places, and maybe she could hide among them. But traveling alone with Benjy would be very difficult.

And how could she leave Aaron? And Corrie and Toby, who had finally come to accept her?

As much as she loved them all, Benjy was the one she must be most concerned with. If Martin ever found the boy, Benjy's life would be miserable, and he would grow up to be a cruel man like his birth father, not kind and good like Aaron.

Janie slid off the bed, reached beneath it, and pulled out the satchel she'd recently put away. The new trunk filled with all of their wonderful winter clothing stood in the corner, as yet untouched. She wished that she could take the trunk, but she couldn't take more than she could carry. With the trunk open, she dropped to her knees and lifted out the new diapers and clothing she'd selected for Benjy, followed by her new undergarments and two warm winter dresses. She might as well take the newer things. She reached for them, then hesitated. Was it right for her to take the things Aaron had bought for her, when she was leaving him?

The thought brought burning tears to her eyes. She'd never fallen in love before, and Aaron meant so much to her. How could she leave him? Didn't he deserve to know what was going on? She should have told him before they married, but she was afraid he would stop loving her when he learned the truth.

If she stayed, wouldn't she be putting Aaron and his children in danger? But her leaving Boston hadn't protected Naomi. Dread swarmed Janie. What if Martin came after her at the ranch and found her gone? Would he harm the children or Aaron as punishment?

"What do I do, Lord?" She dropped her head in her hands and let the tears come. There was no easy answer. No matter what she did, she was sure to hurt someone she loved.

⌒

Aaron set the last crate in the corner, flipped it over, and dropped onto it. This had been one of the most agonizing days of his life. Worse even than the day he'd lost Della.

He'd stayed away from the family as much as possible to avoid their questioning gazes. How could he explain to his children that Janie had deceived him? He shook his head. Della had done the same thing by making him believe she could be happy living in the country, when nothing could have been further from the truth. But they didn't need to know that. Della may not have been a very good ma, but he wouldn't discredit her in front of his children. And if Janie was not really married to another man, things might work out for them to remain together, so he didn't want them thinking badly of their new ma either, even if she had lied to him.

He threw his hat on the ground and forked his fingers through his hair. "What do I do, Lord? What do I say to her?"

He wanted so badly to fix things, but he didn't know how. He wasn't even sure if the situation with his wife was fixable. He huffed a sardonic laugh. Did he even have a wife? If she was already married…

The thought hurt as bad as being kicked in the chest by a horse.

He jumped up and paced the barn, front to back, back to front. Maybe he should just come out and tell her about the encounter with the detective at the depot. She could deny knowing what he was talking about, but he'd seen the picture— of her.

All his life, he'd been fixing things. Helping his brothers out of sticky situations when they were younger. Helping his pa keep the stage stop going, even after the train came through and stole much of their business. He'd helped his ma serve the many guests who stopped for a meal or an overnight stay. As the oldest brother, he was the one who watched out for the younger ones and helped them through hard times. Fixed the things they'd broken.

But he didn't know how to fix this.

He plopped down onto the crate again. "Show me what to do, Lord. How do I trust Janie now that I've learned the truth?"

A sudden thought came to him—what if what the detective had said wasn't the truth? What if he wanted Janie for some other reason, and he'd concocted the story of an employer's runaway wife as a ruse?

Aaron straightened. Had God sent him that idea?

Maybe he should trust his wife—the woman he loved—over a stranger he'd talked to for only two minutes.

For the first time in over a day, peace flooded him. He knew what to do.

Aaron stood, rescued his hat from the dirty floor, and dusted it off. It was time he talked to his wife.

⌒

Janie closed the trunk, having removed only the things Benjy desperately needed and nothing for herself, not even the warm woolen stockings. With the jewels remaining from those Carolyn had given her, she could buy a few new things when she got to where she was going—wherever that was. She laid the items on the bed, wondering how she'd get everything into one satchel. She had to, since she would have to carry Benjy. It meant she wouldn't be able to take more than the dress she wore. Maybe she should leave all of her dresses behind and wear a skirt and blouse. She ought to be able to squeeze one extra shirt into the bag.

Tears blurred her eyes. The last thing she wanted was to leave, but she had to. She still hadn't figured out how she would travel. A buggy was the best choice, but it was slow and easy to track. What she really needed was a horse. But she feared horses almost as much as she did Martin.

She would have to face one fear to flee the other.

The bedroom door opened, and Aaron stood there, solemnly taking in the bed and everything piled on top of it. Janie's heart skidded almost to a stop. She swallowed back her nervousness. What would he think of her leaving?

"What's going on?" His expression didn't look quite as sullen as it had earlier.

She wrung her hands together. Everything within her told her to explain it all to him, but where should she start?

He sighed as he stepped into the room and shut the door. "Janie, we need to talk."

She struggled for something to say—anything to avoid having to tell him the awful truth. "What about the children?" She certainly didn't want any of them overhearing their conversation.

"They're fine. I just checked, and they're all sleeping."

Aaron crossed the room, moved the diapers and Benjy's clothing to the side of the mattress, placed her letters on the side table, and then sat at the head of the bed. He patted the quilt beside him. "Come sit down."

She couldn't move. Her feet were frozen to the ground. What did he know that made him feel the need to talk to her? He couldn't have read her letters, because the seals had been unbroken when she'd opened them. What could have cut the life from him the past day? What had he discovered?

Aaron lifted his gaze. Did she see hope there? "Janie, please. Come and talk to me. There's nothing we can't work out with God's help."

He had to mention God. She might have argued with Aaron, even if she didn't want to, but how did one argue with God? Trembling, she perched at the foot of the bed, leaving as much space between them as possible.

He glanced at the open satchel he'd tossed to the other side of the bed, then looked down at the floor. He'd never had trouble looking at her before. Why now?

Aaron cleared his throat. "Would you mind if we prayed first?"

Janie stared at him. They'd never prayed before a discussion. She was beginning to fear that his news was worse than hers, but how could that be? She nodded, and when he stretched his hand across the bed, she gripped it like a lifeline thrown to someone drowning in the tumultuous ocean.

"Lord, we need Your help. There are things going on here beyond our control, and we can't make it without You on our side, even on a good day. Help us to talk through the problems facing us and unite us as man and wife, as we were before."

Before what? Janie wondered.

"Amen." Aaron squeezed her hand, then pulled his away with a halfhearted smile. Although, if she were truthful, it was more of a quarter-hearted smile, if there was such a thing.

"I reckon you've noticed I've been troubled since yesterday." She nodded, more than a little curious.

"After you and the children left the depot yesterday, a passenger from the train approached me." He stared at her with a look she couldn't decipher. "He had a photograph of you, Janie."

"Me?" She pressed her hand to her heart, which felt as if it were ricocheting around in her chest. Had Martin found her?

"Yes. He introduced himself as Phineas Parker, a detective from Boston. Do you know him?"

"No. I've never heard the name before." She closed her eyes. Martin had hired that man to find her, she was certain, and that meant he was close. She had no time to lose. She jumped up and grabbed for the satchel, but Aaron snatched it out of her reach and threw it in the corner across the room.

"Sit down, Janie. You're not going anywhere until we've talked."

"But you don't understand."

He rose and closed the space between them, taking her quivering hands in his. "Then tell me so I will. I can't help you if I don't know what's going on."

Unwanted tears blurred her vision of the man she loved so much. "There's nothing you can do. Benjy and I must leave and go far away from here."

He tightened his grip, and his expression darkened. "Answer a question for me. When we married, were you already wed to another man?"

She gasped. "What? No! How could you think that?"

His relief was evident on his face. "Because that detective told me he was searching for a man's wife who had run away with his child."

Martin's deception, she had no doubt. "Well, that's a lie—" She halted, suddenly realizing the truth. "The part about me being married was a lie." She twisted her hands, knowing now was the time to reveal her secret. "In fact, I've never been married. Not even once."

Aaron's expression would have been funny if not for the gravity of the situation. "Wait, I'm confused. You weren't married to Phil?"

She shook her head. "He was my brother."

Aaron's brow crinkled, and he dropped onto the bed. "Your brother? Then why pretend you were man and wife?"

Janie sighed and sat on the edge of the bed beside him. "I never wanted to, but Phil seemed to think it was necessary to keep Benjy safe and protect my reputation. I agreed to go along with the ruse, but I always felt guilty about it."

"And you weren't married before Phil?"

"No, I wasn't."

"But what about Benjy? You didn't—"

She pressed her fingers to his lips, unable to bear hearing the accusation that she knew was coming next. "The latter half of what that detective said was true. I did take a man's child, but it was at the request of Benjy's mother." She rose and hurried to the dresser, retrieved Carolyn's letter, and handed it to him. "Please, read this. It will explain a lot."

He took the missive, and she watched the play of expressions on his handsome face as his eyes scanned the page. *Please, God. Help us work this out.*

Aaron folded the paper and blew out a loud breath. "So you think this Martin guy is after you?"

"I *know* he is. Read these letters I opened a short while ago." She handed him the letters that still lay on the table beside the bed, and he read those, too.

"You think—what's Benjy's father's name?"

"Martin Metcalf."

"Do you think he killed this woman?"

"Or paid someone else to do it. That's more like Martin. He's quite wealthy and would probably hire out such a deed."

Aaron pursed his lips and rose, his expression suddenly angry. "You put my children's lives in danger by marrying me, without so much as the courtesy of telling me first that a murderer was after you."

She ducked her head, unable to deny this accusation. "I'm sorry. I didn't know how to tell you. I was afraid you'd leave Benjy and me, and I had no one else to rely on."

"You should have trusted me, Janie."

She stood and looked him in the eye. "I barely knew you. If I knew you then like I do now, I would have told you."

"And yet you didn't."

"I should have. I'm so sorry."

He ran his fingers through his hair. "Is there anything else I need to know?"

She took a deep breath. "Martin pushed his wife—my cousin Carolyn—down the stairs the day she gave birth to Benjy. She died shortly after the delivery as a result of that fall. She must have sensed that her death was near, because she wrote me that letter days before and sent me a bag of valuable gems to help pay for the things I would need to care for her baby." She retrieved the bag from the dresser, opened it, and dumped the contents onto the bed.

Aaron's eyes widened, and he picked up a fat emerald. "Just one of these must be worth more than this whole ranch."

Janie shrugged. "All I know is that I sold two of the jewels, bought clothing and diapers for Benjy, hired a wet nurse, and traveled here, hoping I'd gotten so far from Boston that Martin would never find me. I guess I was wrong." She gazed upon her husband, wishing her story had been a happy one, rather than one that would tear them apart. "So, you see now why I must go, and take Benjy with me. As long as we're here, we aren't safe, and neither are you and the children."

Aaron shook his head. "You know what he did to Miss Carpenter after you left. What makes you think he won't come here looking for you and harm the children anyway?"

She blinked. "I—I figured once we were gone, he would just follow."

"Men like him don't care who they hurt. You're not leaving until I make some decisions."

"What decisions?"

"I don't know. I need some time to sort through all I've learned."

"But if that detective sensed you knew me, he'll wire Martin, and he'll catch the first train out of Boston."

"I'm not the kind of man to make impulsive decisions, Janie. I like to think things out. And pray. I need a little time. You owe me that."

He was correct. She certainly owed him.

"Even if this Metcalf fellow left Boston tomorrow, it would take him close to a week to get here. I need just a day or two."

"What are you going to do?"

"Talk to my parents and Ethan. I want to know what they think I should do."

Janie lowered her head. "They'll hate me for not telling them."

"Maybe." He paused, as if to let that idea sink into her bones. She would deeply miss the loss of his family, too, if she left.

"But I doubt it. You and the kids stay in the house as much as possible. I'll sleep on the settee tonight, but at first light, I'm riding home. I'll return before dark. You make sure you don't leave."

"I would never leave your children to themselves. I hope you have that much faith in me."

He stared at her long and hard, and she felt his disappointment. He turned suddenly and fled to the parlor. Whatever he decided, she deserved her fate. Janie crawled into bed once more, feeling Aaron's absence to the core of her being. She probably never should have let him get close—never should have married him—but he'd stolen a chunk of her heart the first day she met him.

Chapter Twenty

Aaron rode into the yard at his family's ranch, dreading what was to come. The house looked deserted, with no one on the porch or in the yard, no smoke coming from the chimneys, no little boys running about, yelling. Where was everyone?

Part of him wanted to ride off and be alone for days, since his emotions were as raw as a skinned rabbit, but he couldn't leave Janie and the young'uns unprotected. He wanted to believe Janie's story—he actually did, for the most part—but he was so angry at her for endangering his children that he could have fenced an acre with barbed wire bare-handed.

Why couldn't she have trusted him with the truth before they married?

Would he have gone ahead with the wedding if he'd been aware of the situation?

He shook his head. No matter now. He had to make plans—be prepared. Should he bring Janie and the kids here, where there were armed men to keep watch? Or should he send his kids back to Windmill to stay with Josh and Sophie until this thing was settled? But that still left Janie and little Benjy—a boy he'd started thinking of as his own—in harm's way.

After dismounting, he led Outlaw to the barn, where he unsaddled and groomed him while the animal dined on a mess of hay. Then Aaron entered the house, hoping for a good meal;

but instead of the delicious aroma of his ma's cooking, only the faint hint of the bacon she'd fried for breakfast lingered. Another disappointment to deal with.

"Ma?" He hollered her name, even though he knew she wasn't here. Maybe she'd gone to town to visit Josh and Sophie.

He blew out a sigh, snatched a slice of bread from the bread box, and headed to Ethan's house. Sarah would know where his folks were—if she was home.

He knocked on the door, then opened it and stuck his head inside. "Ethan? Sarah?"

"In the kitchen," Ethan shouted.

Aaron made his way through the house that he'd once shared with Della, but nothing was the same except for some of the furniture. Sarah had made the place her own, as she should have.

Ethan sat at the table alone, chomping on a sandwich the size of Texas. He pushed out a chair with his boot. "Join me. Sarah went visiting the new neighbors to the north with Ma and Pa," he mumbled with a full mouth.

"What about Aunt Emma?"

Ethan nudged his head toward the back of the house. "Resting. She didn't sleep well last night and decided to stay home."

Aaron sat, buttered two slices of bread, and layered beef and cheese until his sandwich rivaled his brother's. "Can she hear us?" He took a bite.

Ethan shook his head and swigged down some water. "What brings you back so soon, big brother?"

Aaron chewed his food, using the time to ponder what to tell Ethan and how to word it. In the end, he knew being direct was the only way to go. He explained about meeting the detective and seeing the picture of Janie, then related the story the man had told him. Ethan's brown eyes grew wider and wider.

"Janie's married? I mean, to someone other than you?"

"No. That's the thing. The man lied about that."

Ethan leaned back in his chair. "No wonder you got upset so fast. I couldn't for the life of me figure out what turned your smile upside down that day. What did Janie have to say about the man?"

"She didn't recognize his name, but she also said the part about her taking another man's baby was true."

Ethan's jaw dropped. Then he grinned and shoved Aaron's knee sideways with his foot. "Aw, you're joshin' me, aren't you?"

Aaron remained serious and shook his head, watching his brother's grin wilt. Ethan leaned forward on the table.

"Are you saying Benjy isn't Janie's son? And that she kidnapped him?"

Aaron explained about Carolyn Metcalf and her written request that Janie take Benjy far away from Martin and raise him as her own son. Then he told him about Naomi Carpenter's demise.

Ethan fell back against his chair again and let out a whistle through his teeth. "Great guns, big brother, you sure stepped in a big pile of horse flops. What are you gonna do?"

Aaron shrugged. "I don't know, other than try to get Janie and the kids out of harm's way."

"But you don't know when or if this Metcalf fellow will come here. You can't live your life lookin' over your shoulder all the time."

"I know that. I'm trying to decide if they'd all be safer here or in town."

"Here, of course. Sophie doesn't need the stress of a bunch of people at her house. She has enough to do keeping her asthma under control while being pregnant for the first time."

Aaron pursed his lips, irritated with himself for failing to consider that. "I wanted you all to understand the situation before I move my family here. You have your wife and sons to think of. Where are your boys, by the way?"

"Sarah took them with her to the Barnards'. They have a whole passel of young'uns, and she thought Mark and Jeff would enjoy playing with them. I have an off-season mare foaling in the barn. That's why you found me here."

"My only concern about bringing Janie and Benjy here is that it may endanger the rest of you."

Ethan stuck his fingers in his ears like he had when he was a boy and didn't want to listen to Aaron. "Us Harpers stick together," he said, a bit too loudly. He removed his fingers and gazed at Aaron, all playfulness gone. "If there's danger, we'll circle the wagons. We have a dozen armed men who can help protect your wife and kids. You've got no one in town, except for Josh."

He knew Ethan was right, but he was still hesitant. Bringing Janie here would make it much easier for her to hop on the train when he was busy working. Would she actually leave him?

"What about Benjy's father? Doesn't he have a right to raise his son? Have you thought of that?" Ethan rose, went to the stove, and put the coffeepot on a burner. "I need something stronger than water to get all this straight in my mind." He leaned against the wall beside the stove.

"Janie said this Metcalf fellow is mean—that he even pushed his very pregnant wife down the stairs, causing her to have the baby early. He basically murdered Benjy's mother and probably the headmaster at the school where Janie taught. Do you think a man like that is capable of taking proper care of a baby? And what about the pain Benjy would suffer being ripped away from Janie, when she's the only ma he's ever known?"

"I know you love Benjy as much as you do Corrie and Toby, but you have to look at all sides, Aaron. Are there laws against what Janie did?"

"I don't know. She did have the mother's permission to take him. In fact, her cousin begged her to."

Ethan scratched his ear. "But what if Della had given Toby to someone? You know you'd have risked life and limb to find him."

"Of course I would, but then, I haven't killed two people, either. There's no guarantee this Metcalf man won't kill Benjy." Aaron hoped that the anguish he felt was evident in his eyes. He wanted Ethan to know how much losing Benjy or Janie would affect him.

Ethan pulled out the chair beside Aaron's and sat, resting his elbows on his knees. "I think you need to go into town and talk to the lawyer and maybe even the marshal."

Aaron rubbed his jaw as he considered his brother's suggestion. "That's not a bad idea, but I don't want to be gone for several days."

"Something's bothering me. You said Janie was never married before you, right?"

Aaron nodded.

"Then what about Phil?"

"He was her brother."

"Confound it, Aaron. You sure have gotten tangled up in a barbed-wire mess."

"I know, but I'm not abandoning my wife when she needs me most."

"I'd be disappointed in you if you did." Ethan slapped Aaron's shoulder.

He glanced up, surprised to find his brother grinning again. "What?"

Ethan stroked his jaw with his index finger and thumb, his gaze turning mischievous. "You do realize that you've married a woman who has never been married before. That ought to make you happy, at least."

He couldn't help the smile that tittered on his lips. "It does, and it certainly explains some things."

"Like what?"

"Like none of your business, little brother."

Ethan chuckled and scratched his neck. "So, what are you gonna do?"

Aaron rested one elbow on the table and propped his forehead in his hand. "I don't know. That's why I came here today—to get someone else's perspective on the situation."

His brother picked up his sandwich. "Then you'll just have to stay until they all get back. And you can help with that mare. Eat up. Time for me to head out to the barn."

He didn't like leaving Janie and the kids for too long, but he had to talk to his folks. "I wonder if I should head into Windmill on the next train," he mused aloud. "Even if that detective telegraphed Martin Metcalf, I figure it'll take a good week for him to get here."

Ethan nodded. "That sounds about right to me. Listen, why don't you let Pa or me go to town and fill Josh in on what's going on, and then go visit the lawyer, so you can stay here—just in case? You know Josh is smarter than us in legal stuff."

"I'd appreciate that." Aaron nodded. "That's mighty kind of you."

"Pshaw." Ethan grinned. "We're family." He got up and poured two cups of steaming coffee, set them on the table, and returned to his seat. "I'm thinkin' we ought to send the women and children up to Kansas City for an early Christmas shopping trip. It would give Sarah and her aunt Emma a chance to visit Uncle Bob."

"He was the brother of Sarah's uncle who died, right?"

"Yep."

Aaron relaxed for the first time in hours and grinned at his brother's genius plan. "That would certainly get them all out of harm's way. Let's talk it over with Ma and Pa when they get back."

He liked the idea of getting Janie and the children, as well as Ma, Emma, and Sarah and her boys, out of the reach of this Metcalf maniac. Maybe Josh would send Sophie and Mikey along, too.

He was blessed to have a family who rallied around him.

But even more, he had God on his side.

And for that he was deeply grateful.

~

As the incessant wind buffeted Martin, he wished he was home in his warm house, drinking a whiskey that would heat him on the inside. Too bad that train had been going on to another town and not back to Windmill. He huddled in the uncomfortable duster he'd paid far too much for, riding a nag that made every muscle in his body ache. He chuckled to himself, thinking of how he'd outwitted the livery owner by telling him he needed to rent the horse for a few days. That fool would never see this mount again.

He'd followed the train tracks back to the Harper depot, built a fire inside, and stayed until he'd thawed out. Then he'd made his way to a large homestead, but after searching the big house and finding no one there, he'd been at a loss for what to do.

Then the man he'd talked to at the depot had ridden in from the southeast. He, too, had gone into the large house but soon exited and walked over to the smaller one. Martin had realized someone was there when he heard a yell. He'd been fortunate not to be seen. For as big a spread as the Harpers had, there had been precious few people around.

He was glad he'd decided to follow Aaron Harper's tracks away from the homestead, even though he should have helped himself to something to eat first. His belly whined and complained of hunger, but he was too his close to his son—and that miscreant cousin of Carolyn's who'd stolen the boy—to stop now.

An hour later, Martin topped a hill and jerked the horse to a stop. In the next valley sat a cabin with a barn, and the wagon tracks he'd been following led straight there. He circled around, keeping out of view, and when he reached the far side, he dismounted. He searched for wagon tracks, to see if the driver had continued on, but all he found were tracks where the wagon had stopped in front of the shack of a house and then made an arc toward the barn. This had to be where Janie Dunn was hiding out.

Luck was on his side, because when he ran up to the side of the house, no dog charged him or even barked at him from inside. Harper had left his family defenseless.

Martin rubbed his hands together, sensing imminent victory. Soon he would look upon the child that was stolen from him and avenge the thief.

He peered in through a window to a bedroom. Through the open door, he saw a young girl pass by, followed by Janie Dunn—or he supposed it was Janie Harper now. Excitement made his legs weak. Rarely had he experienced such an overwhelming sense of victory. If only he knew when Harper would return. Martin wished he had more time to plan his escape, but he needed to nab the child before the man came back.

Now, what to do about Carolyn's cousin?

Janie laid Benjy in his bed and covered him with the adorable quilt Aaron had bought for him, then glanced out the bedroom window. Surely Aaron would be home soon. How long did he need to talk to his family? Three hours would be the minimum amount of time he would be gone—an hour to ride over, an hour to talk, and an hour to ride home again. Darkness would fall before too long. If he wasn't home by then, she'd need to light a lantern and hang it on the porch. She peeked at Benjy as she tiptoed from the room, leaving the door open, as usual. It was fortunate that once he went to sleep, the normal noises of the family didn't bother him.

Corrie sat on the sofa, folding diapers they'd rinsed out and dried in the house. The room didn't smell too fresh, but it was better than fighting the chilly wind outside. Toby had begged to flee the stench and was hiding out in Corrie's room, studying his multiplication tables. Janie perched on the sofa beside Corrie and picked up her sewing needle. She pulled a diaper from the pile stacked nearby, then folded down a frayed corner and started sewing.

Corrie cleared her throat. "I've been meaning to ask…is something wrong between you and Pa?"

Janie's gaze jerked sideways, although she shouldn't have been surprised. Corrie was a smart girl and had sensed the tension that had suddenly developed between Aaron and her.

"There are some things about my past that I should have told your father before we were married. He's upset about them. And he has every right to be."

"Why didn't you tell him sooner? I mean, if I may ask."

Janie shrugged. "I should have, but I was afraid."

"Afraid of what? That he wouldn't marry you if he knew?"

"Yes, I suppose. Even though your father was a friend of Phil's and came around frequently, I never got to know him well. He was Phil's friend, not mine. I didn't know how he would react, so I remained silent." She hoped and prayed her decision wouldn't result in Aaron or one of the children getting hurt.

"I'm glad Pa married you, and I'm sorry for causing so much trouble when he first brought us here."

Janie smiled. "Thank you, Corrie. That means a lot to me."

"Pa will come around soon. You'll see. He never stays mad for long."

"That's good to know. Thank you for encouraging me."

"Don't get me wrong, I still miss my friends." Corrie added another folded diaper to the pile.

"I still miss the friends I had in Boston, too, but the pain of separation eases over time."

"I know. Things were especially hard at first when my ma died—" She ducked her head, and her cheeks reddened. "Is it terrible to tell you that I rarely think of her anymore?"

Janie laid her hand over the girl's. "No, of course not. Weeks, maybe even months, go by that I don't think of my parents, but when I do, it's with fond memories."

Corrie frowned. "I don't have many memories of my ma."

"You were only...what? Four when she died?"

She nodded. "I remember that she was very pretty with blonde hair and blue eyes, but that's about all."

"You must have her eyes."

Footsteps sounded on the porch, and she smiled. "Pa's home."

Instead of relief, tension snaked a path down from Janie's neck and shoulders and settled in her stomach. What if Nick and Karen were angry at her for her deception? If Aaron sent her packing, she didn't know what she would do.

The door opened, and a gun barrel appeared, followed by a man stepping into the room. The gun swerved toward Janie as he pushed back his hat, revealing a sinister grin. "Hello, Cousin Janie."

No! Not Martin. She lurched to her feet and stepped in front of Corrie. How could he have possibly gotten here so quickly?

"Cousin?" Corrie whispered in her ear. "Do you know this man?"

Janie's mind raced. If only she had the pistol that she carried in her apron pocket when she went outside, but it was in her bedroom.

Martin shut the door, still grinning, obviously proud of himself for tracking her down. "I can see you didn't expect me. I fooled that husband of yours into believing I was a detective. Got off the train at the next town after I talked to him and rode back. That man of yours sure doesn't have a poker face."

"That's because he's a good, honest man, who's most likely never gambled. But you wouldn't know anything about that, would you?" Janie hiked up her chin.

"Ah, ah, it isn't wise to provoke a man with a gun." He searched the room, and then his gaze returned to Janie. "Where's my son?"

Corrie gasped. "What's he talking about?" She pressed up against Janie's back.

"Shh...not now, sweetie." How could she get Martin away from the children? Maybe if she got him to follow her to her room... If she could distract Martin, maybe the children could get out of the house. "He's—"

"What's his name?"

"Benjamin."

Scowling, Martin shook his head. "That's no name for a Metcalf. I'll call him Martin Junior."

Corrie yanked on the back of Janie's skirt. "What's he talking about?"

Martin's gaze swerved past Janie to the girl. "Obviously, she hasn't told you. That boy is my son, and this woman stole him from me."

Janie stiffened. "That's not true! Carolyn gave him to me to keep him safe from you."

His features contorted into rage, and he moved toward her. Janie regretted provoking him. She had to calm him before he hurt someone. "Never mind that. Come with me, and I'll let you see him."

"Let me?" He barked a laugh. "What a crock. Where is my son?"

"In my room, over there." She reached behind her and tugged on Corrie's skirt, waving her hand toward the small bedroom, then stepped forward. "Follow me, Martin."

He started to, but then the gun swiveled toward Corrie. "She comes too."

Janie shook her head, struggling to keep her wits about her and praying that her fear wouldn't overpower her good sense. "You don't need her. She's just a girl. She can't hurt you."

Martin eyed Corrie, then motioned with the gun. "Sit down and don't move. If you do, I'll shoot you."

Corrie visibly swallowed and did as asked. Her gaze darted to Benjy's room, then over to Janie. Standing behind Martin, she gave a quick jerk of her head toward the back door.

Martin turned and shoved her. She stumbled toward her bedroom, grabbing the door frame to keep from falling. Her heart thundered like the hooves of wild mustangs she'd once seen. How was she going to stall him? He pushed her into the room and followed her.

"Where's my boy?" When he stepped toward the bed, Janie slammed the door shut and reached for the pistol on the dresser.

Gunfire blasted. Her shoulder exploded in fiery torment, and she slumped down, fighting to keep from losing consciousness. Martin grabbed the arm with the wound and yanked her away from the door, dragging her across the floor. She screamed as pain fired through her body. Darkness battled light.

The door hit her in the backside, and he ran out. Janie fought the blackness and pain as she groped around for the gun that had fallen to the floor. She had to protect the children.

Corrie screamed.

Benjy wailed.

Janie pushed herself to her feet, swaying. The gun felt as heavy as a horse. She clutched the door frame, then stumbled into the parlor. Smirking, Martin stopped in the front entry, holding Benjy in one arm and his gun in the other, and stared at her, as if to bask in his victory.

The baby screamed so hard, his face was red. He pushed at the stranger's chest. He rubbed his eyes, then turned, saw Janie, and nearly lunged free of his captor's arms. "Mama!"

Martin shook the boy. "That thief is not your mother."

Benjy cried louder, his shrieks ripping Janie's heart to shreds. She wanted desperately to shoot Martin to keep him from escaping with Benjy, but she was afraid of hitting the boy she loved so much. She stared at Benjy, tears blurring her view. "Please, don't take him."

"Say good-bye, little Martin."

Without taking time to think, Janie lifted the gun, aimed at Martin's foot, and fired. The door frame shattered. Martin cried out and stumbled to his knees, grimacing, but he didn't drop Benjy—or his gun.

Corrie stumbled from the small room, her mouth swollen and bleeding. Tears ran down her cheeks. "I tried, Ma. I tried."

Martin scrambled to his feet, blood flowing from his left thigh, just above the knee, where a large splinter of wood had embedded itself. He raised the gun and pointed it at Janie, but then he narrowed his gaze and swerved toward Corrie. Janie dove at the girl as the room filled with the blast of gunfire and the odor of sulfur. Benjy howled.

Janie struggled to rise. To see if Corrie was hurt. To save Benjy.

But before she could push herself off Corrie, darkness swirled and swallowed her.

Chapter Twenty-one

Aaron rode Outlaw toward home—his home—at an easy lope, his chest warmed by the memory of how Ma and Pa had rallied around him once they'd heard Janie's story. His ma had been quick to defend her, saying Janie had honored the dying wish of her cousin to raise her son. Sarah had agreed, understanding as only a mother with young children could. His pa had commented that while stealing a horse was an offense for which a man could be hanged, as far as he knew, there were few, if any, laws to protect children from cruel parents or caretakers.

He pursed his lips. If he were a more ambitious man with more learning, he would work on getting a law passed to protect children. What kind of country was this when horses were safer than children?

At first, he'd been horrified to learn that his wife had taken another man's son. But after hearing what kind of man Martin Metcalf was, and reading the letters Janie had in her possession, he believed she did the right thing. His biggest concern now was getting her and the kids out of town. He wasn't sure how long they would need to stay away, but his gut told him Metcalf would come soon. He knew his face must have registered shock when that detective had showed him Janie's picture and described her as a wife on the run. What newly wedded man wouldn't react to learning such a thing about his bride? And if Detective Parker was the least bit astute, he would have already wired Metcalf.

Aaron closed his eyes and lifted his face, allowing the sun to warm his cold cheeks. Winter would soon be upon them. He needed to patch some of the cracks in the walls of the house that had been welcome during the summer heat. The cold weather, with its rain and snow, made life harder, but it also allowed him more time indoors with his family. He grinned. Maybe that family would be growing before long.

Come late spring, he wanted to build a nicer home—a two-story one like Ethan's. When everyone gathered in the small parlor and kitchen, the rooms were cramped. He had only one hurdle to jump—a hurdle named Martin Metcalf—and then he could settle down with Janie to grow and raise their family. "Thank You, Lord, for giving her to me. I pray that she will forgive me for my anger over the situation."

"Pa! Pa!"

Aaron's head shot up. He searched the road ahead and spied Toby running toward him. He nudged Outlaw to a gallop, then reined him back as he drew close to his son. He slid off before the horse stopped completely, and ran to meet Toby. "What's happened?"

Toby gasped for breath and pointed back toward the house. "A man...he sh-shot Janie...took Benjy."

Aaron wrapped his arms around Toby, his gut twisting like a cyclone. "You did good, Son. C'mon."

Toby wiped his cheeks and still struggled to slow his breathing. "Is my new ma gonna die like my old one did?"

Clenching his teeth against the pain of that thought, Aaron shook his head. "Not if I can help it." He took hold of Outlaw's reins and pulled out his gun. "Cover your ears. I need to fire off a signal to Ethan."

Once the boy obeyed, Aaron fired three quick shots into the air and then listened for a long minute, his heart throbbing in his ears. Had that detective come and taken Benjy? He'd never considered that scenario. There was no chance Metcalf could have reached Kansas this soon—unless he was already in a nearby town. Aaron hated to think he might have underestimated the man.

Getting no response from the ranch, he glanced down at Toby and pointed to his ears. The boy covered them again, and Aaron fired off another trio of shots. This time, he received a response—two rifle shots from the ranch. He reloaded and holstered his gun, knowing help would soon come. Then he remounted Outlaw and reached down for Toby. The boy put his foot in the stirrup, and Aaron hoisted him up behind him.

"Hold on. Tight." Aaron nudged Outlaw forward and into a gallop. *Hold on, Janie. Please, God, don't take her away, just when I'm realizing how much she means to me. Protect Benjy from that madman.*

The ride to the cabin seemed to take hours, when it was more likely ten minutes. He reined Outlaw toward the cabin and stopped him. Then he reached back, grabbed Toby, and lowered him to the ground. After dismounting, Aaron tossed the reins to his son. "Walk him around for me."

"But Pa—"

"Do as I say. I'll need him to catch that man." Aaron paused at the open doorway to the house. What if the man had returned? He pulled out his gun and peered around the open door. He shoved it hard, just in case Metcalf was behind it.

Corrie squealed, but her features immediately softened with relief. She sat on the floor next to Janie, holding a bloody towel to her shoulder. "Pa! Hurry. Ma's been shot."

He clenched his teeth as anger surged through him at the sight of his daughter's fat, bloody lip. He strode forward, the fact that she'd referred to Janie as "Ma" not lost on him. Kneeling down beside his wife, he held his breath and felt her neck for a pulse. His heart nearly stopped, but then—there! He found it. Not as strong as it should be, but it was there. Swallowing hard, he brushed back the hair that had fallen from her pins. "Janie, can you hear me?"

She fought to open her eyes, then licked her lips. "Yes. Thank God you've come."

"Corrie, get more towels."

The girl hopped up to do as bidden.

Aaron lifted the towel, and rage boiled up within him at the hole in his wife's shoulder. From the looks of the wound and the amount of blood on the rug, the bullet must have gone clean through, which at least spared her the pain of needing to have it dug out. Janie tugged on his sleeve, and his gaze shot to her pain-filled eyes.

"Aaron," she whispered. "Go. Save Benjy."

He was torn. If he left without seeing to her wound, she could die before Ethan got there. But if Metcalf got away, they'd never see Benjy again.

"Go! I'm all right."

He leaned down and kissed her. "I love you, sweetheart. Don't you die on me, you hear?"

"Love you." She nodded. "Please. Go."

He ran his hand down her cheek, giving her an encouraging smile that felt phony as Corrie trotted into the room. *Please, Lord, don't take her from me.* He folded the towel, stuffed it behind her shoulder, and placed a clean one on front. He turned to Corrie. "Keep pressure on this till Ethan gets here. He's on his way, and others will follow. Look at me."

Corrie knelt beside him and met his gaze, her fear evident.

"Do as I said—and pray."

She nodded. "Go on, Pa. Benjy needs you. I'll take care of Ma."

He smiled and stroked the side of her head. "That's my girl."

Aaron rose, filled with purpose. His youngest son needed him, and he wasn't about to fail him. He strode to the cabinet where he stored his ammunition, loaded his pistol, and filled his pockets with cartridges for his rifle. As he tugged the rifle from its rack, he gazed at his girls. "I love you both."

"Aaron. Wait!"

He rushed to Janie's side.

"Martin...pretended to be...detective."

Metcalf had Benjy? His blood ran cold, but he worked to keep his expression neutral. "So, that's how he got here so fast. He probably got off the train at Karsen and rode a horse back here."

Janie closed her eyes. "Be careful. He's dangerous."

"I will." He took a final glance at his wife and daughter, then spun around and strode outside.

When Toby saw him, he turned Outlaw toward the house, jogging to keep up with the horse's long legs. Outlaw whinnied, as if to say he was ready. Aaron hugged Toby. "Good job, Son. Go inside and help Corrie take care of your ma. And pray!" He shoved his rifle in the scabbard and mounted. "Which way did he head?"

Toby pointed to the right, away from the Harper ranch. Aaron reined Outlaw in that direction. "He-yah!" He slapped Outlaw's shoulder with the end of the leather reins and hunkered down as the horse responded.

Hang on, Benjy. Pa's coming.

❧

It took Aaron only a minute to pick up Metcalf's trail on the far side of the house, where the ground had been made smooth by the rain that had fallen earlier. Time was of the essence; the sun would be setting in less than two hours. With Metcalf's record of cruelty, Aaron had to wonder how he would treat Benjy. What if the boy cried the whole journey? Would Metcalf lose patience and slap him like he had Corrie?

Gritting his teeth, he nudged Outlaw into a faster gallop. What kind of man shoots a woman or hits an eleven-year-old girl? The kind that has no business caring for a baby, blood kin or not.

Several miles later, he slowed to a trot, as much as he hated to, but Outlaw needed to rest, and he could do that at the slower pace. Aaron kept his eyes on the trail, determined not to lose it. He knew Benjy's life may well depend on his diligence.

He glanced up at the sky. The temperature tonight would drop, since there were no clouds, and the north wind had picked up, making it feel even colder. More than likely, they were in for a frost. He highly doubted Metcalf had prepared for being out in the frigid weather. The most he might have was a coat and bedroll, maybe some matches. Had he even thought to grab a quilt for the baby?

Aaron reined Outlaw to a stop. The horse's breathing had slowed, and he pawed the ground, as if sensing the urgency of his rider's mission. The wind tugged at Aaron's hat, threatening to steal it away. He cocked his head to one side and held his breath, certain he'd heard something. A wail? Was it Benjy or some kind of cat? It wasn't unheard of for a man to come upon a mountain lion in these parts. Or was the wind merely playing tricks?

He clicked out one side of his mouth, and Outlaw eagerly trotted forward. Aaron kept his ears tuned. There it was again—the same noise, only this time, it sounded like a wild stallion, or maybe a horse in pain. He tapped his heels against the horse's side, and Outlaw broke into a trot, then quickly sped into a lope.

Aaron shifted his eyes from the horse tracks to the landscape and back again. Several minutes later, he reined in the horse as they crested the next hill. From there, he could make out the line of train tracks to the north. Metcalf must have planned to follow them to Windmill—a clever idea, since the man was unfamiliar with this county.

A loud screech and a harsh shout yanked his gaze to a cluster of trees he had scanned a moment ago. There they were! His heart pounded like a locomotive at full speed. He was almost there, but now he needed a plan. How could he close the distance without being spotted by Metcalf? The valley had few trees besides the copse where Benjy's captor had stopped. And why had he stopped? That made no sense—unless his horse had gone lame. If he'd ridden the horse all the way from Karsen without a rest, maybe the animal had given out. If the horse had collapsed, Metcalf might be hurt—and Benjy too.

"Show me what to do, Lord, so that Benjy won't be harmed."

Motion to his left drew his gaze to the hill he'd recently crossed. Two riders—Ethan and Sam—rode toward him. Aaron backed down the hill so Metcalf couldn't see him, and waved his arm, drawing their attention. He pointed toward the valley, then motioned for Ethan and Sam to go around so that they could come up from behind. The duo reined to their left and rode away, just as Aaron had hoped. Thank God that he wouldn't have to face Metcalf alone.

With a plan in mind, he nudged Outlaw forward, riding him a ways to the south and then over the hill. Metcalf wouldn't expect anyone following him to come from that direction. They moved forward at a walk. Aaron started whistling a casual tune, posing as a man moseying along. Maybe Metcalf wouldn't see him as a threat.

A loud squeal rent the air, and Aaron's gaze latched onto Metcalf's downed and struggling horse. His hunch looked to be correct. The man must have ridden it from Karsen—probably close to twenty miles—at a fast pace. Either that or it had stumbled in a prairie dog hole.

Hoping to not be recognized, Aaron tugged his hat down low, but not so far that it prevented him from seeing Metcalf, who sat with his back against a tree. Benjy sat on the ground beside his captor in nothing but his gown. Aaron gritted his teeth at Metcalf's lack of concern for the baby. He pulled out his gun and held his right arm straight down in a relaxed manner. From his angle of approach, the weapon wouldn't be visible. As he drew nearer, Aaron dropped the reins and lifted a hand in a friendly gesture. "Hey there, mister. Looks like you've had some trouble."

Metcalf nodded. His right arm—the one behind Benjy—moved. Aaron suspected that was where the man's gun was hidden. Anger surged. What kind of lily-livered fiend used a baby for a shield?

Metcalf slowly stood, like a man in pain. Then Aaron noticed the blood on his pants. He must have injured himself in the fall. When he lifted his gaze, he realized he'd made a serious error. Metcalf's gun was pointed at him. Benjy rubbed his eyes and yawned, not yet noticing Aaron.

"Get off that horse. I have need of it."

Aaron slid down slowly, making sure to keep his gun out of sight. As he turned, his heart all but exploded. Metcalf had picked up Benjy and now held the gun to the boy's head.

The man let out a harsh laugh. "You thought I wouldn't recognize you? I'm no fool, Harper. Your stupid ploy did nothing but give me a getaway horse. This stupid nag of mine gave out."

"Pa! Pa!" Benjy reached toward Aaron, arching his back in his effort to get away. Metcalf nearly dropped him, and Benjy kicked his feet, one hitting his captor only a few inches above the leg wound. Metcalf cried out and shook the boy, who howled in response.

Aaron couldn't take a chance on Benjy getting shot. "Hey, look. I'm putting down my gun. Take the horse. Just give me the boy."

"No. I'm taking them both."

Chapter Twenty-two

As Aaron dismounted, he struggled to find some fragment of humanity in Martin Metcalf. "You're going to wind up causing that boy's death if you keep him out tonight in the cold with nothing on but a gown. Is that what you want?" Aaron couldn't bring himself to ask if the man was willing to kill his own son. Benjy may be related by blood, but that didn't make Metcalf his father.

"Pa-a-a!" Benjy threw his head back, hitting his captor in the jaw.

"Hold still, you little brat!"

Aaron had never felt so helpless. He did have one ace up his sleeve, but it would endanger Benjy. He held out his hands, palms up. "That wound looks bad. Let me help you."

"Ha! You'd take the boy and leave me for dead."

"No, that's what you'd do. Not me. You need a doctor."

Metcalf staggered back against the tree, obviously weakening.

"I'm a man of my word. I promise I'll help. Give me the boy, and you're free to go after I tend your wound."

"No. Shed that coat and toss it over here."

Aaron did as ordered, immediately missing the comfort of the fleece-lined jacket; but if it would keep Benjy warm, he'd gladly sacrifice it.

Metcalf put Benjy down, and the boy turned and started crawling for Aaron. After shoving his arms in the coat, he lifted Benjy again, who kicked and screamed. Metcalf still managed to keep the shaking gun trained in Aaron's direction.

Scrambling for ideas, Aaron prayed Ethan would hurry, and decided on the only plan he could think of. He watched Metcalf wrestle with Outlaw, who kept prancing away from him. "Get over here and catch this horse before I shoot it."

Aaron headed for Outlaw and walked right up to the spooked horse, murmuring to him and hoping the tone of his voice and nearness would also soothe Benjy. "You're all right, boy."

"Hold him steady, and if you try anything, I'll shoot you." Metcalf attempted to mount, but with his wounded leg, plus holding Benjy in one arm and the gun in the other, he failed.

Stop him, Lord.

Metcalf heaved a loud sigh and turned, keeping the gun trained on Aaron. "Hold the boy while I mount, and don't try anything. I mean it. I'd rather shoot the noisy brat than let you have him."

Metcalf cautiously passed Benjy to Aaron, then limped back to Outlaw. Benjy's face was red and splotchy, his voice hoarse. Aaron cuddled him, hoping to both warm and comfort the boy. Benjy's wails softened to whines as Aaron held him to his chest, and the boy sniffled and shuddered, clinging to him. He patted the boy's back and placed a kiss on his head. "It's all right, pardner."

Metcalf settled onto Outlaw, then held out his free arm. Aaron wrestled with giving the boy up.

"Let me have him, Harper—unless you want him to die."

Aaron took a step back. There was no way he was handing Benjy over to that madman again. If he turned away, Metcalf would shoot him for sure, and he wasn't ready to die. He had a wife and kids who needed him. He had to stall.

"You got my horse. Why not leave while you can? I've got men coming to help."

Metcalf's head jerked up, and he searched the hills. Relief replaced his worried expression, and he smirked. "You had me there for a moment. I don't believe you'd come riding in alone if you had anyone with you. Give me the boy."

Aaron took another backward step. "Better go while you still can. You're a wanted man now. You shot my wife and harmed my daughter. People in these parts don't hold well with men who hurt females."

Unfazed, Metcalf cocked his pistol, lifted it over the saddle horn, and aimed it at him. Aaron spun around and started running.

A shot rang out. Aaron jerked, expecting sudden pain, but none came. He turned and saw Metcalf staring in shock at the red stain growing across his white shirt. The man's expression hardened, and he pointed the gun at Aaron again. Then Ethan and Sam charged toward them. Sam fired, shooting Metcalf in the shoulder. Outlaw reared, and his rider spun sideways and fell off.

Benjy started crying again. Aaron jiggled him, holding him tight, and kissed his head. "You're all right, Son. Your pa's got you."

"Pa." He sniffled and patted Aaron's chest, then laid his head down and released a shuddering breath. Keeping his eye on Metcalf, Aaron clung to Benjy, so grateful to God the child hadn't been harmed.

"You're not...his...father." In spite of the pain he must have been in, Metcalf glared at Aaron from where he lay on the cold ground.

"I'm the man who's going to raise him and the only father he'll know."

Metcalf coughed and grimaced. He lifted his hand from the wound in his stomach, then laid his head on the ground. "I'm dying."

Aaron didn't want to feel sorry for the man, but had he not been raised by godly parents, he well might have chosen a path similar to Metcalf's. "It's not too late to make things right with your Maker."

Metcalf barked a laugh, and blood made a trail down the side of his mouth. "God doesn't want me."

Ethan and Sam dismounted. Sam approached Outlaw and snagged his reins, while Ethan confiscated Metcalf's gun, tucked it into his waistband, and hurried to Aaron's side. "How's Benjy? Is he hurt?"

"Just scared and cold."

Ethan undid his coat. "Here. Put this on."

Aaron nodded his thanks and allowed his brother to help him so he didn't have to give up Benjy. Inside the warmth of the coat, his son relaxed. The boy's trust in him humbled Aaron.

Metcalf's horse attempted to rise and cried out in pain. Sam walked over and stooped down, running his hand over the animal's leg. "Looks like the gelding's broken its right foreleg. Gonna have'ta be put down."

Aaron nodded, hating what had to be done. "Let me get Benjy away first. The gunfire upsets him." He whistled, and Outlaw trotted up to him.

Aaron returned to Metcalf's side, not finished with his efforts to win the man over to the Lord. "God wants everyone, Metcalf. Even you." Metcalf was at the end of his rope. He'd lost too much blood to survive the ride to town. Although Aaron didn't like watching the man die, at least Janie would never have to worry about him returning for Benjy.

"You don't know all that I've done."

Aaron moved a little closer and squatted down, turning away from the wind. "None of that matters to God. When you've been cleansed with the blood of His Son Jesus, it's like you never sinned."

Metcalf laughed, then struggled through a bout of coughs. "I killed my wife. Thought I'd killed my child too, but her cousin...pulled a fast one on me."

"She was only doing what your wife asked of her."

"Ha!" Pain contorted his face, and his breath grew shallow.

"Come on, Metcalf. Repent and spend eternity in heaven."

Martin shook his head. "Too late." He struggled to remove a ring from his left hand. When he finally slid it off, he held it up toward Aaron. "Take this...to my lawyer. Benton Phelps in Bos—" He coughed up blood, then leaned over and spat. He wiped his hand across his mouth, smearing crimson over his lips. "My will leaves everything to my son. I want him to have it."

Aaron didn't want anything to do with this man's property, but that wasn't his call. Benjy was Metcalf's rightful heir, whether Aaron liked it or not. He winced, realizing that if it weren't for Martin Metcalf, Benjy never would have been born, and he wouldn't have the privilege of raising him. "I'll take good care of him. Janie—" Her name caught in his throat. Was she still alive? *Please, Lord.*

"I know." Martin exhaled a loud breath and went limp. Death had claimed him.

Aaron blew out a sigh of relief that the battle was over, but at the same time, he felt remorse for Martin Metcalf's lost soul.

"Sure glad you're all right." Ethan clapped a hand on Aaron's shoulder.

Aaron grinned. "Me, too." Then he remembered his wife, and his grin wilted. "Is Janie—"

"She'll be all right. Ma should be there by now. Pa and I put Janie in bed, and he stayed with her and said he'd tend her wounds so Sam and I could help you. I imagine, though, Janie'll rest a tad better once you and the boy get back. Head on home, big brother. We'll take care of things here."

Aaron nodded at Ethan, his throat tight. "Thanks." He looked at Sam and then his brother again. "I appreciate you two. Things might have turned out much different if you hadn't showed up when you did." Aaron hugged his brother and shook Sam's hand, then mounted Outlaw. "Salvage the saddle and bridle. I have a feeling they belong to someone in Karsen. And that's my coat Metcalf's wearing. I'd like to have it back."

Ethan nodded, then Aaron reined Outlaw around and rode for home. It saddened him that a man could live his whole life and never give a moment of it to God. He had no doubt that as Metcalf burned in the fiery pit of hell, he would regret over and over not calling on God in his final hour.

A short while later, Aaron rode into the yard as dusk set in. The door opened, and a rifle barrel poked out, followed by the aroma of something delicious. "Who's there?"

"It's me, Pa. Aaron."

The rifle disappeared, and his pa rushed out the door, followed by his ma and then Corrie and Toby.

"Oh, thank God you're all right." Ma's hands went to her cheeks.

Corrie hurried to the porch rail. "Where's Benjy, Pa?"

"Right here in my coat. Sound asleep." Aaron slid off his horse, weary to the bone from all the tension of the day.

"Go on in, Son. I'll take care of your horse."

"Thanks, Pa."

Toby and Corrie ran down the stairs and enveloped him in hugs.

"I was so afraid, Pa." Corrie rested her head on his arm.

"How's the lip, sweetie?"

"Sore, but it will heal."

Aaron ruffled Toby's hair. "I'm mighty proud of you both. You did good today."

His ma approached. "Save the compliments until we're in the house. That baby needs to get out of the night air."

Aaron never argued with his ma when she used that tone of voice. Inside, he handed Benjy to Corrie.

"Eww. He's all wet." She kissed his forehead and headed to the small bedroom. "Let's go get you changed, little man."

Aaron hugged Toby again. "I'm real proud of you, Toby, and I don't mind saying it twice."

His son puffed out his chest and beamed a smile. "Thanks, Pa." Then he turned and followed Corrie into his room.

Ma stepped up next and enfolded Aaron in her arms. "Thank you for what you did. I don't know how Janie would have survived if that awful man had gotten away with that sweet baby."

"Well, he didn't, and we'll never have to be concerned about him again. Sam shot him. Twice."

"So he's dead?"

Aaron nodded.

"I can't say I'm not glad. At least you won't always be looking over your shoulder, but I'm sorry that there had to be bloodshed for that to happen."

Aaron kissed her temple. "I need to see my wife, and then I want the biggest bowl you can find of whatever is on that stove."

Ma chuckled and spun for the kitchen while he aimed for the bedroom. The place smelled of medicine instead of Janie's usual flowery scent. He crossed to the bed and sat on the edge of the mattress, grimacing as it creaked.

Janie struggled to lift her eyelids. "Aaron?"

He ran his hand over her soft hair, overwhelmed with love for this woman. "Yes, sweetheart, it's me."

"Benjy?" She tried to sit up, but he held her down.

"Stay still. Corrie has him, and he's safe. Just exhausted from the ordeal."

"He's not hurt?"

"Not as far as I could tell."

"Thank God." She blew out a loud sigh. "And Martin?"

"He's dead."

Janie frowned. "I'm sorry, Aaron. For all the trouble I've caused."

He leaned down and silenced her with a kiss, then pulled away before he was ready to. "Shh...concentrate on getting well. You just about scared ten years off me. I bet if I look in the mirror, I'll see gray hair."

Janie chuckled, then winced and clutched her bandaged shoulder. "Ow. Don't make me laugh."

"All right, but only until you're better. I plan on this family laughing a lot together in the years to come."

She reached for his hand. "I love you so much, Aaron. I'm thankful beyond words that you and Benjy are safe."

"Rest now. I'll be back in later." He kissed her again, slowly, enjoying the softness of her lips, and when he pulled away, he realized she'd fallen asleep. He rose, shaking his head. "Don Juan, I'm not."

He stood there, looking down at his lovely wife. As much as he'd despised Martin Metcalf, he had to admit that if it were not for that man, he'd have neither Janie nor Benjy, and his two children would probably still be living with his brother. He thought of Romans 8:28, "*And we know that all things work together for good to them that love God, to them who are the called according to his purpose.*"

God had certainly worked things out for their good.

Epilogue

Four years later

Reverend Bob Shelton stood at the front of the new church built on the southeast corner of the Harper property and said a prayer of blessing. Janie gazed around at the small congregation made up of her family, their closest neighbors, and the Harper cowboys. The church, which smelled of fresh-cut pine, had been something the Harper family had prayed and planned for, and now that more and more people were moving into the area, Nick and Karen had felt the time had been right to construct it. And one day soon, they would hire a teacher so that the building would also serve as a local school.

The sun shone through the stained-glass window that had been purchased with some of the proceeds from the sale of Martin Metcalf's house. Janie and Aaron had felt it was appropriate to donate the funds, since they had received so much. Most of the money had been put into the bank to save for Benjy when he was grown, but the rest had been used to build a larger house for their growing family.

"Ma! Abby bit me."

Janie rushed to put her hand over five-year-old Benjy's mouth. Aaron winked at her, then grabbed two-year-old Abby off the floor and carried her to the back of the church. With the exception of Abby's penchant for biting, her children normally got along peacefully. Corrie, sitting on the other side of towheaded Benjy, lifted his sore hand and kissed it. Ever since that awful day when Martin Metcalf had taken Benjy, he had basically become Corrie's baby. But Janie didn't mind. She was delighted that her children loved one another.

She heard snickering on the far side of Corrie and leaned forward, looking at Toby and Mikey. She lifted a brow at them, to let them know they would be in trouble if they didn't settle down. The boys ducked their heads.

"Amen!" Reverend Shelton gazed around the group of more than two dozen people. "To celebrate the opening of this fine church, we have a special guest who I understand has the voice of an angel."

Corrie looked at Janie and smiled. "That's you, Ma."

Janie smiled back. "And you," she whispered. She was proud of her daughter's voice and how hard she had been working to train it. One day soon, they would sing together.

"Mrs. Harper, would you do us the honor of singing for us?" The pastor stepped down from the podium and took a seat in the front row without waiting for a response.

Now that the time had come, Janie's knees shook, and her stomach threatened to revolt. But God had given her the opportunity to sing, so sing she would—to Him and to her husband. She rose, stepped up to the platform, and stood behind the podium. As she gazed over the crowd, at the faces of the members of Harper clan who had welcomed her with open arms, she knew that she was blessed beyond words. She'd fled Boston with a baby that didn't truly belong to her. Then she'd met Aaron, and they'd become a family. Her gaze collided with his, and the joy in her heart welled up and overflowed as she opened her mouth to sing.

About the Author

Best-selling author Vickie McDonough grew up reading horse stories and dreaming of marrying a rancher. Instead, she married a computer geek who is scared of horses. But those old dreams find new life as she pens stories of ranchers, lawmen, and others living in the Old West. Vickie is an award-winning author of more than thirty books and novellas. Her novel *Long Trail Home* won the 2012 Booksellers' Best Award for Inspirational Fiction. *End of the Trail* won the Oklahoma Writers Federation Inc. Award for the 2013 Best Fiction Novel. Her books have also won the Inspirational Reader's Choice Contest, Texas Gold, and the ACFW Noble Theme contest, and Vickie has been a multiyear finalist in the American Christian Fiction Writers' BOTY/Carol Awards.

Song of the Prairie concludes her first series with Whitaker House, Pioneer Promises, which also comprises *Whispers on the Prairie* (a *Romantic Times* Recommended Read) and *Call of the Prairie*.

Vickie and her husband live in Oklahoma. Married for thirty-nine years, they have four grown sons, one daughter-in-law, and a precocious eight-year-old granddaughter. When she isn't writing, Vickie enjoys reading, gardening, antique shopping, collecting quilted wall hangings, watching movies, and traveling. She recently took a stained glass class and is working on several projects.

To learn more about Vickie's books or to sign up for her newsletter, readers may visit her Web site at www.vickiemcdonough.com or find her on Facebook, Twitter, and Pinterest. Vickie also co-moderates and contributes regularly to the Christian Fiction Historical Society blog: http://christianfictionhistoricalsociety.blogspot.com.